My Woman His Wife 3:

Playing for Keeps

My Woman His Wife 3:

Playing for Keeps

Anna J.

www.urbanbooks.net

Urban Books, LLC
97 N18th Street
Wyandanch, NY 11798

ISBN 13: 978-1-60162-630-1
ISBN 10: 1-60162-630-4

First Mass Market Printing October 2014
First Trade Paperback Printing November 2012
Printed in the United States of America

10 9 8 7 6 5 4 3 2 1

Distributed by Kensington Publishing Corp.
Submit Wholesale Orders to:
Kensington Publishing Corp.
C/O Penguin Group (USA) Inc.
Attention: Order Processing
405 Murray Hill Parkway
East Rutherford, NJ 07073-2316
Phone: 1-800-526-0275
Fax: 1-800-227-9604

Also By Anna J.

Novels

Hell's Diva 2: Mecca's Return
Hell's Diva: Mecca's Mission
Snow White: A Survival Story
My Little Secret
Get Money Chicks
The Aftermath
My Woman His Wife

Anthologies

Full Figured 4: Carl Weber Presents
Bedroom Chronicles
The Cat House
Flexin' and Sexin': Sexy Street Tales Volume I
Fantasy
Fetish
Morning, Noon & Night: Can't Get Enough
Stories To Excite You: Ménage Quad

Independent Projects

Erotic Snapshots Volumes 1–6
Motives 1 & 2

This book is dedicated to every little girl in the world who dares to dream . . . they do come true!

Acknowledgments

Eight novels later . . . Who knew that little old Anna from Bartram Village would be a writer when she grew up? Just for the sake of remembering the date, I'm writing this on June 13, 2012, two days before my final edits are due to be turned in. I guess I'm amazed that after all of these years I'm still in the game doing it. There are so many authors I've met over the years who aren't producing anymore for reasons unknown to me, and every time I think I cannot write another word or think up another story line, I always find a story to tell. I've come to face the fact that this is how God works. This is *His* plan for me, and it's already been written . . . so I continue to write.

As I was writing this I was thinking about the first day I decided I was going to write a book. I was so hype, but I didn't tell anyone because I didn't want the negativity to mess up my mojo. It took me about six months, and before I knew it I had created *My Woman His Wife*. I was so proud and couldn't wait to get a deal for it. Through a chance meeting I got the deal that I had prayed for, and here I am . . . eight years later . . . still typing away. It makes me smile on the inside to be living my dream. I remember the night I completed my book, and I was reading a novel by the late, great E. Lynn Harris. He had all of these books that he had written listed on the inside cover, and I thought to myself that I couldn't wait to have an "Also By . . ." page to list my stuff under. I didn't even realize at the time that I was speaking it into existence, and the realization of it, all of these years later, moves me to tears a little. Little old me . . . from the projects . . . living her dream!

I have so many people to thank for even making it here, because we all know that being who we are takes a team, and God plants people in our lives for different reasons and seasons. So, I would first like to thank Nakea Murray. You were there when the dream was just that. Not even a word written, just some talk about this hot book I was going to write. Thanks for believing in me, and keeping me in the loop. There's a lot that has been said, and not said, and I'll just leave it there. Do know, if I never told you before, that I appreciate everything you've ever done, and thanks for accepting me . . . flaws and all.

To Mark Anthony, thanks for giving me a chance! My first time out there, and I got a book deal with Q~Boro Books! I still can't believe it! You definitely put me on the scene, and because of you giving me that chance, I'm still doing my thing. Thanks a bunch!

To Azarel, Jamise Dames, Nancy Flowers, and Kevin Elliott: thanks for looking my way when you needed stories for collaborations, especially when there were so many people to choose from. I spent plenty of nights trying to pound out short stories in between projects, and all of that practice helped in honing my craft. Where would the book industry be without opportunities like that? Thanks for looking out for the little people, and helping me build my name. Those opportunities made it possible for me to offer the same opportunities to other authors years later. How hot is that?

To Treasure E. Blue, M.T. Pope, Shakir Rashaan, Jewelze, Charm, Dwayne S. Joseph, T. Real, Zaria, Sabrina A. Eubanks, Aretha Temple, Debra Shade, Candice Marie, Nykole, TP Miller, N'Tyse, La Jill Hunt, Kimber Lee, and Tawana Patrice: When I put the word out that I had an opportunity to shine, all of you guys stepped up to the plate and wrote some amazing stories for my *Erotic Snapshots* line (shameless plug:

available on Kindle and Nook for $1.99). This motivated me to do *Motives* and with the help of Shakir Rashaan I was able to do a second installment with a third on the way. These are the little things that constantly remind me that I can live my dreams and do whatever I put my mind to. Shakir Rashaan & M.T. Pope, thanks, loves, for being just a phone call away when I need to ramble about a book idea that won't let me sleep or just life stuff in general. The life of a writer is a lonely one indeed that only a "writer" understands, but the good thing about late nights is there is always a true writer somewhere in the world losing sleep right along with you. I love all of you, and thanks for everything!

To Allison Hobbs, Cairo, Candace K, Erick S. Gray, Kwane, Tu-Shonda Whittaker, Daaimah Pool, Brittany Williams, Anya Nicole, Blair Pool, T. Styles, Ken Divine, Marlene Ricketts, Dwayne Birch, Anthony White, and every other author that I've been blessed to have met over the years. I see y'all still doing it big! It ain't that many of us left who are still doing it from back in the day, and so many of you are an inspiration to me. Tu-Shonda, I still can't rise at five in the morning with you to write, but at seven I'm there! (LOL) Kwan and Treasure, y'all are still killing the game. Keep doing it big babes!

To my family: so much has happened in the past year, and I'm smiling and sad about a lot of things. Uncle Herb (aka Uncle Deacon), I'm happy to see God working in your life the way he is. I mean, Deacon? That's huge, Uncle! I'm happy for you, and I'm glad to see you doing what's necessary to take your life in the direction you want it to go. You have definitely made me proud, and I see good things in your future. Mom Dukes, thanks for your constant support. The family is small, and we all have to stick together, even when we don't want to. Thanks for everything. Tiff, how 'bout that driver's license? I steadily see you growing, and I'm happy that I've been able to be an example of what can happen in your life when you put your mind to it. I'm looking to build a house from the ground up one day, and I know exactly who I need to call!

Tisha, you know we grew up like sisters. I don't know if you know it, but you are an inspiration as well. We lost five family members in a matter of six days. Four in a fire, and one to God knows what happened. I was so nervous about seeing my father's family after all of these years, but you and Shar told me it would be cool and it was. Thanks for being there, cuzzo, no matter what it is. I see you with those kids, and I know you wish that you had done things differently in your life. If no one has ever told you, you are one of the best single mothers I know. Life lessons happen for reasons that we don't know or understand at the time, but we need those experiences to grow, and when we get that moment when it finally clicks and makes sense it makes it all worthwhile. You are doing a damn good job to be doing it without help from their dad, and I'm proud of you. I'm glad that we are still close enough to have heart-to-heart talks, and I'm glad that I have you in my life. I love you, cousin! Keep doin' ya thang, cuz you know I will!

To my babe: it was a few years ago when I first saw you, and I was saying to myself, "who is that with those pretty eyes?" Even after seeing you a few times here and there, I never knew that things would be like this with us. After so many heartbreaks and heartaches in both of our lives, I'm glad that we were able to leave all of that behind and do us. Things get rough sometimes, and we want to call it quits but never do. LOL. It's like, where you think you going? I just want to thank you for putting up with this temperamental "writer's personality." I'm always talking about how I need some alone time, but as soon as you try to give it me I'm all up under you. A lot has happened in the past year or so, and even if by the time this book hit the streets and things have changed I still love you for the time and experience. We both said we wanted this to be a forever thing, and I pray every night that God sent you my way, and that it would be. No one wants to keep starting over, and even though I didn't know what I was looking for would come in this form, I'm glad it did. I love you, chicken noodle! LOL. And thanks for always being there when I need you. Remember our first date at Joe's Crab Shack and they sat us near the playground, and the kids were throwing rocks at us while we were eating? Ahotmess.com! (LMAO) That's just one of the many things that we still laugh at, and I'm looking forward to many more to come.

To my fans: THANK YOU! THANK YOU! THANK YOU! For so many things I'm thankful. I've been in the game for eight years because of you, and even with those that let me know that *"I wasn't feeling that one, Anna J.!"* I still love you for keeping it real, and constantly supporting me throughout the years. Over the years I received so many e-mails asking me for another Monica book, and finally here it is. I love that I can switch up my style and write about different stuff, and all of y'all hang in there for the ride. Thanks a million, and I hope to write a million more books for you! Okay . . . maybe not a million, but I'll get as close to it as I can before my time is up. Thanks for everything, and I love you all.

Don't forget to leave a review whether you liked it or not, and I'm always reachable at www.allthingsannaj.com!

Now, go ahead and turn the page and get this book started. That's what you've been waiting for right? LOL.

Happy Reading!
Anna J.

Chapter 1

Jasmine Cinque

All I asked James to do was pick up the kids from the afterschool program. I mean, how hard was it to take responsibility for your own damn kids? It made no sense to me that I was called out of a business meeting because it was after six and no one had gone to claim my children yet. I say *my* children because it'd been years since James acted like they were *ours*. How embarrassing is that? This wasn't the first time this had happened either. Another reason why I was so irritated right now. You could mess with me all you wanted, but do not jeopardize my job or the safety of my children. It would quickly become a sticky situation for the accused.

What worked me the most was that I had to make two stops. Monica's son was a bit of a problem child so I had him in an entirely separate program from Jalil, Jaden, Janice, and Jordan (my two sets of twins). That meant I had to go get my kids first, and then go and get James's son. Now, I know that sounds harsh, but I really don't give a damn. I refused to take any claim to that boy. He belonged to James and Monica. The rest of these kids were mine.

To make matters worse, it was pouring down raining like we were in the middle of a tsunami, so visibility was down to practically nothing. It was a cold January night, and I hated driving in these types of conditions. When I got to Junior's program the instructor threatened once again to kick him out because he refused to just follow directions from either him or any of the aides who worked there. I wanted to snatch his ass up right quick and check him, but I told James that Junior would be his responsibility, and I was standing by it.

Every time I saw his face in the rearview mirror I wanted to pull over and choke the shit out of him. He looked so much like Monica, and he had her "I don't care" attitude as well. Why didn't she take her bastard son with her? I thought if enough time had gone by I could grow to love him like my own, but I just couldn't feed into the lie. He was conceived by my husband and birthed by a woman I'd once loved . . . still did. I hated myself for missing her, but my heart did what it wanted to do, so what could I do about it?

I hated the fact that I could still picture so vividly everything we'd done sexually. I'd given up on James a long time ago, so all I had was memories of Monica during quick masturbation sessions when I finally got some alone time. Hell, I had five kids to raise, so any "me time" I might have had in the past was a done deal now. I was okay with that sacrifice years ago when I was hype about being married and starting a new life. Now, I wished I would have just stayed the single whore I was. Life was much simpler then. Don't get me wrong, I love my kids, but I didn't sign up to be a single parent. That just wasn't a part of the deal. Now I had James to thank for this bitter-ass attitude. *Thanks, James!*

I'm not even going to go in on Monica's trifling ass. She got to live a carefree life doing whatever, wherever she lived, and I didn't even get to sleep in late on a Saturday morning because I had responsibilities. Then she had the nerve to send us checks like we needed them. Now, I'll be truthful and say that I had no problem cashing the $3,000 checks she sent monthly like clockwork for her son (which later turned into $5,000 as he got older), because that money got me a new Benz that I drove when weather permitted and Jalil and Jaden a new wardrobe. If she thought I was using it for him then shame on her simple ass for leaving him here. I didn't want her son feeling anywhere near comfortable at my house so he got to wear hand-me-down clothes that Jordan could no longer fit into or I no longer wanted him to have, and if you had a problem with that you could feel free to come get him. I'd have his shit packed by the door ready for your arrival.

Time certainly did fly, though. With Jalil and Jaden being the oldest at eight years old, I had some help with my four-year-old twins and Monica's four-year-old, but there was only so much they could do. I refused to bog them down and burden them with the responsibility of taking care of a child at their age when all they wanted to do was have fun and be kids themselves. Janice and Jordan didn't know that Junior had a different mom, and it was really hard to tell considering they all looked like James. I mean, Junior had a little bit of Monica in his features, but those were definitely James's kids. Where as the other kids looked like a combination of me and James, it was clear that Junior had a different mother. There was no denying it. So, I just left that bit of information on a need-to-know basis. Even with Jalil and

Jaden, Junior came along when they were pretty young, so it just sort of worked out.

I wanted all of this Monica business to stop, and I hated that every time I walked into my house I could still smell her scent. When I walked into my kitchen I could almost see her perched on top of the table while James and Sheila joined her in a twisted orgy that almost got their asses killed. When I went into my bedroom my clit pulsated as I thought about the things she did to me on my bed. I could feel her hands touching me in places that James knew nothing about, and when I closed my eyes real tight I could almost feel her warm tongue kissing my nipples and trailing kisses down my stomach. Hell, on a good day in my imagination I would have her and the twins all at the same time. A pure mess, I tell you.

I had to get out of that house or I would've gone crazy, and so we did. We packed up and moved and I threatened James to not tell Monica a damn thing. I promised him I would set up a post office box so that her mail would be directed there, but I never did. We didn't need shit from her. The only reason she would need to know where I lived was to come and get her damn son. You can judge me all you want, but until you've walked in my shoes and lived my life for me there is nothing to discuss. I don't care how you feel about it. Point blank period.

I had been dialing James's cell phone for the past hour and it went from ringing to going straight to voice mail. That just pissed me off even more because that meant he was definitely ignoring my calls. The same damn way he had been ignoring his responsibilities for the last two years, but I had something for his ass though. Payback is a mutha, and when it all came down to it I would be cracking the hell up in the end.

That's exactly why when he got paid I made sure to only leave him enough money in his account to get gas and maybe buy lunch if I felt like being nice that week. Occasionally I would let him go down on me, but as soon as I was pleased and able to release he just ended up beating off in the bathroom to relieve himself. I did that shit to him every time, and his simple-ass constantly fell for it. It would be a cold day in hell before he would warm his dick with my walls again, and the sooner he realized it the better off we would be.

That's not to say that I didn't get it from elsewhere. Best believe I had a lineup if ever I needed a tune-up. I didn't have time to be fooling around with a maybe from James when I could get a definite from any given person on my contact list. Male and female included. My time was precious, and I didn't have a lot of it to be wasting on nonsense.

Most of the time I would get a quickie in my office from the secretary on the second floor in my office building before I left for the day, or I would meet up with any given person at this little hotel I found over in Mount Laurel, New Jersey when I really wanted to dip off and enjoy myself a little before it was time to pick up the kids. James never knew about it, and I just kept all that on the inside, hoping all of my secrets wouldn't just bust out one day. You can't keep everything in the dark for too long. It's just designed to come out in the light eventually. That's just the way of the world.

I had this little issue with those twins from Bally Total Fitness that I couldn't shake as well. They wanted a paternity test to see which one of them was the dad, but I wanted to leave well enough alone. I didn't bother either of them for child support so what was the big deal? It was a one-night stand, for heaven's sake. There was no need to go any further. Anything that happened after that was on me, and those were James's kids. All five of them. I didn't want nor did I need to prove anything otherwise. I thought I had gotten away with it until Monica wrote that letter, and even though James didn't deny Janice or Jordan, he had to think in the back of his mind that there's a possibility that they may have belonged to another man.

We weren't exactly the best of friends or on speaking terms around the time of conception, and we might (and that's a very strong "might" because I really can't remember that far back) have had a quick night of makeup sex, but the timing was certainly off, and he always felt like I was trying to get him back for bringing Monica into the picture. It was one of those never-ending situations that guys take you through when they wrong for doing some dumb shit, but want to drag you through the mud forever because they can't deal with it. Typical male bullshit.

He did have a kid outside the marriage, but it's not the same thing as what I did, and my love for him wouldn't allow us to go through that kind of pain. Yeah, I still loved him, although the way we acted toward each other now you wouldn't think so. He just got on my nerves so bad sometimes. We had a lot of work to do, and had strained so far apart that neither of us really knew the first step to bring this thing back together. At this point did I really want to? Did *we* really want to? Was there anything to come back to?

After Monica wrote that letter to James telling him about the twins I had the threesome with to get back at him I wasn't sure where this thing with us was going to go. Dudes run they mouth too much though, and can't never keep nothing to themselves. A woman will cheat forever and never say a word. A man wouldn't even be out the pussy good before he ran running his mouth to anyone who would listen.

James didn't really react as bad as I thought he would. He could have very well just packed his stuff and rolled out, but guys will be miserable just for the sake of not wanting to pay child support. That was exactly why I ate his check up every time. I told him there was no truth to the letter, and at the time he seemed to believe me, but my gut told me that he really didn't. I guess he figured since he had done so much dirt himself he couldn't rightly crucify me for my shit, but he just never let it go. That's part of the reason why we were where we were in our marriage now, and another thing added to the list of why I hated Monica's simple ass.

The rain was coming down harder and I felt myself hydroplaning as I cut through small streets to avoid the end of rush-hour traffic on the expressway. My wiper blades weren't doing shit against the amounts of water that were beating down on my car, like the elements were angry at the decisions I'd made. I told myself to slow down when I slid through a stop sign and almost caused a major pileup a few blocks back. The kids looked scared and helpless, and I knew I would have to deal with my issue with James at a later date. The first thing I needed to do was get everyone home safely.

I called his phone again and this time he answered, but all I could hear was loud music in the background. I was steadily saying hello, but all I heard was a bunch of females laughing, and then the phone call disconnected. When I called back again the phone went straight to voice mail once again.

I was beyond pissed, and it took everything in me not to drive around the city and look for him so that I could string him up by his testicles and dangle him from a utility pole. He made me so sick! This weather was unbearable, and this twenty-three-degree temperature did not make January feel inviting, letting me know that 2008 just may be a difficult year to get through. I needed to make it home because the wind was starting to whip up something serious, and the rain started turning into sleet as we drove. I could see the fear in their eyes, and I knew it was time to wrap it up until I got to a safe place.

The combination of the horrible weather and my reckless driving wasn't a comfort to anyone, considering that the car had already almost failed to stop and I even fishtailed a little a few times. Normally the car would be full of chatter from the kids talking among each other about their day, but on this day there was a deathly silence surrounding us.

I tried getting through to James a few more times as I half watched the road and typed him a misspelled text message at the same time. The angrier I got, the harder I pressed on the gas. I wanted him dead, and just as I sent him the message I looked up to see through the rearview Junior pulling at Janice's ponytail.

"Sit y'all asses back or I'll—"

Before I could finish my sentence I realized that I had pressed the brake, but the car was still moving. Everything seemed like slow motion as I slid out into the intersection and my Jeep was hit first on the passenger side by a Hummer that was taking its turn at the stop sign, and then by another Jeep that collided into my driver side in the back, causing us to spin out of control. I couldn't control the wheel.

The Jeep did a few quick spins, and all I remembered hearing was the collective scream from my kids as we crashed against the telephone pole. I hit my head so hard on the steering wheel right before it crushed me in, and I was seeing stars. My legs felt jammed under the dashboard, and the wheel was pressed so tight against my chest I could barely breathe. I heard the kids crying loudly, but then everything started to sound muted and all I saw was black.

Chapter 2

James Cinque

This chick looked just like Monica. Chocolate-brown skin, kissable nipples, and all. She'd been gyrating and popping her pussy in my face for the last five minutes . . . working hard for this twenty I was holding in my hand. I was contemplating how long I should make her sweat, because if I added just ten more dollars I could get me a VIP session that would mean more than a mere lap dance. The J Spot had some of the best girls in the tri-state area doing a lot of strange shit for some change, and I contributed to their bills more often than I wanted to admit. Fuck it, I was a man after all. What did she expect me to do if I wasn't getting it at home? Keep stroking one out? There wasn't an ice cube's chance in hell that I was going to keep going out like that.

Jazz was messing up my groove though, just like she messed up everything else. I could hear my phone vibrating on the bar next to my shot of Hennessy, but I refused to answer it. I didn't feel like hearing her bitch because I didn't go and pick the kids up. I didn't feel like it. She was being a smart ass claiming she had to stay at work late, but I was sure she'd figure it out when the after-school program called her because she was late. There was a fee to pay of five dollars for every five minutes you were late, but she had the money. Shit, she practically had my entire check so she'd just have to handle it. I knew she would be at least forty-five minutes late, so she could just spend some of my hard-earned money on something other than shoes and overpriced handbags.

Mocha, the Monica body double who was dancing in front of me, was a snake charmer. The way she moved her body made me sway with her. I couldn't help it. I knew she had to have a juicy pussy, too, and the more I sat there and thought about it the more I knew I had to get at it before I rolled out tonight. It was only right. She entertained me relentlessly every time I came here, so why not test the goods to see if it's worth it? I'd have been a fool not to.

There were two other girls dancing on either side of me, and the one girl picked up my phone while it was vibrating and pushed the talk button. I wasn't even fazed by the shit. I gently took the phone out of her hand, and when I saw that she had answered Jazz's call I just hung the phone back up. Fuck it. Shit was going to be off the chain when I got home anyway, so I might as well have enjoyed myself now. Only God knew when the next time would be that I would be able to get out and have fun after the all-night argument that would go down tonight, so there was no use in rushing home to the bullshit. Feel me?

Mocha bent down and took my phone out of my hand and inserted it in her juicy pussy. Climbing down from the bar she made her way over to the VIP room, and I had no choice but to follow her. After all, she did have my phone. The right thing to do would be to get it out before it started ringing again. My dick was straining against my Sean John slacks, and I couldn't wait for Mocha to release it. She had a wicked smile on her face that let me know I was in for a treat. I paid at the window and was escorted back to one of the many used rooms where I had a ball fishing my now dripping-wet phone from out of Mocha and filling the void with my stiffness. I wore her ass out for the entire thirty minutes I paid for because I knew once I got home it would be awhile before I could come back this way again.

It took me a little longer than it should have to get home because there was a real bad accident blocking Ford Road. The expressway was still a little backed up from the rush-hour traffic, so I had to sit in traffic either way until I found a street I could turn off on. The accident was indeed horrible. A utility pole was knocked down almost completely, causing downed wires on that block. You could see the medics working to get out whoever it was who was trapped inside of the wreck, and it didn't look like there would be any survivors. That just made me wish these people would move so I could get home a little quicker. That was someone's family in that Jeep: a loss no one was ever ready for.

It took me an hour and a half to get home, a trip that would normally only take me about thirty-five minutes. I didn't see Jazz's Jeep in the driveway, so I figured she might have gone to her mom's house before coming home. It was slushy and hailing outside, and I knew how she hated to drive in this kind of weather. I was still feeling a little tipsy from all the drinks I downed at the strip joint so I mellowed out on the couch for a minute before I went upstairs. I knew Jazz wouldn't be out too late so I at least wanted to be in comfortable clothes because I was sure we would be up for a couple of hours arguing.

I must have dozed off on the couch because when I woke up the nightly news was on, and someone was banging on my door. Jazz still hadn't come home, and I got an instant attitude because now she was taking shit too far. She was probably going to stay the night at her mom's, but the least she could have done was called. It was just like Jazz to be on some self-centered bullshit, so I wasn't surprised.

The banging on the door was persistent and I figured maybe she decided to show up after all, and needed help bringing the kids in. I took my sweet old time getting to the door just to piss her off even further. That accident that I went past earlier was being discussed on the news, but I had the television on mute so I couldn't hear what they were saying.

I had my screw face on when I opened the door, only to be greeted by Jazz's brother punching me in my face. He, along with a few of her uncles and her dad, took time to beat the shit out of me in front of my own house. I couldn't swing back if I tried because they were swooping down on me. The cold numbed my body just as fast as the blows from their fists and Timberland boots, so I balled up in a fetal position until they were done.

Her father grabbed me by my bloody collar and pulled me up to a wobbly standing position. *I don't know what I did to deserve this, but Jazz has a lot of explaining to do. Damn, is not picking up the kids worth all this?*

"It's because of your stupidity that my baby girl is in the hospital," her father yelled at me before tossing me into the living room like a rag doll.

"What are you talking about?" I asked as I wiped blood from my mouth with my shirt. I was thinking I might have lost a tooth in the scuffle; I just couldn't tell at this moment.

Instead of answering, Jazz's brother picked up the remote and un-muted the television. I watched in horror as the accident I couldn't get by earlier was played again. I could see what I now recognized as Jazz's truck smashed up against the pole as the newscaster warned us that the scene would be graphic. They showed the Jaws of Life trying to pry open the roof of the car. Even though her license plate was scrambled I knew it was her car. I instantly felt like shit. *Why didn't I just go and get the kids?*

"Where are my kids?" I asked, my stomach feeling weak like I was about to vomit. Here I was out having sex with strippers and my wife was wrapped around a damn telephone pole. The look on their faces said it all. *Did my kids die? What happened with Jazz?* I broke down and cried like a baby. Was I such a horrible person that I would be punished like this?

"Save all those bullshit tears and go clean yourself up. We need to get down to the hospital as soon as possible," Jazz's brother barked at me as he watched the news play back the accident for what seemed like the hundredth time within minutes. I dragged my sore body from the couch, and went upstairs to get myself together. They really did a number on me, but I wasn't concerned with that right now. I needed to see what was up with my family.

When I got back downstairs I could see Jazz's uncles trying to console her father, and I didn't think I was ready to face the situation just yet. What if Jazz had died and they didn't want to say it right now? I felt myself hyperventilating as I was squeezed between the other men in the car. All kinds of crazy thoughts ran through my head as the drive to the hospital seemed to take forever.

"You better hope for your sake that everything is okay when we get there," her father warned from the passenger seat. I couldn't say a word; I just closed my eyes and tried like hell to rewind the day so that I could do things differently. I knew we were going through shit, but my wife was all I had. Furthermore, and what seemed a whole lot worse, if something was indeed wrong how was I going to explain it to Monica?

Okay, so she rolled out on her son years ago, but that didn't mean that she didn't have the right to know that he had been harmed or even killed. No one could consciously deny anyone that right. I was a lot of things, but heartless wasn't one of them. If something happened to this woman's child then I would have to call and let her know. Simple as that.

Chapter 3

Monica Tyler

Philly was a mess. Even more so was the flight over. There was so much turbulence I thought for sure we were goners a few times. I was so tense the entire ride, and as I looked around and saw people sleeping I couldn't understand how they could be. Were they at peace with God to the point that if they died it didn't matter? I had years of praying to catch up on, and I wasn't ready to go just yet. When the plane finally landed at Philadelphia International Airport and we had clearance to exit I was one of the first people off that joint, almost forgetting my carry-on.

I was glad to be back for a few reasons. For one, there was nothing like Philly. The air was different down here. The people were different, and the atmosphere just screamed pride. I loved it, and was seriously contemplating moving back.

It'd been four years since I'd been home, and I couldn't wait to get back into the scene. The few times I did come back were to do exhibits, but that was work and I didn't get a chance to chill. I did meet this chic though, Jaydah B, and letting her come to Atlanta and stay at my place was a huge mistake.

Who knew she would be so clingy? She's this famous author right here from Philly who was killing the charts with her erotic novels. She was nasty too, and proved to be a bit of competition in the bedroom. Oh, some of the things she did to me had me like damn! I was giving her all I had and she was giving that shit right back like she knew what she was doing.

For some reason she thought we would just be laid up for two weeks, and that I didn't have a company to run. Besides, the Safe Haven and my art gallery didn't run themselves. Who did she think did all the leg work? Robots? In addition to that, I still photographed for several well-known magazine publications, and they paid me well so there was no way I was missing out on any of that money. When she wasn't out doing book signings she was on my damn phone wanting to talk and have phone sex. I had the lives of damaged teens in my hands that needed my attention, and possible buyers of my art so that

I could make money. I didn't have time to fuck all day whether it was by phone or otherwise. She was on fire, and for the first time in never I didn't think I had what it took to turn her out. She wasn't shit like Jazz and Sheila; she knew what to do in the bedroom. She was just a tad bit annoying though so we cut that trip short. It was time for homegirl to go on home and write another book or something. Anything was better than her being in my damn face.

Needless to say, I was not happy when we arrived in Philly and the city was practically shut down. There were normally cabs lined up outside of baggage claim waiting for people, but today they were few and far between, and the line was extra long. I just needed to get to the Embassy Suites so that I could fall back for a second. Jaydah invited me to stay at her condo, but I declined. I had enough of her for the last week and a half to last a lifetime. Sexually, I would definitely hook up with her again, but right now she was riding hard on my nerves and I just needed some space. This was just a chill thing, but she was already acting like we were in a relationship.

The crowds of people who were stranded at the airport were nothing but a huge ball of frustration. People were ready to go home, and from the looks of it they would be sleeping in these hard-ass chairs at least until the morning. I barely made it here myself, and for a lot of people who were on the same plane I was, it was a connecting flight. All the boards had delayed signs coming in and going out, and the chatter of cell phone calls being made to loved ones was almost deafening.

I had no loved ones to call. My sister was out in Atlanta, partying hard as shit, and I'd been having trouble catching up with her for the last few weeks. I thought she would be cool once she made the Falcons cheerleading squad, but all she seemed to do was step her party game way up, and I knew she was sleeping with a number of the players on the team. Those eight balls she loved didn't seem to be enough for her anymore either, and her habit was out of control. I offered help, but she didn't think she needed it so there was nothing I could do but wait and see what happened.

My sister was the truth, too. I'd even have gone so far as to admit she was even prettier than me. Where I was dark chocolate, Yolanda was a smooth, flawless butterscotch. I had a nice ass, but Yolanda had a donkey that many a video chick was jealous over. She had a nice full D cup that could go braless, and her jet-black hair reached damn near to the top of her ass, and it was all hers. She was the shit, but you could almost see the effects of her lifestyle wearing away at her face . . . almost. Yolanda stayed on point and you would never catch her half ass, and I just hoped she stayed that way.

After standing in line for more than an hour, pissed that I let Jaydah leave, not taking her offer to drive me to the hotel, I finally got a cab. The gypsy driver couldn't stop staring at my ass long enough to put my shit in the trunk, and I let him stare, too, because I knew this ride would be on him.

"Where are you going?" he asked me in a thick Indian accent, and I flirted shamelessly as I gave him directions. His cab smelled like a mixture of Old Spice and an Italian hoagie with all the fixings, but I thugged it out until I got to my destination. I didn't have a choice, being as cabs were scarce at the moment, and I didn't feel like waiting on another one after the rough flight I just had.

"I'm staying at the Embassy Suites on Bartram Avenue," I flirted shamelessly with the cab driver. He looked like he wanted to climb in the back seat and fuck me against the glass, and in my earlier days I probably would have let him. The Embassy was literally only about five minutes from the airport, and would cost no more than ten dollars to get there, but I didn't pay for anything I didn't have to.

This was going to be a quick ride, so I knew whatever I was going to do had to be done if I was riding for free. Searching the outside pocket of my carry-on, I pulled out my trusty pink vibrator. It looked like a thick plastic spoon that had a little dip in the middle of the circle for lubrication. It wasn't shaped like a dick or anything, so unless a person owned one, you wouldn't know what it was.

I turned the tip of it to the left, hoping my battery hadn't died. The buzz coming from my little toy indicated that I would be cool at least from here to the hotel, but I would need some batteries soon. The sound caught the driver's ear, and I saw him through the rearview mirror as we sat at the red light waiting our turn to go. Moving swiftly yet elegantly, I pulled my long dress up around my hips, and slipped one leg out of the tights I wore underneath to cover my bare bottom from the cold. The look on the cab driver's face showed that he was happy to see I didn't have any panties on.

After placing a small drop of KY Warming Liquid directly on my clit, I gave the driver a show as I slowly ground against the pulse of the vibrator. I used my free hand to spread my lips open so that he could get a good view, and I closed my eyes and leaned back as I worked magic on my quickly approaching orgasm. I moaned and licked my lips as thoughts of James, Jasmine, and Sheila took turns licking my pussy and fingering me. It was weird because I hadn't thought much about them in a while, and I guessed being back in Philly conjured up those feelings.

I was so lost in thought, I didn't even realize that we had already reached the hotel and the cab driver had pulled up behind the building instead of at the door. I could see slight drool form on the side of his mouth through the mirror as his right hand moved in a quick up and down motion indicating that he was jerking off. This was going to be easier than I thought. I noticed that the meter was still running, and he had to know I wasn't paying a dime if he got one off too.

"Miss Lady, your pussy sure looks like it tastes good. How can I find out?" the cab driver asked, his accent not as evident as when I first got in. That led me to believe that he only used it when necessary, and that this might not be his first time witnessing a masturbation session in the back of his cab. Eyeing the meter, I saw that it was now up to about fifteen dollars. Now, I was willing to pay ten if I necessarily had to, but anything more than that was not going to happen.

I let the thought spin around in my head for a second as my orgasm approached, and figured what harm could it be to let the man taste the best pussy in the world. After all, he probably never had anything like it before and wouldn't ever get the opportunity again. The look on his face said that he might tear it up, too. Shit, if he was any good I might have had to get his number before he pulled off.

"Okay, I'll let you taste it," I answered seductively while I removed my tights completely and slid my feet back into my Ugg boots so they wouldn't touch the dirty floor. "But this ride is on you. Understand?"

He simply smiled and got out of the car, exposing his rock-hard dick to the rain and sleet that was beating Philly to death. I turned sideways in the chair, and opened my legs wide for him to eat, lifting my dress up over my hips so that only my ass touched the seat. I didn't want to have to get out with a wet spot on my ass. He opened the back door of the cab, and his smile got wider when he saw I wasn't playing. He was working with some shit himself, and if it weren't for his foul body odor I might have entertained the thought of finishing this up in my room.

Depending on how he handled his business I just might . . . after he showered of course.

The cab driver scrunched his tall frame into the back seat, and wasted no time placing my legs on his shoulders and devouring me. He practically sucked my entire pussy into his mouth, and I must say I wasn't ready for a beat down like that. If there were walls in the cab I definitely would have been climbing them.

He used his entire tongue to massage my clit, and took the liberty of inserting three of his huge fingers into my tight walls. I flinched a little because I didn't get a chance to see if his fingernails were clean, and I doubted if he had washed his hands at all today. My body paid my thoughts no mind as I bounced up and down on his hand uncontrollably, my pussy begging for release.

"Yeah, just like that," I moaned as I tried unsuccessfully to hold my orgasm a little longer. My walls began to clinch and I could feel my clit pulsate against his tongue as my honey ran out of me and soaked the back seat. The cab driver dove deeper between my legs, lapping up all of my juices from the inside of my thighs, and afterward his fingertips.

"Damn, that was good," he said right before his body stiffened, and he released all over the back of the front seat. The sight of his babies sliding down the faux leather backing and onto the floor made my stomach do a flip, but I kept my composure.

He took a minute to catch his breath, then without a word climbed out of the back, and took his position back in the front seat like he was a limo driver, and I was a high-profile client. I smiled as I watched him use his tongue to taste what was left of me on the corner of his mouth. When we pulled around to the front of the hotel, he jumped out and got my bags out of the trunk while I gathered my stuff in the back seat. He even insisted on taking my bags all the way inside.

"How much do I owe you?" I asked him with a sly smile on my face, needing to make this quick because I could still feel my honey running down the inside of my legs.

"Just take my number, Miss Lady," he said as he gave me a business card to the cab company he worked for with his number written on the back. "You can pay me back another time."

I just smiled, and waited for him to leave before I gave the receptionist my room information. I didn't need him trying to creep back up here later on for payment. The bellhop looked rather tasty, and I could feel him watching my ass as I sashayed to the elevator. He never took his eyes from my behind as we made our way to the top floor of the hotel, and I made sure he knew to come back after his shift was over once I was situated.

After I got comfortable in the room I looked out at the snow that coated the city, and the mess that it was creating for everyone. The real purpose of my being here reminded me that I had to get on the horn and make some calls. I had some business that I needed to handle, and first on the list was finding out where my son was.

Chapter 4

James: A World Apart

I can't breathe. I feel like the oxygen was taken out of this car, leaving me to suffocate in silence. I mean, I know there is air in here because the people surrounding me are breathing like it's nothing to it. For me, anxiety has my heart in a death grip and I can't . . . breathe. I'm spiraling out of control right now with madness, not knowing what to expect and how I'll react once I get to the hospital. What if Jazz and the kids are dead, or on their way to dying? What will I do without my family?

It's funny how they say in your last moments of life you see your entire existence flash before your eyes. I didn't think these were my last moments, but the past ten years ran in front of my eyes like a Lifetime movie. All of the ups and downs, and everything in between. The good, the bad, and the ugly. The most joyful times of my life, and the times when I didn't think I would make it through. I really wasn't that bad of a husband and dad, was I? Shit had been crazy at home and I needed a minute to regroup; I deserved that, right?

Okay, so I didn't need to unwind with a stripper, but when I couldn't even get some in-house ass what was I supposed to do? Not to blame it all on Jazz, but if she was handling her business the way she was supposed to we wouldn't have been at each other's throats right now, or ever for that matter. It should be included in the marriage vows that fucking your husband on a consistent basis is a must do. A lot of turmoil would be avoided in the long run, trust me. A little pussy and good head goes a long way in my book.

So I invited another woman into our bed. And? Don't judge me. I simply did what most men only wished they had the balls to do and the wife to go along with it. Now, I'll be the first to admit that things got out of control and a lot of skeletons had to be thrown in the closet. More so to the point where we now had to push the closet door closed with force. Maybe I was a *little* wrong for entertaining Monica's wild ass, but she made me want to do all kinds of freaky shit and I couldn't help myself. Hell, I did what any straight and sane man would have done. Took advantage of the opportunity. The things she could do with her mouth had me like, *oh shit!* I couldn't turn good head down; that's like against the law or something.

Let it be known that I never stopped loving my wife regardless of whose mouth was on my dick. Jasmine gave me the gift of children, and a loving marriage at least for a few years. We had chemistry, and a genuine feeling of peace with each other. We could talk about anything, and our dreams were that much easier to achieve because we had each other. The key word was *had,* just in case you didn't catch that. We just lost our way kind of, and I was hoping God was as merciful as everyone kept saying He was because I needed her. I had been wilding out, and acting a fool, but I was done with all that now. I was ready to be a good husband, and bring all this mess to a standstill. I wanted our lives to go back to when shit was good and we had no worries. *I swear if Jasmine makes it through this I'll stop fucking other bitches . . . I think.*

Hell, who was I kidding? I thought I'd definitely need me a good therapy session to get rid of some of these demons. I was not on no Eric Benet shit with a sex addiction, but I liked me a fine-ass woman who was willing to fuck the shit out of me until I didn't have an ounce of cum left in my body. I couldn't help it, and I didn't think I really wanted to fix it. Shit, Jazz used to be that woman, but all the fussing and the cheating and the nonsense just got to be too stressful. She didn't desire me, and I no longer wanted her . . . it was bound to get crazy eventually. I just never thought we would be here at this point like this.

I couldn't think right now. It looked like we were heading toward University of Pennsylvania Hospital, judging by the houses that we were passing, but I couldn't concentrate on anything but breathing at the moment. *What if this is it? For real this time. Like what if this is the fucking end? I need space, but these goons ain't budging. I feel like I want to make a mad dash for it, and I'm feeling antsy.* The ride over to the hospital was the most agonizing ever. I felt like a piece of me faded away with every block we went by. This could really be the end for us. I mean, what if Jazz didn't make it through? What was I going to do without her?

On the way there we passed by the accident scene, and at that moment I wasn't so sure about my family making it out alive. The car was moved from the pole, but was almost folded in half where the middle seats were crushed in and things didn't look good from here. The tension in the car smothered me, and I wanted to break free but I couldn't. I was stuck between Jazz's uncle and brother, and they already warned me that if I cut up they would cut me up into little pieces. I had no reason not to believe them, because they were very protective of Jazz, and had warned me of that early on. I'd seen them knock out other dudes for being the slightest bit disrespectful to the women in their family, and up until now I hadn't given them a reason they knew of to go off on me.

Honestly, I felt sorry for the kids. Anything that happened to me I probably deserved it, but the kids were innocent in this situation. *Speaking of the kids, how do I explain this to Monica if something happened to our son? She's going to wild all the way the hell out. I already know it.* I often wondered why she just never took the boy with her, but Monica was not the mothering type so I understood her motive. It was a bullshit move, but probably for the best in the long run for the kid.

From my position in the back seat I could see Jazz's dad in tears, the sobs racking his body as he tried to control the pain he felt. What did I do? Why didn't I just bring my ass home and deal with my family like a real man? The honest answer would be because I didn't feel like it. I felt like we'd been beyond repair for years. All because I let my lust come before the love I had for my wife. Dealing with Monica was a bad move, but I couldn't honestly say I wouldn't have done it again if I'd had the chance. I had yet to meet a woman who could satisfy me like her, even Jazz. I might have done things differently, but I wouldn't *not* try it again. That opportunity would be too good to pass up.

We pulled up to the hospital after what felt like days later, but we could only drive but so fast due to the nasty weather outside. I felt myself hyperventilating, but Jazz's brother gave me a look warning me to pull it together. I took a deep breath, and straightened my shirt after rubbing my temples. I didn't know what I was about to walk into, and I suddenly didn't want to be here. I was not ready to face the music just yet, but Jazz's father was looking like he was daring me to make a wrong move. Her country-ass uncles looked like they would willingly break every bone in my body on command, and on the real I didn't want it with these dudes by any means.

I could hear the receptionist asking something inaudible because I was in a daze and she sounded like the teacher off of *Charlie Brown* at this moment. My palms were sweating, and I felt overheated despite the cold chill that rushed in every time the automatic doors opened. *I'm not ready for this.* I thought for a minute to just break the hell loose and make a mad dash for it, but where would I go? I was miles away from home in nothing but a sweat suit and Timberland boots with no coat in sight, and not a dime in my pocket. I could have gone to the police station, but what would I say? "I'm running from my wife's family because she almost died in a car crash worrying about me because instead of picking up the kids and doing what I'm supposed to do I'm out paying strippers for sex that I could be getting at home if I could just act right?" They'd have probably slapped the cuffs on me just for being stupid. So I stayed, and braced myself for the unknown.

The ride up to the intensive care unit felt like forever, and I was kind of hoping that the elevator would just pick up speed and go straight through the damn roof. I didn't feel like this shit right now, and I was starting to get pissed off. *Why the fuck didn't she just pick up the kids and go the hell home? I've told Jazz time and time again to stop texting and driving, and when I didn't answer the phone the first million times she called she should have just let the shit rest until she at least got everyone home safely. What the fuck? It's like why? Why the hell is this shit happening? Where the hell are my kids?*

"What exactly happened at the accident scene?" I asked everyone, but it was like talking to empty air. No one even bothered to acknowledge that I was even standing there except to ensure that I hadn't run off. I was irked beyond belief, but I didn't feel like these fools jumping on me again so I let it go. Someone would have to answer me eventually.

The dinging of the bell indicating that we reached our floor stirred me from my ranting thoughts for a second. I was actually sizing these dudes up, trying to see who I could knock the hell out first and get away, but I was outnumbered and I really didn't want to make a scene at the hospital. I didn't want to see my wife like this. The last time I was in a hospital to see her it was because she was in labor and I had to be here. Jazz didn't just get bumped and bruised just for the hell of it, and up until now the kids didn't have anything major going on that required hospitalization. If I had to pick between the hospital and home, the crib would win every time hands down.

I didn't see any kids in the waiting area, and I was scared to ask of their whereabouts so I decided to just wait it out. I would cold snap if my kids weren't alive, and a selfish part of me just didn't want to know that truth if that was the case. Not right now, and not like this. I saw Jazz's dad conversing with a fine-ass nurse at the nurse's station, and my mind wandered to her riding my dick, her huge ass smothering my balls and smacking against my thighs as she comes down on me. *What am I doing? My wife is in ICU . . . Focus, man, stay focused.*

"Let's go," Jazz's father said to me with a straight face, looking like he would hate to have to repeat himself. I struggled from my seat, not even remembering sitting down, the effects of the ass-whipping they gave me earlier starting to show in a small limp and a thumping pain behind my right eye. I was sure this was probably nothing compared to what Jazz was feeling, so I wasn't about to complain.

"Were you in the accident as well?" the nurse asked me as I walked by, but all I could do was shake my head no as I moved toward where I assumed Jazz and the kids were located. I couldn't breathe, for real this time, and I was starting to feel lightheaded as we headed down the hall.

"Are you okay?" the nurse asked as she stopped to prop me against the wall. I didn't answer, instead shaking my head in a quick side to side motion in an attempt to gather myself, and I could see Jazz's uncles looking like they were ready to jump on me if I didn't get it together quick. Taking heed to the threat, I straightened up and got it together.

"I'm fine, just take me to my wife," I managed to squeak out in a low tone as I stood up on wobbly legs and forced one foot to step in front of the other.

The tension in the hallway was so thick you could cut it with a knife, and I was sure both the nurse and the doctor felt it. I was psyching myself up so that I could face the inevitable, trying to make myself believe that it's not that bad even though we're in the intensive care unit. It could just be that they wanted to keep a close eye out on her. All of that went out the window when I got my first glimpse of Jasmine through the glass separating her from the hall traffic. Damn, I wasn't prepared at all for this.

"You're in the right place to die, homeboy," Jazz's uncle said close to my ear to ensure that I heard every word. "Straighten the hell up before you go in."

Nothing could have prepared me for what I was going to see when I approached Jazz's room. I knew she was going to be a mess, but this was nothing like the stuff I saw on television. I was expecting a bandaged head, maybe a little bruising on the jaw line, and even a cast-covered leg being supported by something hanging from the ceiling. I would have even gone for the arm being wrapped up and looking like a chicken wing. Just looking through the glass, all the tubes and bandages brought tears to my eyes. This shit just got serious real quick. With blurry vision I stumbled over to the bed where my wife lay comatose, and cried. Her face was covered with twisted shades of blues and deep purples, and her lips appeared to be sliced to shreds. I held her hand in mine, and kissed every scar from her bandaged fingertips up to where her elbow and hospital gown met. What the hell did I do?

"Jazz, if you wake up I promise to make everything right. I love you, baby. Please don't leave me like this," I whispered in her ear as my tears soaked the material covering her shoulder. This was crazy, and I just couldn't believe it.

I wished I had the power to change places with my wife. Only difference was I would have wanted them to pull the plug on me. She didn't deserve a constant fuckup like me in her life, and I was even considering leaving the marriage once she came through. Jazz deserved someone who would love her unconditionally and would be there for her always. At one time I thought I was that man, but now I was not so sure.

Chapter 5

Monica: Bird's-eye View

Standing on the balcony, taking in the sights of the city, I gathered the fluffy terry cloth bathrobe around my shoulders courtesy of the hotel, as I sipped a cup of mint tea from a cute little coffee mug I found at the airport gift shop on my way to Philadelphia. Every so often the wind would pick up, violently swirling the snow around as sleet turned the streets into a humungous ice skating rink. My mom used to always say that when the weather was bad like this, God was angry with us. I could definitely see the truth in that. I personally played a lot into His anger as an adult.

My mind was spinning with all kinds of thoughts, and I didn't know where to start. What if I never found them? What if Jazz decided to try to fight me or something? Furthermore, what if we fell back into the same situation we had before? It was different, kind of, when it was just the two kids, but a five piece? That was a lot to juggle, and I wasn't willing to stretch my time or patience like that no matter how good the orgasm was. Furthermore, I couldn't bear being that close to my son without parenting him either. That was just too much at one time.

It'd been four years since I'd laid eyes on my son, and to be perfectly honest, I was scared of the outcome. Did he even know that I was his mother? He was practically forced on the Cinques, so if they never divulged that information to him it's only right, and there wasn't much I could say about it. They'd been more parent to him than I ever could've been then and now. I had the papers drawn up granting sole custody and everything. All they had to do was sign on the dotted line.

When I first split, James would send me picture messages of my boy growing up and walking around. I would cry just looking at them because I should have been there for all of those moments, but I was selfish and scared. What was I going to do with a baby? I was a mover and shaker, and I couldn't do that with a diaper bag on my hip. It got to be too overwhelming watching the videos and looking at the pictures, so without notice to him I changed my number.

I couldn't deal with the constant reminder that I might have made the biggest mistake in my life. The easiest thing to do was ignore it, and so I did. I'd lived my life for the last four years like I didn't have a child. I saw sending out checks to the Cinques for him like a bill I paid monthly. It was nothing to it: write the check, address the envelope, lick the stamp, and drop the shit into the mail. Easy as 1–2–3–4.

Pretty soon he wasn't even a thought and I moved on autopilot. Making sure my sister didn't crash and burn was a job in itself, and with running Safe Haven and my new art gallery my life was pretty full. A child wouldn't have fit in my plans anyway, or so I kept convincing myself. Yeah, leaving him here was the best move possible. Jasmine would love him like her own, and James would show him the ropes. Just the way it should be.

Why did the checks start coming back though? That was like the million dollar question in my head right now. Up until a few months ago the checks were being cashed and everything was good. I sent them more than enough to make sure my boy was properly fed, and clothed. Hell, the Cinques weren't exactly broke so he would have been good regardless of whether I sent a check or not.

I was even more surprised when I called James for the scoop and the number I had for him didn't work. Feeling desperate, I called Jazz already knowing the answer . . . Her number was changed as well. I had a friend of mine—more of a spy than a friend, honestly—go over to the house to see if they even lived there and it was reported back that the property had a for sale sign on it and the house was already empty. That was nothing but Jasmine's doing, but "why?" was the question.

So I called myself, using the voluptuous Jaydah B as a distraction, but she proved to be more of a distraction than I wanted her to be in an annoying way. I really couldn't enjoy her company the way I wanted to because I was trying to decide if I needed to show my face in Philly. She was just interested in achieving multiple orgasms. Rightfully so, after all, that was what she came to the ATL for, but damn. *Who knows, maybe I'll give her another chance when I'm less distracted, but I feel like my son needs me. I've never felt like this before, and I'm not sure why I'm feeling this now. I just hope I won't have to act a fool down here. Right now I come in peace; let's just hope I can leave the same way.*

Chapter 6

James: A Midwinter's Night Dream

"James, pull some of it out, baby. I'll let you put it back in," Monica moaned into my ear while I deep stroked her to death. She wanted me to go deep, and I had no problem meeting her request. The warmth that surrounded us was like we were wrapped in a cocoon near a hot spring, and the shit was driving me crazy. I hadn't had Monica in ages, and I almost melted when I slid into her.

"James, pull it out, baby. Please, pull it out," she pleaded into my ear, following it up with a low moan that made goose bumps crawl down my back in the same spot where her nails just scratched my skin. I wanted to oblige, but it felt so damn good. Jasmine's pussy never felt like this.

"I'll pull some of it out, but I have to push it back in, understand?" I spoke into her ear as I went deep one more time.

"Yes . . . yes . . . yes. I understand, James."

She tightened her walls around my length, and wrapped her legs around my back, pulling me in deeper in spite of her request for me to pull out. I pushed her legs back so that she could let me go, and after scooting up on my knees I slowly slid my snake from her cave, causing her to shiver all over. With the head of my dick sitting just at her opening, I felt her pulsate as honey oozed from her opening, making the head feel slippery. I had to count sheep to keep my cool, and take control of the situation before we crashed it. She was about to get dicked down something serious, whether she was ready or not.

Monica held on to the headboard for dear life, tapping out because she couldn't handle it. I ignored her taps, slowly inching myself back into her wetness. My dick was brick hard right now, and I swore it felt like it was still growing the closer I got to an orgasm. I would push it in a little more each time, and pull all the way out until just the head was in. The feel of her opening clinching the tip and trying to suck me back in was driving me crazy. She was losing her damn mind, and on the low so was I. I loved a kinky chick in the bedroom, and Monica was all for it. All this shit talking and ass smacking had me feeling some kind of way. Damn, I think I love this girl.

"James, push it deeper, baby," Monica requested in between pulses. She didn't know what the hell she wanted me to do, and from the way she thrashed back and forth, causing her hair to halo around her, I could tell she was in on the verge of an explosion and that shit was turning me all the way the fuck on. I leveled my body above hers and used my feet to brace myself as I pushed into her until it felt like my balls could squeeze in. A gush of warmth coated my dick with a gooey stickiness that made me moan out loud my damn self. Oh, she was playing hardball tonight, but I was ready.

"You like this dick all up in you?" I asked her as I slow stroked her into another orgasm. The light scratching of her nails against my back, and her pleading for me to "take it" was answer enough. I went from an extremely slow pace to almost pounding her brains out, back to a slow crawl. I hadn't gotten fucked good by my wife in years, so I was going to make this shit count.

"James, please . . ."

"Please what?" I asked her, pulling all the way out. I stroked my dick in a lazy up-and-down motion as it pulsated in my hand. This bad boy was about to blow! Rubbing her creamy juices

in, I leaned back on my knees so that I could catch my breath. I wasn't ready to bust just yet, but if she kept clinching up on my dick the way she was it was about to be a wrap.

"Please put it back in," she responded, panting loudly, trying to catch her breath as well.

Damn, she still had a gorgeous body, and I still loved her dark-chocolate nipples. She palmed her left breast, and pulled her nipple into her mouth, circling the tight bud with her tongue. I wanted so badly to be her tongue at that moment. I remembered when Jazz used to be freaky like that. Monica was making it her business for me to forget Jazz, if only for this moment, and I was all for it.

"What else you want to do with that tongue?" I asked her, pulling my legs from under me, and lying back on the bed, stretching out so that she could see all this dick up close and personal. Oh, I was gonna wear her ass out!

She had a wicked grin on her face as she switched positions in the bed, and rested her body between my legs, taking me all the way into her mouth down to my balls. I loved that she didn't have a gag reflex. Closing my eyes I let Monica enjoy my chocolate stick, pumping slowly into her mouth as she slurped me in. I cupped the back of her head to maintain control, but that shit wasn't working at all.

"Yeah, suck daddy's dick," I said in a low tone as I took hold of the back of her head a little tighter and guided the way. She ran a finger up the crack of my ass and pressed into the space under my balls, causing me to practically jump up from the bed. Damn, that shit felt good. Yeah, she's definitely a keeper.

Releasing the vacuum-like suction from the head of my dick, Monica stood up on the bed with her legs on both sides of me. Squatting down, she took me into her tightness, accepting my girth on the way in and juicing my dick with her walls on the way out. Lawd, how did I luck up on this?

"You gonna cum on daddy's dick?" I asked her while lightly pinching her nipples with one hand, and fingering her clit with my other. She was sloppy wet, and the friction from me smearing her juices across her clit was causing her body to tremor slightly. Seemed as if Miss Lady was losing her composure.

"Yes . . . yes . . . yes," she moaned as she swirled slowly on my pole. The heat emanating from her core had my dick like ten degrees warmer than the rest of my body.

"Yeah? Am I the best?" I asked her, taking full advantage of her weak state. She was grinding down hard, and I could feel my cream slowly

rising to the top. She would rise up off of it, and then grind down onto it in a beat that was probably in her head.

"Yes, James, you're the best," she responded in a low tone that sounded extra deep for some reason.

"The neighbors can't hear you," I threw out there as I pinched her clit between my thumb and forefinger, causing her body to convulse uncontrollably until I let it go.

"James, you're the best, baby," Monica moaned out, trying to catch her breath in the process.

"Damn, girl, take that dick," I responded as I tried to keep my nut in my sac a little longer. I was about to plant a thick nut up in her that would permanently knock the back out her pussy.

"Mr. Cinque, it's time to wake up," Monica spoke to me, but her voice sounded like a man's.

When I opened my eyes everything was a blur, and all I could feel was the warmth of her pussy wrapped around my dick. I didn't know what was going on, but I was still trying to get my nut, fuck that.

I felt a hand on my shoulder and it felt like someone was shaking me, but I refused to open my eyes. I hadn't been stroked like this in ages, and I was going for mine. I could hear a man's voice talking to me, and Monica was steadily slipping away. I tried to hold on to her, but I couldn't.

"Mr. Cinque, wake up."

When I opened my eyes, standing before me was the doctor that was handling Jasmine's case. I was fully clothed with an evident hard-on. Sliding up into the chair, I tried to hide my erection and my embarrassment as he updated me on my wife's status with a look of disdain on his face. I already felt bad about what happened, and this man frowning down on me didn't make me feel any better.

Through the room I could see Jazz's family still sleeping on the uncomfortable set of chairs just outside the room. I guessed we all eventually dozed off some time during the night. Taking a peek at my watch, I saw that it was now seven o'clock in the morning. Looking over at Jasmine as the doctor listed her prognoses, I felt a little better knowing that Jazz had a good chance of survival, and that they were keeping her heavily sedated until the swelling around her brain went down.

"We will have to take her into surgery at the end of the day to wire her left jaw. The bone was dislocated in the accident, and will need to be mended in order to set properly. I do want to make you aware that Mrs. Cinque may be a little out of it when she first awakens because of the impact to her left frontal lobe," the doctor explained as I went into a zone.

As I listened to him tell me how the quality of life for Jasmine may potentially change, all I could do was stare at her. I mean, Jazz could be a real bitch sometimes, but she handled her business almost effortlessly, and I couldn't imagine her operating in any other fashion.

"Because of the head trauma, she will have pain accompanied by the discomfort from wiring of the jaw. We will have to assess her motor skills once she is awake and moving around, but she is responsive to touch in the state that she's in now," the doctor informed me as he continued to write in her chart, periodically making eye contact with me.

"There's a possibility that she may not remember who you are at first. In cases like this we often see some short-term memory issue that may or may not correct itself. Either she will remember you, or most of her memories will be from things that happened years ago."

He droned on and on about what to expect, and what type of help was offered to make the transition smooth. I wanted him to stop talking, but for a second I couldn't form any words.

"There is therapy for people with head injuries that will definitely aid in getting your wife's mind back on track, but as already said, we have to wait for her to wake up to see where she is in her mental state."

"Doc, I just need to know . . ." I said to him in a solemn voice. All of this was too much to handle at one time.

"What is it, Mr. Cinque?"

"Can you tell me where my kids are?"

Chapter 7

Monica: Plan A

Morning came all too soon, and I hated that I neglected to pull the shade closed all the way. A sliver of sunlight beamed through the crack, and right into my eyes. I usually slept with a mask covering them, but I had forgotten to pack it in my haste to get Jaydah out of my house, and back in Philly. I decided, since my sleep was disturbed, I might as well get up and get going with my day. I had some investigating to do, and I wouldn't get anything done being laid up in the bed all day.

It was early, but I knew if I made a few phone calls I was bound to get things moving at least. I didn't want to do it, but I knew Judge Stenton would have to be my first call. Not that I planned to disrupt anything at the Cinques on purpose. If I needed to get my son and roll out I knew I would need some paperwork. Was I ready to be a mom? Hell no, but if I had to step up to the plate it was a now-or-never situation.

I had the number to his home, cell, and office, and I wondered briefly if Sheila would answer the phone at the courthouse. Still knowing the number by heart, I dialed the ten digits that could possibly connect me to the answers I needed. To my dismay the phone continued to ring, and I really hoped that maybe I had dialed the wrong number by accident. When the district court answering machine finally picked up, I hung up in disgust. After all, it was a week day; why wasn't anyone picking up?

Chancing a look outside, I immediately got my answer. Overnight the city got covered with snow up to our ears. I couldn't believe the amount that had fallen in that little bit of time. Trust and believe I did not miss all of this mess. Turning on the television to see what was going on in the world, I didn't need Fox News to tell me that the city was shut down. Such an inconvenience.

As I listened to the television, I gazed through the menu to see what was offered for breakfast. I contemplated whether I want to hit the judge on his cell phone, but I really didn't have a choice. I wasn't sure if he was with his wife and kids, or if he would throw shade since I didn't make it to the city the last time he wanted to see me. I also didn't know how much access he had to city business from home, but it was worth a shot. Just as I was going to pick up the phone, something on the news definitely got my attention. A car wreck flashed across the screen, followed by a picture of Jasmine. Grabbing the remote, I turned the volume to the max:

"Prominent Philly lawyer Jasmine Cinque has been reported to have been in an accident that has her in the ICU. Due to the quick dropping of the temperature last night, it appears that her car spun out of control and smashed into a utility pole in the Bala Cynwyd section of Philadelphia after slipping on an ice-covered roadway. The medics had a hard time getting to her due to the inclement weather, and had to use the Jaws of Life to extract her and her five children from the wreck. It has been said . . ."

At that moment my mind went numb. *Jazz almost died? Or did she die? Wait, the newscaster didn't say she was dead, so she's still breathing somewhere. What happened to the kids?* They didn't say anything about the children, and when I opened my eyes to look at the TV they were showing footage of her car wrapped around a pole, and you could see the medics trying to open her car like a can of tuna.

I was instantly sick, and had to rush to the bathroom before I vomited all over my nightgown. What happened? Furthermore, why was she out in that mess yesterday? Jazz hated driving when the ground was wet, so I needed to know what or who forced her out yesterday in the midst of a storm. My eyes burned from the tears that I refused to let roll down my face. *Damn, did I still love this chick? And where the hell is James?* They didn't say anything about his whereabouts. Did they divorce? Maybe that was the reason why I couldn't get in touch with either of them.

Pacing back and forth, I knew I had to get out of this hotel and on the street. I needed to see about renting a car, and I needed to call the hospitals to see where they were. *Wait a minute . . . let me slow down and think rationally.* I needed answers, and being in a panic was not going to help.

The ringing from my cell phone startled me out of my thoughts, and I dived across the bed to catch it before it stopped, wondering who it was. The only other person who knew I would be in Philly was my sister, and I hadn't spoken with her since I landed so I hoped nothing happened. I wrapped up business before I left Atlanta so I knew the call wouldn't be directly related to that either.

"Hello?" I answered without looking at the screen. My heart was racing a mile a minute. Did something happen to my sister? Was it a company issue? Did someone break into my house and the alarm company was contacting me? All kinds of bad thoughts ran through my head as I waited for the caller to respond.

"Hello, stranger." The voice came through the other end and I couldn't help but smile.

"What a pleasant surprise. I was just thinking about calling you."

"Is that so? My wife told me she saw you in the hotel lobby checking in yesterday, and it made me wonder what brought you back home."

Was it coincidental that just the person I needed to talk to was calling me? When I changed my number I made sure Judge Stenton, among others, knew how to reach me for whatever reason. Hell, he was a very influential man to keep around. Aside from spectacular sex, he donated a lot of money to both my art gallery and Safe Haven, a girls' home for teenagers who had been sexually molested.

"And she didn't say hello? That's odd."

"So what are you doing back here?" he asked, cutting the small talk short. Everyone needed someone of power in the tuck just in case shit got crazy or something against the law had to be done. He was that person for me.

"Well, for some reason I've been getting the checks back that I send out to the Cinques, and . . ." I explained everything to the judge, even what I just saw on the news about Jasmine being in the hospital. I needed answers, and I needed to know what was going on.

"As far as your son goes, Monica, you gave him up so I don't know what can be done there unless he's being abused. What exactly do you want from them? They stopped accepting your checks? So what! They just may have needed to move on, and didn't need a constant reminder of the role you played in their past."

"But they were cashing them up until recently. It doesn't make sense," I screamed into the phone. He tried to make it seem like I was the crazy one, but in knowing the people I was dealing with, I knew there was more to the story than that.

"How long are you staying here?" the judge asked in a nonchalant voice like he was done with talking about the issue. We were going to talk about it, but I had to play things cool if I was going to use him later. I had to make him think we were doing things on his terms.

"As long as it takes."

"Okay, you can't possibly stay in a hotel that long so as soon as the streets are cleared and I can get out I'll have a car come to get you. You can stay in the hideaway until you get what you came for. For now, just lay low. The city is shut down, so you can't go anywhere anyway."

"Thanks for everything. I owe you one!" I said into the phone as I calculated what my next move would be.

"You sure do, and I plan to collect on it. We'll talk by the morning."

After I hung up with the judge, I decided to at least put something in my stomach as I continued to watch the news. Jazz's story was top news, and I was just waiting for James to show his face. I knew I would need to speak with him, and I wasn't too sure if I was ready for all that. After all, I did wreck what was left of his marriage and dropped an unwanted baby on him. His reaction to me being here would determine if I kept my cool. Hopefully he would just be cool about it and give me the answers I needed. I had no problem going away quietly like I was never here, provided that everything was in order. Now, if it was not in order, then the circumstances of my visit would not be pleasant.

Ordering breakfast was a breeze, and I was elated to see that fine-ass bellhop when I opened the door. He must have held a couple of jobs at the hotel, but I wasn't mad about his hustle. I opened the door wider to invite him in to set up my food in the kitchen area of the suite. Damn he was fine, and I know you're thinking how I could be thinking about sex at a time like this. Easy, my pussy had a mind of her own and she liked to be fed as well.

"Are you the dessert?" I asked him in a seductive voice as I came out of my robe and stood there naked, allowing him to take in all of my curves. He looked like he had hit the jackpot! His eyes seemed to glaze over, and the way he licked his lips was like he was ready to eat me up.

After securing the door, I sauntered over and climbed up on the counter, putting my pussy at mouth level. All he would have to do was bend at the waist and taste it. He seemed to be in shock, so this had obviously never happened to him before. He would surely tell the entire hood about it later on. Grabbing him by the collar and pulling him closer, I leaned back on my elbows to balance out.

"Eat up," I practically whispered to him. Sparks shot through my body when his tongue connected with my clit, and I knew I was going to wear his ass out before he left. I just had to dig out my condom stash from my luggage and it would be on. That didn't mean I forgot about Jazz and James. I'd most definitely be dealing with them later.

Chapter 8

James: Live at Five

Since Jazz was a prominent lawyer in the Philadelphia area, I was asked to speak to the public on her behalf, giving everyone an update of her condition. The conference was scheduled to be held later in the day. The city was snowed in overnight, and I was starting to get cabin fever since we were all stuck in the hospital until the cleanup of the city was over. Between trips to the cafeteria, and avoiding the looks of hatred I was getting from Jazz's family, I was ready to blow this joint. True story. It wasn't until the doctor left that Jazz's father decided to clue me in on my children's whereabouts.

"So where are the rest of my kids?" I asked once again when Jazz's dad walked into the room. After getting over the initial shock of seeing my wife in her condition I needed to do a headcount of everyone else.

"The kids are with their grandmother at your brother-in-law's house. All of them were discharged shortly after they came in, except for Jordan due to his injuries," he explained in a sympathetic voice.

"So why did it take so long to get an answer? I've been asking about my kids since last night!" I came back even more frustrated.

"James, you needed to focus on one thing at a time. Trust me, it was for your benefit."

I looked at him like he was crazy. I was guessing that he had already talked with the doctor about who would break the news to me about my son, but it pissed me off that he waited this long to even say something to me. I could have gotten this info on the ride over here. After all, I'd only been asking about them since they dragged me out of my house hours ago. The look on his face had me holding my breath, and I broke down in tears when he told me that all of the kids were okay, but Jordan was in intensive care in the children's ward of the hospital. Children's Hospital was in the next building, but because of the time they came in and the extent of the injuries they kept both him and my wife in the same facility. He asked the doctor to allow him to tell me because he figured I probably wouldn't be able to handle dealing with both Jasmine and one of my kids being near death at the same time. That was hilarious to me that he all of a sudden was concerned about how much I could handle, considering they tried beating me to a pulp not too long ago.

I fell to the floor in a barrage of tears as I curled up in a fetal position wondering what I had done that was so bad that the karma would come back and destroy my family. I mean, I wasn't a monster. I wasn't molesting little kids, and robbing banks or anything like that. I just stepped out on my wife sometimes to be with other women, but what man didn't? Did I really deserve all of this? I asked God why this was happening, and I needed answers now!

"Mr. Cinque." I heard the doctor's voice as I gathered myself from the floor and sat back down in the chair to catch my breath. "Mr. Cinque, I'm sorry about all of this, but I need to talk to you about your son. I'll need you to come with me."

I didn't have the energy to respond, and on weak legs, I got up and managed to drag my body down the hall after him. It was like my body was numb, and I couldn't form any logical thoughts. I wanted to break loose from this place and go back to the day before yesterday so that I could do it all over again. I thought about making a break for it and jetting from the hospital, but where would I go? Jazz's family would just come find me and beat the shit out of me again. I just wasn't ready to deal with all of this, and although I was sure leaving the situation wouldn't make it better I just didn't want to be around. I needed a do over.

When we got to the doctor's office, I took a seat in one of the leather chairs that sat in front of his desk. Eyeing the photos of his family that were strategically placed around his office made me sad. The smiling faces of his wife and kids made me pray even more that everything with Jazz and Jordan would come out okay. I just couldn't take any more bad news.

Looking through the file, the doctor looked like he was trying to formulate the right words to let me know what was going on with my family. I wondered if he ever cheated on his wife. From the pictures he looked to be in love and living a happy life, but I knew enough to know that a picture didn't tell the entire story. A picture was just a snapshot, a brief moment in time that was captured by chance that we could never get back again. It wasn't real life, it was just a moment.

"Mr. Cinque, your son will need a blood transfusion," the doctor explained in a sympathetic voice. "Since your wife is already in a fragile state I'm suggesting we get the blood donation from you as opposed to getting it from the blood bank and risking your son contracting hepatitis down the line," he explained to me. I could see the sorrow in his eyes, and I wondered briefly if it was genuine or if he was just doing his job.

"That's not a problem. How is my son doing? Can I see him?" I asked, trying to control the tears that made my chest ache all over again.

"You can see him, but I have to warn you that there are a lot of tubes exiting his body. He is on a breathing machine as he cannot breathe on his own from the puncture wound that has been fixed in his right lung. He got the worst of the damage because his side of the car was the side that struck the pole and was wrapped around it. The other kids got some bumps and bruises, but they were able to be released and are with your wife's mother."

I felt like I was going to pass out. If I would have just taken my ass home instead of sitting up in that damn strip club none of this would be going on right now. I should have just gone to get the kids. I wasn't built for this kind of shit, and I knew I had to get some strength from somewhere to deal with it. Accepting a tissue from the box the doctor held in my direction, I got myself together so that I could handle my business. I had to be strong for my family.

"Thank you for everything you've done so far. Can I please see my son now?" I asked in a voice that I didn't recognize.

"Yes, I'll take you out to see your son, but we need to stop past the outpatient lab first to collect your blood so that we can get it ready for him. Do you know your blood type?"

"No, I actually don't," I responded, feeling stupid that I didn't know that information. I didn't regularly donate blood or anything like that, and before now I had no real reason to be up on the kind of thing.

"No problem, we get that a lot. We will get all of that information once we send up the samples."

I followed the doctor into a sterile lab that was on the next floor down, where several tubes of my blood were taken. They could have taken every drop of blood from my body at that moment if it would save my son. I remembered it like it was yesterday when I saw him come into the world. His tiny hands and feet, and those eyes . . . it was something about him that I just couldn't place, but the joy of seeing him replaced all of the questions I had in my head. Our family had grown, and that's all that mattered.

The phlebotomist expertly drew my blood, and I could tell she tried not to stare at the scars on my face. When she inquired if I was in the accident I just told her I was to keep down the confusion. She didn't need to know my business. Once I was bandaged up I was escorted to my son's room, where the doctor waited for me outside. The curtains were drawn so that I couldn't see inside, and I was grateful for that. I wasn't prepared to just walk up on him like I had been forced to do with Jazz. I needed to get myself together for this one.

"Mr. Cinque—" the doctor began, but I cut him off.

"Please, call me James," I insisted.

"James," the doctor continued with a look of concern on his face, "your son is in critical condition, but he is stabilized. You're going to get emotional, but please be aware that although he is sedated he can still hear you. I'll be standing right out here if you need me."

He gave me a reassuring smile, and backed away from the door, allowing me to enter on my own. I stood at the door, trying to steady my breathing and brace myself for the unknown. I never imagined having to see any of my kids like this and the shit was really tearing me up on the inside.

When I opened the door tears flooded my eyes, and my feet felt stuck to the floor. *If I could only trade places with him.* There were tubes everywhere pumping different colored fluids into his little body. The machine that controlled his lungs made a soft swishing sound and a small beep permeated the air every so often. My baby . . . he was only four years old. If he didn't come out of this alive I couldn't possibly keep living.

As I finally crept toward him I wondered what Janice would do without him. They'd been joined at the hip since conception, and moved like synchronized swimmers, often finishing each other's sentences. She was too young to understand death, and I hadn't the slightest clue how to get a four-year-old to understand that her best friend would be gone forever.

Placing those thoughts aside, I went over and took my son's small hand into mine. Looking into his swollen face, I could hardly recognize him beyond the bruises. He had his mother's lips though, and I leaned down to brush my lips against his cheek to let him know I was there. Placing the chair next to his bed, I took a seat and leaned into the bed so that I could whisper into his ear. I needed him to come back to me as soon as possible.

"I love you, son," I began, getting choked up immediately. "And I want you to know that we're all waiting for you."

I held his hand as the tears cascaded down my face and wet the side of the bed. I promised God that if He pulled my wife and my son through this I would be the man He intended me to be. I had promised Him this many times before, but this was the straw that broke the camel's back. I had to get my family unit back together.

"Mr. Cinque." A nurse came to the door, interrupting my racing thoughts. "The news vans just arrived. Do you want to get cleaned up a little bit? One of your associates from TUNN brought you a change of clothes for the press conference."

Looking down at my son, I gave him a kiss on the cheek, hoping it wouldn't be my last. Letting his hand go, I followed her to a private room where I was able to shower and change my clothes, afterward meeting back up with Jazz's family right outside of her room. There was nothing I could do about the black ring that had formed under my right eye, or the scratches along the side of my face and neck, and at this point I didn't care what the media thought. I just needed to update the world on my wife and keep it moving.

"Is it possible for me to have a minute alone with my wife before I go out?" I asked one of my associates, who came to capture the story among the other news stations that would be present.

"Sure, but we go on in ten."

Nodding my head, I stepped into my wife's room, closing the door behind me. As I looked down at her I remembered our wedding day, and how hype we were about getting back to the hotel to consummate our vows only for us to fall asleep when we got there. I remembered how she went from having a flat belly to carrying a huge beach ball that held our first set of twins. I remembered how much I loved her, and how I needed her in my life.

"Jazz, I need you back," I spoke into her ear as I held her hand. "Our kids need you . . . and I need you. Please, make it back to me."

Kissing her on the cheek, I dried my eyes with the back of my hand and straightened my tie in the reflection off the glass. Getting myself together as best I could, I went out and prepared to talk. Jazz's family seemed less angry and more supportive, and I was relieved that they were no longer throwing daggers at me with their eyes. We were all scared, and concerned, and I understood how they felt.

When I stepped up to the podium in the hospital's conference room I trained my eyes on the camera and tried to check my emotions. The tape hadn't even started rolling good, and I was already in tears.

"I regret to inform you that my wife and son are both in intensive care from the accident. From what I understand, the car slid out of control on an icy street in last night's storm, causing the accident," I explained to the media, getting choked up and having to stop several times. I tried my best to continue, but it got extremely hot all of a sudden and I felt like the room was closing in. All I heard next was somebody call for a doctor as I hit the floor, and the room went black.

Chapter 9

Monica: Let the Truth Be Told

My eyes were glued to the TV as I stopped mid-pack to listen to the press conference that James was giving on Jasmine's status. My heart sank when he said that his son was hurt as well, but he passed out before everyone could get the rest of the scoop. Was that my son he was talking about? They had three boys; which one was it?

I sat on the bed and waited for them to come back with the broadcast, but it seemed as though that fool might be out for the count for a while. The accident site from the previous night was shown again, and I cringed on the inside at the sight of the Jeep wrapped around the pole and the medics working the Jaws of Life to get them out. They all could have died, and from the looks of the tragedy many people might have thought they already were dead if they hadn't seen the news coverage.

Just as I grabbed my phone to call the judge it rang, flashing the judge's name and picture across the screen. The car he sent for me must have arrived, and I wasn't even halfway packed because I was distracted by the breaking news. The judge didn't like to be kept waiting, and I knew I had to get moving or he would get an attitude.

"Hey, baby," I spoke into the phone in my sweetest voice.

"Monica, the car is outside. Time is money, and I've been sitting here with a brick-hard dick for way too long."

My smile was wiped away immediately, and I started to give it to his arrogant ass and read him his rights, but I still needed him. *This one I'll let slide, but I can't say I'll be that nice the next time.* The judge knew who was really running this show, but I let him feel like he had the upper hand so that I could keep getting my way. It was so much easier and stress free.

"I'm walking out the door now," I responded through a forced smile.

"That's what I like to hear," he said in a deep voice, sounding like he might have been stroking himself in anticipation. "Oh, and Monica?"

"Yes, Judge?" I responded as I threw the last few things I owned in my bag.

"Wear a trench coat and red heels . . . nothing else."

"Yes, Judge," I responded flirtatiously and began removing my Ugg boots from my feet. The judge had long money, and for him nothing was off-limits. Never mind it was dead winter and about five whole degrees on the outside. He always got what he wanted . . . and I got whatever it was I wanted. *This time, it's for my son.*

After quickly changing my clothes, I called to have my bags taken down to the car. Of course my sexy little bellhop friend showed up looking sad because I was checking out, and I wished I had a few extra minutes to break him off before I left, but money called.

Once my bags were stacked neatly into the trunk I was whisked off to what would be my home while I was here in the city. I tried to bring up the news on my phone just in case James came back to finish out the report, but I couldn't get a live stream. While I was riding, I couldn't help but wonder what my son looked like now. He probably looked like James, as the rest of his kids did.

Honestly, I wondered if I was doing the right thing. Who was I to come and disrupt this boy's life after I abandoned him like last season's Louis Vuitton? Did I even have the right to be here preparing to wreck shop? Like I had that right . . . I entertained the thought of just spending the week with the judge until the coast was clear and I got enough money from him, but that tight feeling in my gut told me I needed to be here. Something was about to pop off, and I felt like my boy needed me. Pulling out my iPod to sooth my nerves, I connected it to the USB port in the stereo system, and turned up my Floetry CD. I needed to get my mind off of the problems I was having because I knew once I got to the judge I would need to focus all of my attention on him.

I must have nodded off, because when I opened my eyes again the car was pulling up into the circular driveway of the judge's getaway spot. It looked like they might have gotten some outside landscaping down, and I was impressed at what I could see since everything was covered in snow. The brick facing on the house looked new, as well as the door. There was also a cute gazebo that looked like in the warmer months it would be surrounded by a flower garden. The grassy area in the center of the circular driveway had a cute fountain that wasn't there before, and I could only imagine the serenity of the running water during the warmer months.

The driver came to a gentle, rolling stop, and jumped out to assist me in getting out. Gathering my trench coat around me to protect me from the wind, after checking that my face was still intact, I slipped a Tic Tac in my mouth and strutted up the walkway to the door like I was on a runway in Paris during Fashion Week.

Taking the steps one at a time, I knew I looked scrumptious, and felt sexy as the crisp air caressed my moist clit when my legs parted to take a step up. Before I could touch the knob, the judge had swung the door open and was standing there himself in a house robe and slippers with a tobacco pipe dangling from his mouth. Damn he looked good.

Forever the distinguished gentleman, he smiled as he stepped back and removed my bag from my hand. I sauntered past him, knowing his eyes were traveling the length of my body, and he was removing my trench coat in his mind. I turned to face him just as he was giving the butler orders to take my belongings up to the master bedroom, and to leave out of the back door. Finally facing me, I did just as he did and took all of him in.

He was still extremely sexy. Smooth skin, thick lips to match his even thicker dick, and a fresh cut. He looked a little older . . . wiser, most would say, and I could see a little more gray peeking up at his temples and throughout his beard. Yeah, he still had it. He walked over to me with a confident swagger like he already knew he had me dripping wet. Once he got over to me, he took my hand in his and raised it above my head, turning my body in a small circle. Stopping me when I was facing him, he planted a sensual kiss on my lips, stepping back only to untie the sash on my coat.

He looked pleased as he slowly opened my coat to reveal the surprise inside like he was unwrapping a Hershey's Kiss. Of course I kept a flawless body, and the look in his eyes let me know that I was indeed the truth. He ran his tongue across his lips, tasting the corners like he was hungry and ready to eat. Leaning forward he took one chocolate nipple into his mouth, moaning out loud, and then took the other doing the same. I kept a serious face, thankful for the heat on my back from the fireplace. I didn't want him to know he had me open that fast.

Turning in my heels, I stood still as he removed my coat from my shoulders and allowed it to pool around my feet in a soft puddle of cashmere and silk. Stepping over it, I cat-walked toward the chaise longue because it was closest to the fire, making sure he saw my plump ass bounce with each step. He always told me I could have been a model, and I kept a flawless tight body just to keep him guessing.

Stretching out on the chaise with one leg bent at the knee, and the other on the floor, my legs were partly open waiting for him to come and taste me. He circled the chair smoothly, stopping to take in the vision. The flames cast shadows all over my body as I glistened like a shiny new penny. I could tell he was trying to go slow with the flow and not bum-rush me. It had been awhile since he'd had me like this, and he was savoring the moment.

As he got closer he came out of his robe, revealing a tight, muscular chest and flat tummy that I didn't quite remember him having. Somebody had been working out, and I liked it. He had the body of a man in his early thirties, and it was too bad he didn't have the stamina to match. He was usually known for only lasting a good ten minutes; that's why I would always milk the hell out of a foreplay session. *Who knows? Maybe this new body came with new dick control?* I smiled, showing him I was pleased.

He moved toward me, kneeling beside me, spreading my legs wider. My pussy glistened with a sticky wetness that he wasted no time sticking the tip of his tongue in. Catching my clit between his lips, I gasped as he sucked and slurped me into his mouth causing my body to convulse. His huge hands delicately caressed and pinched my nipples sending shock waves through my body. I couldn't control my pelvis from grinding into his face, smearing a glazed layer all over it. I moaned and bucked under him as he lifted my leg up and placed it over his shoulder so that he could get closer.

An orgasm started building up in my gut, and I was trying my best to hold it in, but the judge was steadily dragging it out of me. He fucked my pussy with a stiff tongue that had me ready to pass the hell out, and just when I thought I couldn't take any more the floodgates opened, and I released a river of honey down his throat and all over his neck.

"Please, let it go . . ." I begged as he held my clit captive, forcing wave after wave of orgasmic pleasure to crash against it, making me delirious. I must say I didn't remember the judge being this phenomenal orally, and I silently gave kudos to whoever taught this old dog some new tricks.

His fingers invaded my space, and caused me to jump as he stuffed two of them inside of my tight, wet hole. I bounced up and down on them like I was riding a good stiff dick, bringing myself to another mind-blowing orgasm that almost wiped me out. Somebody was playing for keeps, and I was not mad about it at all.

He licked me slowly from my opening to my clit allowing me to calm down and control my breathing. I swear if he had a close neighbor they would have thought someone was trying to kill me with all the hollering and screaming I just did. I felt like he literally sucked the life out of me, no pun intended. I knew for sure I was going to have to put in some work after that performance.

He rose up from between my legs with a glazed but a happy look on his face. His pajama bottoms tented in the pelvic area letting me know he was ready to go in. I sat up and took hold of it, stroking it through the material of his pants, causing his eyes to close and his head to lean back. A small circle started to form from the pre-cum that I was pulling from him, and I hoped he would last this time.

Using my feet to pull his pants down, I continued to stroke him, taking the liberty of tasting the clear fluid that dripped from the head of his dick. He seemed to have gotten bigger, the mushroom head barely fitting in my hand. Closing my mouth around the head, he moaned as I took him into my mouth an inch at a time until he was balls deep into my throat. I had learned a trick or three myself, and I was more than willing to show him.

Massaging his balls, and inserting a finger into his asshole at the same time, had the judge screaming louder than I was as his legs began to tremble. He tried to back away from me, but the sensation was too good and he leaned toward me instead. Releasing him, and gargling his balls in my mouth had him on opera status and I knew I had him just where I wanted him.

Letting him go completely, I leaned back in the chaise and massaged my swollen clit, palming my breasts with the other hand as I leaned down to take my nipples into my mouth. The judge struggled to get to his knees, and came down into a kneeling position on the chaise right in front of me. Just as he was aiming his dick for the target, I stopped him.

"What's wrong, baby?" he asked between gasps as his dick twitched in his hands. I simply swung my legs around him and stood up.

"We can get back to this in a minute," I told him in a serious tone. "Right now, I need to know what's up with my son."

Chapter 10

James: Day-mares and Night Dreams

When I came to I was stretched out in a hospital bed with a bandage on my head. The last thing I remembered was doing the press conference, and everything went black. I couldn't even remember if I got everything out, but I knew for sure that my head was pounding like crazy. When I opened my eyes a nurse was leaning over me taking my vitals, and shining a light in my now open eyes.

"Mr. Cinque, that was a pretty nasty fall you took," she said, smiling down at me while checking my head dressing. My dress shirt was now gone, and all I had on were my slacks and a wife beater. Through the window I could see Jazz's family talking with the doctor.

"What happened? All I remember . . ." I began, but she cut me off.

"Don't talk. I just gave you pain medicine for your headache so let it kick in. The doctor will be in to talk to you shortly."

Taking her advice, I nestled into the pillow and closed my eyes, trying to slow down the drums pounding on my temple. What was going on in my life? I said a quick prayer, hoping some mercy would be thrown my way. When they say "what goes around comes around" they weren't lying.

"How are you feeling?" Jazz's brother asked as he entered the room. My head began to pound more upon seeing him. When were they going to leave?

"I'm okay. Head killing me." I gave a dry response. It was obvious that my damn head hurt considering it was bandaged up. I wasn't sure of what happened but I must have banged it up when I passed out.

"Yeah, that was a pretty nasty hit. They had to wheel you out on a gurney and everything. Of course the media was snapping pictures left and right, but they got you out fairly quickly. Glad to see you awake."

"Thanks, man," I responded before closing my eyes again, hopefully indicating that I was done talking. Too much was happening too fast, and I just needed some quiet. That was short-lived once I heard the doctor enter the room.

"Mr. Cinque, glad to see that you're up. That's a nasty bump you have on your head there, but the CAT scan came back normal, and there are no signs of any internal damage. You just have a pretty nasty gash where your head struck the podium," the doctor spoke to me in a calm tone as he looked over my chart.

"Thanks, Doc," I spoke to him in a groggy voice. "Is the media still here? I need to finish the update."

"What you need to do is rest. You've been through a lot in the past twenty-four hours, and you need to relax yourself. I need you to be on your A game for your wife and son."

"And how are they doing?" I asked, hoping nothing drastic had happened while I was unconscious.

"Your wife and son are still in stable condition. The blood that you gave is in the lab being tested for any trace of disease as well as to identify your blood type since you didn't know that information just as I explained to you earlier. It shouldn't take much longer, and as soon as everything comes back clear we will proceed with your son. I'm thinking everything will come back okay."

"That's great to hear," I said while gingerly touching the side of my head. "When will I get to see them both?"

"In a little while, the medicine you were just given may put you to sleep in a little while depending on how your body reacts to it. Once you awaken I'll allow you to see your family. Also, you're scheduled to do another press conference in the morning, and I don't want you passing out again," he said with a gentle smile.

"Thanks for everything, Doc," I responded, feeling the effects of the medicine kicking in.

"No problem, Mr. Cinque. I'll be here in the morning. If you need anything, my brother will be covering the overnight shift and is aware of your situation. He'll do anything that's needed to make your stay comfortable."

I couldn't keep my eyes open to respond and found myself drifting off. *It felt like I was still awake, because I was sitting next to my wife's bed watching her sleep. She didn't look as beat up as I remembered, and almost all of her scars were gone. The kids, even Jordan, were sitting out in the waiting area outside of the room watching TV, and I wondered when Jordan had gotten out of the ICU. Jasmine's mom and dad were out there, and everyone looked happy.*

Just when I went to get up to use the restroom, Jasmine's hand shot out and grabbed a hold of my wrist. When I looked at her, her eyes were bloodshot and she had a sad look on her face. I was scared, and I knew my face showed it but I couldn't move or speak. All I could do was look her in her eyes.

"James, I'm sorry this happened to us," she spoke in a sad tone as tears streamed from her eyes.

"Honey, it's okay," I responded, finally finding my voice. "Just let me get the doctor, and . . ."

"I have something I need to tell you about the kids," she replied, the tears turning a crimson red as they ran down her face and soaked the sheet that was tucked in around her neck. I wanted to call to get the doctor but she had a death grip on me.

"Jazz, let me go get the doctor. You're bleeding."

"But the kids," she said through her tears. "I need to tell you about the kids. The second set of twins . . ."

Before she could say another word I managed to snatch my wrist from her grip and run to the hall to get the doctor. It felt like the hallway was the length of a football stadium as I ran down it in slow motion to reach the doctor who was standing at a nurse's station. They looked animated as they laughed out loud at something they were reading in a chart. When I finally got close to them, they stopped briefly to look at me, and then burst out laughing again.

"Doctor," I said out of breath as I leaned against the counter. "My wife opened her eyes . . . She's bleeding everywhere!"

The doctor didn't say a word, and simply walked around me and headed down the hallway toward Jazz's room. I followed him, but my feet felt like I was walking through quicksand. I hoped Jasmine didn't bleed to death by the time we got back there because we were moving slow as fuck. Why hadn't anyone called for the EMT or anything yet? I knew for sure that if my wife was dead when I got to her room all hell was going to break loose.

Both the doctor and I arrived to the door at the same time, and I was preparing to see blood everywhere and my wife to look like a shriveled-up prune. To my surprise Jasmine looked like I remembered her: bandaged up with scrapes and bruises with her eyes closed. There was no blood anywhere, and the beep from the life support machine could be heard.

"Mr. Cinque, your wife looks fine, but you look horrible on the other hand," the doctor said in an animated voice like you hear in those scary movies.

"Excuse me?" I asked, wiping the moisture from my eyes only to find blood on my hands.

"Mr. Cinque, you're bleeding all over the place," the doctor said, followed by laughter. As I looked around, everyone, including Jasmine and the kids, was pointing and laughing at me as my blood oozed out of my body and created a puddle on the floor.

The puddle began to swirl around me and create a black hole that I began to sink into. I was calling out for help, but couldn't hear my voice, and everyone was still just pointing and laughing like I didn't need help. I could see Jasmine getting out of the bed and walking toward the door as my body sunk lower into the floor. The look she gave me could have killed me alone if looks could kill. She gave me a sinister snarl as flames began to lick at me feet.

"Thanks, Doc, for helping me with this," she said as she smiled down at me. "Now, me and my kids can live our lives with their real father."

I began to scream, and just as the hole was closing over my head I woke up. The nurse was standing next to the bed checking my vitals. My heart had to have been beating a million miles a minute because I was sweating profusely, and my head pounded more than it did earlier.

"Must have been having a bad dream, huh?" the nurse asked as she removed the blood pressure cup from my forearm. "Try to relax, Mr.

Cinque. The morning will be here before you know it."

I couldn't form any words as I lay on the bed with my eyes closed trying to figure it all out. I'd had the feeling before that the second set of twins were possibly not mine, but I never brought it up because of my own dirt. Was the dream revealing something to me that I knew all along? This was just too much for one person to deal with, and I just needed to rest. After the nurse left I twisted around in the bed until I found a comfortable position and willed myself to go back to sleep, hoping my dream didn't pick back up where it left off or got worse off than it was before. Too many skeletons in the closet lead to nightmares, and I knew eventually once things got back to normal that Jazz and I would have to hash it out. That was if we both wanted to sleep peaceful at night. I knew I did.

Chapter 11

Monica: Taking Care of Business

"Monica, do we have to talk about this now?" the judge asked me as he sat with a look of disbelief. His once erect penis was now starting to shrivel back down to a soft lump in his lap. I knew he wanted to hurt me at the moment, but he was a smart man. He still had some pussy to get.

"Not in its entirety, but I do need you to understand a few things," I responded as I turned and moved back closer to him. "I'm certain that the city will be up and operating by the morning, so I'll need you to get on it with info about my son."

"Okay, but that's in the morning. What does that have to do with what's happening right now?" he asked in a desperate voice as he began to grow again.

"Just in case I have to take my son back with me, I need things to be handled properly," I said as I kneeled down in front of him, and began to stroke his erection. I was really rooting for the Cinques and hoping that everything was on point so that I could just go back home. I was in no way, shape, or form ready to be on mommy duty, and the sooner I found out that everything was good the faster I could roll out from this dreaded city. Watching his eyes roll up into the back of his head made me smile a little. Yeah, I definitely still had it.

"Monica," he said through deep breaths as he grew longer and began to pulsate, "you have to keep in mind that you gave up all rights when you left four years ago. You can't just swoop back in and take him away from the only family he's ever known."

"But he's my son," I argued as I cupped his balls in my warm hands and continued to stroke him.

"But he doesn't know that."

It felt like all the sound in the house went mute. I could no longer here the logs crackling in the fireplace, or the desperate pants coming from the judge's mouth. The truth of the situation hit harder now than I thought it would after hearing someone else say it out loud, and he was right. My son thought Jasmine was his mother. It was different when I said it to myself a hundred times a day for three years straight, but from out of the mouth of someone else sealed the deal and brought it all into perspective. Sensing the change of the mood, the judge looked down at me with a confused look on his face.

"Monica, come on. You knew all of this would happen. The bigger question is, why after all this time have you shown up? Why are you trying to disrupt everyone's lives?"

"Because I feel like something is going on," I responded as I let go of him and brushed tears from my eyes.

"And why do you feel that way? The Cinques are a good family."

"Well, if they are a good family, why did my checks started coming back with no forwarding address?" I questioned, getting more upset by the second.

"They probably felt it was time to move on, Monica. Damn, did you forget all of the nonsense and headaches? The real reason you are here is not for your son, anyway," he said, standing and grabbing his pajama pants from the floor. Stepping into them hastily, he reached for his robe and slipped it on, leaving me naked and frazzled.

"What other reason would I have to be here?" I asked, confusion lacing my voice. I was not ready to be a mom, I had to admit that, but I felt like my son needed me.

"You're here," he said in a matter-of-fact tone, "because you're hoping that Jasmine still loves you."

Boom!

That shit felt like a slap in the face, but was it truth to that? I did still love Jazz. I'll admit that, because you don't just stop loving someone. I dreamed about her plenty of nights, and I could still remember how her body felt in my hands. I closed my eyes and pictured my tongue exploring her body, and my pussy got wet all over again.

"That's not why I'm here," I responded weakly.

"Listen, I'm going to have a cigar and a little bite to eat. Go ahead and get yourself together and meet me back here in an hour. I'll have some food sent up to you to get your strength back up. When you come back I don't want to hear anything more about the kid or the family he's with. There is nothing that we can do about that today. We will handle it in the morning. Understand?" he asked with a stern look on his face that said he meant business.

I didn't bother to respond because he had already set the rules. Grabbing my bag from the couch, and my trench coat from the floor, I made my way to the master suite where I would be spending the week, permitting I found out what I needed to know about my son in that amount of time. After I got myself situated I took a quick shower, where I allowed myself to cry for the first time in years. I felt so confused about being back home in Philly, but I knew there was a reason why I had to be here. It was hard to explain, and I didn't expect the judge to understand, but I needed his help.

A mother, regardless of any situation unless she really doesn't care, has a connection with her child. Even more so when she has to get rid of the child for whatever reason she has. Although the child isn't in your possession, you can still feel if the child needs you. It's a gut feeling that can't be ignored. I believed it may have been different had I never held him, or if I had cut all ties and just rolled out, but because James kept in contact with me up until I changed my number, I saw all of the things that I would have otherwise missed out on. No, I didn't see him take his first steps in person, but a hundred times I played the video that James sent me as I cried myself to sleep feeling bad about what I had done.

That was only to get up in the morning with puffy eyes, convincing myself that I had done the right thing. No, I wasn't there during the teething process, but when that first little Tic Tac–shaped tooth showed up in his mouth, I got the picture message of my smiling baby showing off his new tooth. On his first day going to daycare I got the picture of him with his cute little outfit, and matching book bag. All of these things took a toll on me, and I just couldn't keep torturing myself. I had to move on, and I needed closure. I was doing good, too, up until that first check came back with no return address and I found out that the numbers I had for James didn't work. That feeling in my gut told me I needed to be here, and I didn't regret the decision I made at all.

By the time I got out of the shower, there was a tray resting on the side of the bed with food on it just as the judge said. I took the time to dry off and moisturize, tucking the towel under my arms. Taking a second, I enjoyed the fruit and cheese and spiced meats that were there for me. I knew I would have to come correct when I got back downstairs so that the judge would cooperate.

Going into my stash, I dusted honeydew powder all over my body. It added a nice shimmer, and tasted sweet. So wherever the judge kissed me he would taste it. I slipped into a lace red boy short with matching bra, and blood-red pumps to match. Checking my hair in the mirror, I was satisfied as I applied a neutral coat of lip gloss to my plump lips. I had pissed the judge off, so I had to bring my A game this time around.

As I walked through the house back toward the chimney, I found the judge sitting in a cushioned chair by the fire smoking a cigar. I would have to work through the wall he undoubtedly had up, but the judge couldn't resist me so it shouldn't have been too hard. As I rounded the chair I stood posed in front of him with my back facing him so that he could take it all in. I could feel the heat from his eyes as they traveled my body from head to toe. Doing a slow spin, I faced him with a mischievous look on my face, ready to handle my business.

He didn't crack a smile, and actually looked disinterested, but that didn't discourage me. He was playing hardball, and I was cool with that since it wouldn't last long. Stepping toward him, I leaned down and kissed him on the mouth where we intertwined our tongues in a seductive dance. Continuing my kisses down the side of his neck, I made sure to pay special attention to his nipples because that would definitely start the melting process. I could feel his erection press against my stomach as I drew circles around his nipples with my fingertips, lightly scratching his chest as I continued to travel south.

Caressing him through his silk pajamas turned me the hell on, and I had to catch myself from drooling on them. When the head peeked through the slit in his pants, I didn't hesitate to put my mouth around it, and take as much of him in as I could. I convinced myself that I just needed to enjoy this and not think about anything else. The anxious feeling in my stomach started to subside as I worked the judge into a frenzy.

Standing up, I allowed him to remove my bra and panties, and I took a seat on the lounge chair so that we could pick up where we left off. He came over behind me and took his time tasting my body. He licked and nibbled on me like he was starving, and I could tell he was enjoying the taste of the honeydew dust that covered me. Pushing my legs back, he captured my clit and slurped all of me into his mouth. I could feel my body reacting, and an orgasm quickly approaching, but I couldn't stop it. I wanted to make him work for it, but that plan didn't seem to be going so well.

By the time he got done with me I was begging him for the dick, and he was more than happy to oblige. Placing my legs on his shoulders, he took his place in between my legs, transfixed on the bull's eye just as he was earlier. My juices were steadily gushing out in anticipation, and he looked like he couldn't wait to get wet.

"Don't think you're going to stop me this time. Once I get in there I'm in it until it's over. Understand?" He spoke in a husky voice that meant business. I didn't even get a chance to answer before he shoved himself inside of me.

I was sloppy wet as he pushed and pulled in and out of me. I was sure my moans could be heard for miles as I stroked his ego with my words and tight pussy. He was killing it though, and for a second there I couldn't handle him pounding into me. He took my legs and positioned them at his side, and flipped me over on my side. I was nervous about falling off of the chaise, but he held on to me as he positioned himself under me so that I could ride him backward. I had to steady myself on my knees, and once I got my shoes off I was ready to go in.

"You miss this pussy?" I asked him as I slammed down onto him, making my ass bounce around for his viewing pleasure.

"You miss this dick?" he countered as he met me thrust for thrust. We were playing a wicked game, and I was betting that I would get him to bust first.

"Yes, baby, I missed it," I responded as I tried to control my orgasm. I couldn't let him win, but he got me when he reached around and circled my clit with his fingertip. That shit sent me over the edge, and I almost lost it.

"See, your problem is you're always trying to control everything," he spoke as he forced my body to lean back and connect with his. "You never want to let go and enjoy the moment, do you, Monica?" he asked as he pulled on my clit, and palmed my breasts.

I couldn't answer if I wanted to because my body was feeling something I never felt before. He had me stretched out on his legs, but he was still penetrating me to the fullest, slow grinding me into convulsions. I was also surprised that he hadn't crashed it yet, and was thoroughly enjoying the ride.

He lifted my body up and bent me over, standing behind me on the side of the chaise. Easing himself back inside of me, he went at a steady rhythm, speeding up a little more as he got closer to exploding.

"I've been waiting for too long to have you like this. You ready for me to explode, baby?"

"Yes, I'm ready," I replied as I braced myself for him. I was spent, and really couldn't take any more of the pounding he was putting on me. Hell, maybe he was taking vitamins or even Viagra, but whatever it was I was happy that he was doing it. The judge I knew from back then would have been crashed. Even when we hooked up after one of my benefits not too long ago, it wasn't this good.

"Yeah, take that shit," I moaned out, causing the scene to intensify. He grabbed my hips, and zoned in causing another explosion to build up in me in the process. We were both gasping for air, and I could hardly contain myself. Just as I was reaching up, I turned in time to see the judge grab his chest and fall back. Was this man having a heart attack?

"Call . . . call the butler. Tell him to get help," he gasped as he held his chest. The look on his face was excruciating, and I started to panic. I knew I had a killer pussy, but damn.

Running toward the kitchen, I grabbed the phone and dialed the numbers next to the word "butler" on the call log. Once I informed him of what was happening, I raced back to the judge to check on him. He was in the same spot I found him, barely breathing and still holding his chest. I did my best to get his pants back on him, and even once the butler showed up a few minutes later I was still naked. There was a separate smaller structure on the side of the house, so I assumed that was where the butler stayed on the property. He didn't seem to notice as he dressed the judge in sweats and sneakers. I took the liberty of jetting upstairs and throwing on sweats and my Uggs so that I could travel along.

I found it weird that an ambulance wasn't called, but I didn't say a word as I held his head in my lap all the way to the hospital. I assumed his wife wasn't called, and I didn't ask. I wasn't even sure where we were going, but as luck would have it we pulled up to the University of Pennsylvania Hospital, the same hospital where the Cinques were. *Let the games begin . . .*

Chapter 12

James: Ghost of Ménage à Trois Past

I had a splitting headache. It seemed worse now than it did before I went to sleep. It could be from not eating or the bump I got on my head, but whatever it was drained the hell out of me. I sat up on the side of the bed just as the nurse was coming in to take my vitals. Too many events happened within the matter of a day and a half, and I was over it.

"Good morning, Mr. Cinque," the jolly nurse said as she scanned my chart. This nurse was different from the one who was taking care of me last night. She was cuter, too. My eyes traveled her curves, but I forced my mind to go in another direction.

"Good morning," I managed to mumble as I held the side of my head.

"Seems like you still have a headache, huh?" she replied, finally looking me in the face. "I'll get you something for that to go along with your breakfast. Sit back on the bed for me so that I can take your vitals."

Scooting back on the bed, I chanced a glance out the door, hoping Jasmine's family was gone. I was contemplating making a dash for it, but to my dismay her brothers were resting in chairs just outside the door. This shit was like a never-ending nightmare. I felt like I was in jail, and her family were the guards making sure I stayed in place.

I closed my eyes for a split second just as a "code thirty" was announced over the loudspeaker. I could see the nurses rushing, and I wondered if it had anything to do with my wife or my son.

"What does that code mean?" I asked as she quickly took notes in my chart.

"Someone came in under cardiac arrest," she replied nonchalantly as she continued to write in my chart. Soon after I could hear the commotion in the hallway as people started running by. I got a glimpse of a person on a stretcher, but what caught my eye was the woman running beside it. *Was that Monica who just ran past?* I shook my head and rubbed my eyes. The crowd had already passed, but I was still stunned. If it was her, what was she doing in Philly? When did she get here?

"Mr. Cinque, your tray should be arriving soon. I'll put in an order for your pain meds as well. Continue to rest, and I'll be back in a little while."

I shook my head, acknowledging that I heard her, but my mind was gone. Was that really Monica? I had to get a look, but I knew I would have to wait. Everyone would want to know why I was looking around the hospital for a strange person.

Just as I settled back into the bed my breakfast was brought in by a dietary aide. She was even cuter than the nurse who was there, and I had to keep myself from staring at her as well. *What's wrong with me?*

"Good morning," she said with a smile. "Fill out this menu card for your lunch and dinner and I will collect it from you when I come back for your tray."

I gave her a warm smile as she positioned my tray in front of me and made sure my bed was adjusted. I wanted to see my son, and my wife. Did I have to wait for the doctor to see them? Just as I was going to buzz the nurse she came in with a woman from venipuncture.

"Mr. Cinque, she's going to draw some blood from you this morning," the nurse replied as she looked through my chart.

"What for?" I asked her as I held my arm out to be punctured.

"The doctor will be in shortly to discuss that with you."

I tried not to watch because I hated needles, but I couldn't help it. The phlebotomist was quick with drawing the seven or eight tubes of blood that she was instructed to get from me. I didn't think anything of it. I always protected myself whenever I stepped out on Jazz so I wasn't worried about any disease. Once the young lady was done, I went back to eating my food, totally forgetting to ask the questions I intended. I still had to report the news on my wife, and TUNN was giving me another chance to do so, considering I didn't pass out again in the process. My wife's family, or even the doctor for that matter, could have done it but I wanted to be the one to deliver the news. She was my wife, and as her husband I felt like that was my responsibility. That's what she would have wanted.

I was done with my breakfast and watching the news by the time the doctor came in to talk to me. He had a look of concern on his face that got my attention. Pushing the tray to the side, I sat up on the side of the bed to brace myself for whatever he had to say. Maybe something slipped by that I didn't know about. I had a few wild nights, and a few broken condoms along the way. Although I'd never been burned with a sexually transmitted disease, I know enough to know that some diseases lie dormant and can show up at any time. What if now was the time? How would I explain it to everyone? I was nervous instantly, and needed the doctor to get to the point ASAP.

"Good morning, Mr. Cinque. How is the headache coming along?"

"Pretty good. Hurts less now that I've eaten," I responded as I looked around the room. "Ummm . . . there was more blood drawn this morning. What's wrong?"

"Nothing's wrong. I just want to make sure that everything was drawn correctly. There was a mishap with your blood in the lab yesterday, and the results were tainted. In order to give your blood to your son we have to ensure that everything is on point or it could prove fatal for him," the doctor responded as he made notes in my chart.

"Okay," I responded in confusion. "So, how long will it take for the results to come in? Did I test positive for a disease?" I asked on the verge of panic.

"I sent your blood up stat so it shouldn't take long being they messed up in the lab yesterday.

The ABO blood group typing test, which is a type of paternity/DNA test to determine your blood type and to ensure you are a match for your son, was compromised and that's an important factor to ensure that your blood type matches your son's for the transfusion process. If you are an O blood type, you are a universal donor and can donate to anyone, but only A types can go with other As and Bs can only go with other Bs, et cetera. If the blood type is not compatible very dangerous results will occur," he responded with a gentle look on his face. "In the meantime, you should prepare for the announcement. The news team is gathering in the auditorium, and the public is being let in. Your clothes are behind the door and toiletries have been set aside. If you need anything else the nurse will get it for you."

"Can I see my son and my wife before I do all of that?" I asked desperately.

"Sure you can. I'll have transport take you to both rooms."

After pushing my now empty tray to the side, I made use of the facilities and got myself prepared to stand in front of the camera again. Although I wasn't being released from the hospital just yet, the doctor gave me permission to make the announcement; then I would be right back in bed. By the time I finished getting dressed, transport was there to take me to see my family. I protested about the wheelchair, but was quickly reminded that it was hospital policy, so I gave up the fight and let them wheel me around.

We went to see my wife first, and I was sad to see that she looked exactly the same. The bruising and all. From the hall the machines could still be heard beeping, and the wires were still coming out of her like octopus tentacles. I checked my tears this time because I needed to stay strong for everyone, and I remembered that the doctor said she could still hear me. Not sure what I was expecting, but I guessed I was hoping for her to be a little better than the last time I saw her.

Bending down next to her ear I told her that I loved her, and I couldn't wait for her to wake up. Her fingers flinched a little, but her eyes remained closed. That was enough for me to know that she heard me. What if she didn't recognize me or the kids when she woke up? That was a possibility that the doctor discussed with me regarding her condition. How would the kids handle it? Especially the younger ones? How much different would Jazz be? After taking my seat back in the chair, I hung my head deep in thought and with a heavy heart as an escort wheeled me down to see my son.

The results were just the same with him. Nothing had changed since the last time I was here. I held his little hand in mine, and rubbed my thumb across the back of his hand. This was so unfair! Why didn't God just take me instead of taking my family through all this turmoil? I kissed him on his forehead and stared at him for a few more minutes with no response from him indicating that he knew I was there. Not a twitch or anything.

Taking a seat back in the wheelchair, I prepared myself for the update. It still didn't make sense to me to have to be wheeled around, and I figured I would have to get up and walk to the podium anyway. Once I got to the auditorium I could see a crowd gathering of news reporters and spectators, and I noticed that the podium was more wheelchair accessible and I wouldn't have to stand. In my eyes that painted a picture that I was more hurt than I was, but I guessed they were being cautious of my possibly fainting again.

The escort wheeled me up to the podium, and quietness went across the room as all eyes fell on me. Scanning the crowd, I saw the faces of my fellow coworkers from TUNN, and the good doctor was standing in the back. As I prepared to address the crowd, I could see the reporters from surrounding news stations getting their notepads together, scribbling down questions for me to answer. I was a nervous wreck, but I took a deep breath and pushed forward. Once I got through this I wouldn't have to do it again.

"I would like to thank you all for coming back out," I began in a shaky voice. All of a sudden this was too much to bear, and I didn't think I could do it.

"Take your time, son, and get it out," I heard Jazz's father say from behind me, and I wondered briefly when they had all appeared.

"Thank you for coming out," I said again in a clearer voice. "My wife, Jasmine Cinque, is a prominent lawyer here in the Philadelphia region, and I am sad to report that some time during the night a day ago she was in a really bad car accident that may have caused a bad brain injury. She is being kept asleep until the swelling in her brain goes down, and it will not be until the point that she wakes up that the doctors will be able to determine the true extent of the injuries."

A collective gasp filled the room as pens and pads connected and my every word was recorded. The news stations that were following the story had done a great job reporting Jazz's progress, and the spectators who were in the room only hyped the media up. I guessed it was one of those things where once information is confirmed to be true the weight of it all settles differently in people's minds, and it becomes real. Several microphones sat in front of me in a cluster from different news stations and newspapers alike, and I knew everyone was dying to be the first to report the news on my wife.

"Although she is on life support, she is in stable condition and the doctors believe that she will pull through just fine once the swelling goes down," I continued as I held back my tears. Simply saying out loud the state of my wife's condition brought me to tears. What if she didn't make it out? What would I do with all of these kids by myself?

"Was your wife speeding?" came the first question from the audience. I immediately got on the defensive. Even if she was, that didn't mean she deserved to be where she was now.

"I can't say for sure because I was not there when the accident took place. I met my wife and son here after the fact."

"Why was she out traveling in such horrible conditions?" Question number two came from the audience, and I zeroed in on the person who asked. He looked rather young, and may have been fresh to the reporting business. His goal,

I was sure, was to get the "drama" aspect of the story to print scandal. I refused to aid in the tainting of my wife's name.

"She was picking up our kids from afterschool care."

"Well, from my research here, it was understood that she was called out of a meeting because you hadn't gone to get them yet. Do you agree that all of this could have been avoided had you just stepped up to the plate?" the fresh-faced reporter responded as he flipped through a few pages of notes. Stunned, the audience turned from him back to me like we were in a tennis match. He caught me off guard with that one and I was sure it showed.

"I'm not too sure of your sources, nor are we here to discuss this in detail. The point of the fact is my wife is upstairs in a room fighting for her life. Those who know and love her deserve to know at least that much, and any scandal you are trying to dig up won't be addressed at this time," I responded in an even tone, although I was ready to come up out of this wheelchair and toss it at his big-headed ass.

"Which son is it? The adopted son or the biological?" came a feminine voice that I recognized immediately. Everyone's eyes, including mine, raced to the back of the room and landed on

Monica. I thought I'd seen her fly past my room earlier right after a man came by on a stretcher. Now my suspicions were confirmed, but I did not feel like dealing with her right now. What in the hell was she doing here?

I could see the pens scratching across pages, and a slight buzz could be heard as the element of surprise died down and more questions were thought up. Gripping the side of the wheelchair, I cleared my throat before answering. I had to keep my cool before I ended up doing this interview via satellite from prison.

Chapter 13

Monica: Answer That!

The look on his face was priceless, and I'd be lying if I said I wasn't enjoying it a little. Hell, the news weren't the only people in the world who needed answers. Did my son need me as much as my gut was telling me he did? I needed to know, and when I saw people gathering up in here, I was just being nosey while I was waiting on the verdict from the judge. Who knew I would walk in on the Cinque press conference? This was supposed to happen, and I wanted answers . . . now!

"It's my biological son," he responded in an even voice. "One last question and the interview will be closed."

He was pissed!

I was loving it!

Let the games begin!

I heard some reporter present him with another question, but I dipped out the back. I got my answer. It wasn't my son on his last leg, so I was okay for now. I would just need to find out where they lived so that I could make my next move. I would need the judge for that, and he needed to come out of this mess alive and alert.

After grabbing a cup of coffee from the cafeteria, I circled back around to the judge's room. I figured James would be awhile wrapping up the news conference after the last of the questions were answered, considering when it came to interviews one last question could turn into ten more , so I decided to stop past the patient information booth to see what I could find out. When I walked up I was greeted by an extremely attractive woman who looked to be in her thirties. Judging from her appearance, she definitely took pride in how she looked, even though she was sitting at a desk. She showed a bright smile through thick lips, and I briefly wondered how they would feel on my body. Deciding to test the waters, I stepped up next in line. Just in case I needed to use her later, I wanted to get her in my pocket now.

"How may I help you?" she asked with a wide smile and bright eyes. A closer look revealed a nice pair of kissable breasts. A little more than a handful . . . Made me wonder what color her nipples were.

"Hi, I'm here to see my brother. I believe he checked in yesterday. I can't remember what my mom said on the phone," I responded with slight embarrassment in my voice, the actress in me in full motion.

"That's not a problem. What's your brother's name?" she asked as she flipped through a few screens on her computer.

"James Cinque," I answered with confidence.

She took a few minutes to search the system, and after a second or two came up with his room number. Taking a piece of paper from a stack, she wrote down his info and passed it across the desk to me.

"Here you go," she said with a jolly tone in her voice. "Do you have a parking ticket? If so, I can validate it for you to get a discount on your parking. It's not a lot, but every little bit helps."

"No, I was dropped off," I lied, "but thanks for letting me know. I love your lip gloss by the way."

"Oh thanks." She smiled at me.

"Thank you."

After tucking the info in my back pocket, I backed away from the station, deciding to leave her be. I wasn't certain about her, but if I ran into her again I would definitely give her another try. What *did* disturb me a little was that anyone could walk up and get info on you, and the people at the desk didn't ask for identification or anything. I knew not to check into U of P if I was ever hiding out.

On my way back upstairs I got off of the elevator, and took in the scenery as I walked down the hall to the judge's room. The nurses bustling up and down the halls and in and out of rooms added an energy to the place that is only welcome in this type of setting. The sorrow seemingly saturated the walls as hushed tones and looks of grief painted the faces of family members who were awaiting the fates of loved ones. There were a lot of frowns around. Not one smiling face, except for the gentle, concerned looks of nurses and doctors in hopes of offering some comfort to the weary.

It was interesting to see people in their element, moving around and accomplishing whatever the goal of the day was. Halfway down the hall I came upon the section where the seating area for families was, and there were a group of kids sitting with an older woman who looked just like Jasmine. I almost tripped over my own feet when my eyes landed on the children. I mean, there they were . . . all of them. They were just sitting there in their own little worlds looking just as exhausted as everyone else. The scene tugged on my heartstrings something serious, and made me sad.

The last time I saw the Cinques' older two they were just toddlers. I couldn't believe how much they had grown. Just the daughter of the second set of twins was sitting there, which meant her twin brother was the one in the ICU. I couldn't believe how much they all looked like James. There were two younger children sitting there, and they didn't exactly look alike, which meant the other one could be none other than my son.

I was face to face with him and I couldn't believe it. I tried to point out features of mine, and I noticed immediately that although he looked like the rest of the kids he had my mouth and nose. He had the same complexion as James, and he and the other little boy definitely looked like brothers. I resisted the urge to scoop down and take him into my arms. My eyes misted up, and I had to get it together considering Jasmine's mother was staring at me strange.

"I'm sorry," I apologized as I willed my feet to move forward again. "I thought I recognized these kids," I said to her.

"It's not a problem," she offered with a kind smile.

"It's just that," I added with dramatic flair, "this little girl looks like the daughter of a friend of mine from a few years ago, but she had a twin brother. My friend's name is Jasmine, and I haven't seen her in years."

"Well, if you are speaking of Jasmine Cinque, these would be her kids," the woman offered with a sad smile.

"For real? Oh my goodness, where is she? I haven't seen her in so long," I gushed as I played into the vulnerability of the woman. I was going to juice her for as much information as I could before James popped up.

"Well, unfortunately she's in the ICU. I'm surprised you haven't heard because it's been all over the news. She was in . . . Well, that's not really a conversation to have in front of the children," she stopped herself, and then looked around at their sad faces.

"I totally understand," I offered with an equally sad look on my face. "I'm here visiting a friend as well, but if I could leave my number with you could you text me or call me later with the information so that I can maybe stop by and see her at a better time?"

"Sure, I don't see that being a problem. I'll give it to James whenever he comes back from downstairs."

"Thank you so much," I responded as I scribbled my phone number on an old Michael Kors receipt from my purse. This was working out better than I thought it would. James would be upset, but he would call me if for nothing else but to tell me to back off.

I thanked her again as I handed her the slip of paper, and watched as she secured it in her pocketbook. Turning on my heels, I chanced a glance at the little boy once more, taking in his face for memory one last time. A smile spread across my face as just a tear slipped from the inside corner of my eye. How could I have given up such a precious little thing? Seeing him made me happy, but I was so confused at the same time. Would I have been a good mom to him, and how different would my life have been if I had kept him? I wasn't the type of woman who could take care of someone else by myself, and I just wasn't confident that it would have been a fairytale setup.

Kids need a lot of love and attention, something I just didn't think I was capable of giving. Especially considering I never got it. I came from a broken home where my mother was beat to death right in front of me and my siblings. We always had to be quiet and stay out of the way of our drunken father's rage. My mother was too busy trying to survive to give us hugs and kisses, and shit just got worse as I got older and other family members got a hold of me. I was damaged goods, and I felt like my son needed at least a fair chance at a good life with a loving family. Something I just couldn't give him.

Stopping in the restroom just past the judge's room, I sat down in a stall and bawled my eyes out. It caught me by surprise because I didn't think I would be so emotional upon seeing him. The last time I looked at him face to face he had a little round face that looked like James's . . . Still did, and now he was inches taller and into his features. Seeing him instantly took me back to the videos that James would send me of him crawling and eventually walking. I erased the voice recording of his first words because I couldn't handle not being there. My thought process: *he's not my responsibility now. He's with his father, where he belongs.*

My question now was did he belong there, and if I did indeed have to take him how would it work out for both of us? My place wasn't exactly kid friendly, and I wasn't 100 percent sure that I was ready to make the necessary changes for him. What if he hated me, and despised me for giving him up? Did he know that he was adopted, better yet thrown on the Cinque's because his real mother was a selfish bitch who didn't want the assumed inconvenience of having a kid around? This was too much at one time, and I couldn't control my sobbing. It took me about ten minutes before I was able to control the tears that were invading my face and racking my body with grief. I had to play this the right way, and I needed to get back to business.

Coming out of the stall, I took a few minutes to wash my face and get myself together at the sink before I went into the judge's room. Just in case he was up and noticed I was crying, I would just tell him I was concerned about him and thought that I had lost him. He was so self-centered his egotistical ass would believe it.

After applying a fresh coat of lip gloss, I stepped out into the hall just in time to see James reunite with his family. From what I gathered, he must not have seen his kids since the accident. The group hug and the way all of the kids screamed out "Daddy" when they saw him was a touching moment. He looked drained and pissed at the same time when he exited the elevator, but when he laid eyes on his kids the expression changed to one of love and relief. I got misty-eyed again, but kept it moving before Jasmine's mom pointed me out to him. I wasn't ready to meet him up close and personal right now, especially considering I crashed his press conference. I knew I wasn't his favorite person in the world at this moment in time.

Stepping into the judge's room, I could see that he was still asleep. The nurse informed me that he was on private status in the system so no one would be popping up unexpectedly. She addressed me as his wife, but I didn't bother to correct her. I didn't need a scandal breaking out at this time. I needed him to do some shit for me, and I needed everything to run smoothly. There was a bodyguard at the door twenty-four/seven, and I was simply waiting for him to wake up.

"So . . . ummm . . . how long will he be down for?" I asked the nurse to gauge how much time I had to sit in this dreadful place. Maybe I could go shopping in the meantime and check back.

"He should be waking up by tomorrow morning, Mrs. Stenton. We gave him drugs to keep him asleep until the test results come back, and to keep him comfortable. The doctor will be making rounds soon, and should be able to explain everything better," she responded as she read from his chart.

"That sounds like a plan," I responded as I pulled my Kindle from my bag and got comfortable. I was going to have his driver take me back to the hideout, but I didn't want to risk leaving and on my return not be able to get back in for any reason. I mean, I wanted to go shopping to waste some time. Instead, I took the pillow that the nurse offered me, and enjoyed the food off of the judge's tray. I didn't even know why the shit was in his room. The man was unconscious, and couldn't eat a thing.

The image of my son's face popped back in my head and brought a small smile to my face. I was happy and nervous at the same time because I didn't know what the outcome would be. A huge part of me was hoping this was just a big misunderstanding, and I could just go back to the "A" without any regrets. Something told me it wouldn't be as smooth as I thought, and I was preparing myself for the ride.

Chapter 14

James: Picking Up the Pieces

I swear she's just as messy now as she was back then. I knew I saw Monica fly past my room earlier, but did I think that she would show up at my press conference? Hell no! Then she came in there asking questions, and stirring up shit for no reason. *Why is this woman constantly trying to wreck my flow?* If I would have known that a night of great sex with a sexy-ass woman would lead to all of this mess years later, I would have stayed faithful to my damn wife, or at least used a condom. Maybe we wouldn't have been in this shit now. As a matter of fact, I know we wouldn't. Hindsight is a bitch in a sexy dress and heels, and whatever lesson she intended to teach had been well learned. Trust me on that one. After all of these trials and tribulations I couldn't even be sure that I would even want to touch my wife.

I left the press conference feeling defeated, but I was glad that it was over. Now that the deed was done I could concentrate on my family. I was wheeled out of the room before things got too heated, and held my head down as various reporters from the news took pictures to no doubt post as headline news. When I got up to my floor, I removed myself from the wheelchair and began walking down the hall. I just needed to stand up because the wheelchair made me feel more helpless than I already was.

Halfway down the hall I looked up and made eye contact with my oldest daughter. It was like everything started moving in slow motion as tears made my vision cloudy and I started running toward her.

"Daddy!" my daughter screamed out as we collided in a tight embrace in the middle of the hall. Pretty soon, I could feel the arms of all of my children wrapped around me in a tearful embrace. I didn't think this day would ever come. Every time I asked about my kids I got the grizzly.

When I stood up, picking up my youngest daughter and Monica's son, my mother-in-law walked up to me with tears in her eyes. I knew she would be in my corner regardless of the mess that was going on now. When I reached her, I sat the kids down, and she gave me the tightest hug her small frame could manage, letting me know everything would be okay. Taking a seat in the waiting area, the kids continued to cling to me for dear life as we discussed the goings-on of my wife and son. This was a major stressor for all of us, and we were all waiting for one of them to wake up.

"So what did the doctor say about Jordan?" she asked just as Jazz's dad, brothers, and uncles walked up. Everyone stopped to give out quick hugs before I updated them on what I knew.

"I gave blood this morning because Jordan will need a transfusion," I replied, not letting on that an error had occurred with the previous sample. I didn't want any cause for alarm to upset anyone.

"And what about Jasmine?" she asked as she blinked back tears.

"Jazz is the more stable of the two. They give her meds to keep her asleep until the swelling goes down. She whacked her forehead on the steering wheel pretty hard, and although it doesn't look like a lot is wrong, they just want to be sure," I responded as Jaden cuddled up closer to me. We sat and conversed for a while, and just as Jazz's father offered to take the kids for something to eat in the cafeteria the doctor walked up and greeted us.

"It's nice to see everyone here." He spoke with a gentle smile that one couldn't help but return. "Despite the circumstances, how is everyone holding up?"

"Pretty good so far, Doc," I responded for everyone. "These are my children, and this is my mother-in-law."

"Nice to meet everyone," he responded. "James, I need you in your room so that I can check you out, and discuss some things."

"No problem, the kids were just going to get something to eat."

After they all left, Jazz's mom slipped me a piece of paper that I stuck in my pocket on the low. I knew she didn't want the others to see it by how she handed it to me in a hug, and winked her eye at me afterward. Following the doctor into the room, I took a seat on the side of the bed, preparing myself to be checked out so that I could sit next to my wife and son.

"So how are you feeling now that the press is done with you?" he asked as he checked my vitals.

"Pretty good, considering the circumstances."

"That's good to hear," he said as he scribbled something in my chart. "You will be free to check out today, but I need to talk to you about your blood test, and your son."

"Ummm . . . okay? Is everything all right? Do I have a disease?" I asked, borderline panicking.

"No, you don't have a disease," he responded with a kind smile as he pulled up a chair. *This shit must be about to get deep.*

"Okay, so what is it? Just give it to me straight."

"Well, after sending your blood up to be tested yesterday I thought it was weird that your paternity type didn't match your son. That was the reason why I had it redrawn this morning, but when I got the same results I knew then we had a major problem."

"What are you saying, Doc?" I asked, already knowing the answer.

"I'm saying that Jordan is not yours, and if we are going to do the blood transfusion using a family member's blood we have to act fast. I can take it from your wife, or the child's twin. I just need to know what you want to do."

Boom!

The other shoe had fallen, and it's safe to say a bomb was just dropped on me. Did this man just tell me Jordan wasn't my son? I felt myself hyperventilating, and the last thing I heard before I blacked out was the doctor calling for a nurse. Why was this happening to me?

When I finally came to I was stretched out on the bed with my family surrounding me. This was all just a bad dream . . . it had to be. I knew it wasn't when the sad look on my mother-in-law's face came into view. So it was true. Jordan wasn't my son. And if Jordan wasn't my son, that meant that Janice wasn't my daughter. It didn't make any logical sense because they looked just like me, just like my other kids did. If I wasn't the father, then who was?

I was pissed, confused, hurt . . . hell, all of the above! Did Jazz really do this to me? To us? To our family? Yeah, I did my shit too, but nothing of the magnitude of this. Some would think that I was justifying my wrongdoings, but in *my* head our situations were *not* the same. She knew I was sleeping with Monica except for the times that I crept out, and when Monica turned up pregnant there was no way it belonged to anyone else but me. Jasmine, on the other hand, had sex with someone I didn't know about, passed the kids off as mine for years, and never admitted to it. That, in my opinion, was hardly the same thing. Call it biased, a double standard, an excuse . . . I don't care. I needed her to wake up *now!*

"Mr. Cinque, I'm glad you're awake," the doctor spoke from the door as the nurse took my vitals. It was kind of hard to do with my oldest daughter wrapped around me, but she managed. Hopefully they didn't tell the kids the God-awful news I just heard.

"Do you guys mind if I speak with him alone?" the doctor asked. Jaden protested at first in a tearful fit, but I promised her it wouldn't take long before she was right back in my arms again. She was comforted by Jalil, and it made me proud to see my son step up to the plate at such a difficult time. Once everyone was out, he took a seat on the side of my bed to talk to me. Tears flooded my eyes instantly.

"Mr. Cinque, I'm sorry I had to give you that type of news at a time like this, but we need to make a move if we are going to save your son. Do we take the blood from your wife or the twin? I know it's a lot to digest right now, but I need an answer or your son may die."

I was still speechless. He just told me that Jordan wasn't mine, but he still referred to him as my son, and honestly I didn't know how to feel. *Is this shit really happening?* The look on the doctor's face confirmed that it truly was. The look of genuine concern and understanding made me feel like he understood where my head was at in this moment. He was a man and a father as well. If he all of a sudden found out that his kid wasn't really his he would surely feel the same as I did. Betrayed. Confused. Hurt. Uneasy . . . The list just went on and on. I had so many questions, but I knew I needed to sort my thoughts out, and now wasn't a good time.

"Whose blood would be better?" I asked as my thoughts swam around in my head, colliding into each other. Jordan wasn't mine . . . and the thought echoed in my head over and over again.

"The twin's blood would be an excellent choice since they share everything already, and we would only need three pints. The procedure for testing is the same to make sure they will be compatible, just as a precaution."

"Will it hurt her?" I asked, concerned about my baby girl. I had the overwhelming urge to hold her in my arms and look at her face. The needle that was used to collect the blood was huge, and hurt me, so I could imagine the pain in the arm of a toddler.

"Since she's so young we will put her to sleep, because I doubt she will sit there for the procedure," the doctor stated truthfully as he looked me in my face. I must have looked a mess.

"And what if you got it from Jasmine? Will it put her at risk?" I wondered. I was seeing her in a totally different light at this moment, and I needed answers from her.

"She's already out, so it's just a matter of obtaining permission from you and we can get the blood from her now."

I thought about it for a second, and I knew I didn't want to put my daughter through that kind of mess. My daughter . . . or whoever she belonged to. This shit was crazy, and I found myself getting more pissed off by the second. How was I supposed to be acting now?

"Let's get it from Jasmine. I can't take my baby girl through that kind of pain if it's not necessary," I responded, trying to sound sure. "When will the surgery take place?"

"I'm going to send someone in now to get the blood, and as soon as the blood is run for testing we will begin. Everything is being done stat so that we can move quickly."

"Do what you have to do to save my son."

The doctor nodded in understanding, and exited the room to start the process. In the meantime my head was spinning, and I was confused. Almost immediately after the doctor was gone, my children busted into the room and surrounded me. I grabbed Janice into my arms and stared into her face, trying to see something different. All I saw were my eyes looking back at me. Cuddling her to my chest, I placed my free arm around Jaden, and made room for Jalil and Junior to embrace me as well. I didn't know what Jasmine did, but this was my family, and I was not going to trip.

If nothing else, I knew I needed to have a talk with some twin trainers from Bally Total Fitness.

Monica warned me of this in a letter years ago, and I didn't have cause to believe her until now. I guessed it was time for me to investigate the truth.

Chapter 15

Monica: If It Ain't One Thing It's Another

It felt like I'd been at the hospital forever waiting for the judge to wake up. This was some bullshit! I'd never had to sit in on a heart attack victim before, so I didn't know exactly what it was I was supposed to be doing at this moment. I found myself staring at him, and he looked a hundred years older than he did hours ago. I still hadn't found out the cause of the cardiac arrest, and the beeps from the monitor he was hooked to were driving me crazy.

The time on my watch read 4:00 p.m., and I was wondering if the Cinques were still gathered in the hall. I needed to get out of this room before they would have to check me into the psych ward. Deciding that maybe I could go out for a little while and come back, I gathered up my things and kissed the judge on the forehead, whispering in his ear that I would be back. I couldn't really go far since I didn't have a vehicle, so my first stop would be to hail a cab to the Enterprise center located on Market Street so that I could get some wheels. I had to be able to move around.

What I loved about University City was that at any given time of the day there was a Yellow Cab waiting to make money. Upon leaving the hospital, I was able to walk right out the door and into the back of the cab. To my surprise, it was the same cabby from the airport. Looking at my watch again, I knew I wouldn't have time today to let him hook me up, but maybe he would go for an IOU. He smiled immediately when I closed the door, asking me where I wanted to go.

"Where to, pretty lady?" he asked, minus the accent that I was sure he used with other customers. Surprisingly, he smelled like he might have actually showered today, and the Old Spice and bologna stench in the cab itself was faint.

"Enterprise," I spoke with a smile on my face as well; afterward confirming my rental on my iPhone. I figured I'd hit the mall, find something good to eat, and check back to see what the judge was up to before deciding where I would lay my head for the evening. I'd be damned if I was staying in this hospital all night. Since his condition had changed, I wasn't 100 percent sure that staying at his place was the best thing to do. As far as I knew, his wife didn't know about that piece of property, but somehow she found out he was in the hospital, so who knew how much information she was able to gather up? I just wasn't in the mood to figure it out, and would rather just play it safe in the comfort of a hotel. I would just get the cash I spent for it from the judge at a later date.

He must have taken other patients there because he didn't even bother to ask which location as he drove a few blocks down and over. The meter didn't even reach twenty, but I held the bill in my hand to see what he would do. To my surprise he didn't take it.

"You still have my number, right?" he asked, looking at me through the rearview mirror.

"Yes, I do," I replied.

"Good, this ride is on me. The next *ride* is on you."

The cabby definitely had me intrigued, and once again I thought about giving him a chance to prove what he could do. If his head game was any indication of what else he had in store, it might just be worth a try. Shaking my head, I exited the car and made my way inside the building to pick up my reservation. The more I moved about the more I started thinking about moving back to Philly. It didn't take long for my car to be brought around, and once we did the visual inspection, I was behind the wheel and on my way to find something to get into.

Deciding to take a ride through the old neighborhood, I first went through my block to see if it still looked the same. What I thought would be happy memories were shut down as soon as I pulled up to the door. Instead of the soft pastel pink comforting me, all I could see was those bastard-ass cops rummaging through my personal space and taking my shit. My stomach cramped up as my mind flooded with memories of my first abortion, and how I was tortured when I got pregnant the second time around.

Blurred snapshots of Sheila, Jasmine, James, and that weird-ass cop made me clutch my stomach as I shook, feeling like I was about to vomit. Snapping my head up, I glared at the house, happy I left this place. Since I was a kid, my entire existence in Philly had been nothing but turmoil. Going back from my childhood up until I left this wretched place . . . everything was just pure hell.

Gathering myself, and catching my breath, I took one last look at the place I called home. I was almost certain of my feelings up until I saw a child run out of the house. His laughter carried across the yard to my ears as he jumped head first into the snow bank on the side of the house. Shortly after, a tall man came crashing through the door with a huge smile on his face, following the child into the snow, and soon after that a petite female rushed through the door carrying scarves and gloves.

It was a nostalgic moment. One I totally missed out on when I gave my son away. It was too cute how the mom fussed at both of them about not being prepared for the cold, and how they both had solemn looks on their faces as she fixed their scarves around their necks and scolded them about not having gloves on. The moment she was done, they resumed play, and she stood on the step staring lovingly at who I assumed was her family . . . until our eyes met. She looked at me curiously for a second, and then a huge smile spread across her face as she waved at me like I was an old friend.

It caught me off guard, and I looked behind me, almost forgetting that I was intruding on their private moment. When I turned back around she was off the steps and walking toward me. My God . . . she was gorgeous.

"Hi, how may I help you?" she asked me in a pleasant tone.

I was speechless for a second because my eyes were transfixed on her full lips, which looked soft as pillows. It took me a second, but I finally found my voice as my eyes traveled up to meet hers. Soft pools of chocolate with hints of caramel swirled throughout.

"I'm sorry. I used to live in this house," I finally responded, cheeks beat red from the cold and embarrassment.

"You gave this up?" she asked in a surprised voice. I guessed because I sold it for way below market value in excellent condition, I practically gave it away.

"Yeah," I replied. "I moved to Atlanta and wasn't able to really get back here enough."

"Oh, I understand," she replied, a smile still plastered on her face. "Would you like to come inside and see what we've done with the place? I'm Logan by the way, and that's my husband, Kenneth, and our son, Sage."

"Hi, I'm Monica. Nice to meet you." I held my hand out to embrace hers, and her skin felt so soft . . . like it would melt in my hand.

"Nice to meet you, Monica. Well, come on in out of the cold, and I'll give you a tour."

After setting the car alarm, I followed Logan up to her house, stopping to meet her son and husband. They made a very cute family, but I wondered briefly how they ended up here. There was no sign of an accent or anything, but folks from Philly didn't invite strangers into their homes. We just didn't do that kind of thing. Regardless of that, I followed her inside and was surprised at what she had done to the place. The splotches of color that I had in the living room were now covered by plum-colored paint. The room had splashes of celery green and chocolate throughout in the form of throw pillows and artwork that gave it a warm feel.

The night of my abortion played out again in my head, and all I could smell was the old stench of blood in the air that James attempted to clean up while I was gone. Shaking my head back and forth, I focused on the various pictures of the family that rested neatly around the living space. There was art going up the staircase, exactly where my art previously hung, but I didn't see me in any of the pictures. Following her up the stairs, I peeked into the master bedroom, and the night I first had Jasmine came to mind, stirring up butterflies in the pit of my stomach that settled down around my clit.

This shit was too much to deal with right now. As we neared the room where my son's room would have been, it was set up for a toddler. All I could see was the knife that was stabbed through a baby doll that was placed inside with red paint all over it. I shuddered at the memory. We came out of the room and walked toward the back, the last room in the house. When she opened the door it was like déjà vu . . . The camera set up, the easels with half-done paintings, splatter sheets, and tubes of paints lined up on the floor . . . It was overwhelming. She walked into the room and picked up an old-school flashbulb camera and told me to smile, snapping my picture within a second. I was dazed and amazed.

"So, as you can see," she began with a slight giggle, "I'm an artist. I paint, take pictures, all of the above."

"I see." I smiled at her. "What's under the sheet?"

"Oh, this is a treasure. I scored this puppy at an exhibit I went to a few months ago, but before I could get a picture with the artist she had already left for the evening."

She pulled the cover back, and it was an original painting I had done my first week in Atlanta. I was so trying to get over all of the nightmares I had left here, and trying to cope with the thought of leaving my son to be raised by someone else. The swirls of dark blues and blacks in combination with bright yellows and bursts of orange represented me trying to break free from my past and walk a straight path into a promising future. It was a very emotional time for me.

"*Peace and Remembrance,*" I spoke just above a whisper as I viewed the painting.

"Yes, how did you know?" she asked with a look of surprise on her face.

"I'm the artist. I painted this when I first moved to Atlanta. I must have left before you got there."

The look on her face was of pure disbelief. And the scream that came for her mouth . . . like she hit the lottery. It was entirely too cute. Just like her. A few seconds later two sets of footsteps could be heard barreling up the steps toward the back room, and I was instantly embarrassed.

"Honey, what's wrong?" her husband asked with a concerned look on his face. Their son could be seen peeking out from behind his father's legs.

"Babe, do you know who this is?" she asked while holding her chest.

"Ummm . . . no, I don't. You said your name was—"

"It's Monica! *The* M. Tyler!" she shouted in excitement. He, on the other hand, still had a confused look on his face.

"She painted this painting, and the one in the den!" she shouted again. When her husband still didn't respond, she reached to take her cell phone out of her back pocket, and pulled up my Web site. When the picture of me came into view, the husband's face changed immediately.

"Oh, snap . . . You're her . . . You're you!" he spoke in an excited voice.

"Yes, I'm sorry. It's just that I used to live here, and—"

"Oh my God! M. Tyler is in our house!" they said in unison. I wanted to laugh at the duo, but I just kept my composure while they lost their minds a little.

"I'm sorry I didn't recognize you," Logan apologized. "It's just that you look different in person, and . . . Oh my God! This was your house?"

"Yes, it was," I replied through a forced smile, ready to go. This was definitely too much at one time.

"Honey, go check the stove while I find a brush. I need Monica's autograph before she goes."

He didn't even put up a fuss, giving me one last smile before grabbing his son's hand and leaving the room. Meanwhile, Logan had already gotten a brush and paint out so that I could sign her picture. I found a spot on the bottom and autographed her picture adding a personal touch only for her, giving her back the brush when I was done. She stood there staring at me in an uncomfortable silence that made me feel awkward.

"Listen, I have to give you my number," she gushed as she scribbled her name and number on a piece of construction paper. "Don't tell my husband, but I've had the biggest crush on you for years. Your paintings are so . . . provocative, and although I've never been with a woman, if I had the chance it would be someone like you."

Yep, I was speechless. Tucking the number into my pocket, I thanked her for the tour and said good-bye to her family and made my way to the car. *Did she just come on to me? Yeah, I think she did.* Deciding to keep the number for later, I secured it in my phone and pulled off. She was cute after all, and you would think I'd had enough of dealing with married couples. *Guess not.*

Pulling off, I made my way to the Cinques' old house to see what was going on over there. Seemed to me Philly hadn't changed a bit. As I drove I noticed a black car following me, and at first I paid it no mind. No one knew I was in Philly, so I wasn't too concerned. However, I did become more concerned when every corner I turned the car turned. I even went around a block twice just to see if they would follow and they did. Whoever had a tail on me wasn't doing a good job being inconspicuous. I didn't panic though; I was too smooth for that. Instead, when I got to the Cinques' old house I pulled over into their garage like I lived there and shortly after I could see the car pass me by in my rearview. Whoever that was, they were on my ass, but I was ready. Philly didn't know what it was about to get itself into. *Monica's back, and holding no punches.*

Chapter 16

James: For Better or Worse

The surgery started exactly two hours later. I sat by my son's bed the entire time leading up to it, wondering who his real daddy was. I mean, I'd been there since the beginning, so I was technically his dad, but who created him was the real question. Me and dude must have looked alike because Jordan had all of my features, from my thick eyebrows to my full lips. Jasmine hated that none of the kids looked like her, and I often teased her that I did all the work and it showed. Those were the days when we were in love, and nothing could have come between us. Before Monica came and poisoned everything we worked so hard to achieve. That bitch! Honestly, the poison had to have already been in the works for her to come and mess everything up so bad, but I didn't have the energy to contemplate all of that at the moment.

What was she doing back in Philly was the next question. I hadn't heard from her in months. Even after we moved and I tried to get in contact with her I couldn't. The cell number I had for her changed and she never responded to the letters I wrote and sent to the return address on the checks she sent us. I used to send her pictures and videos of Junior all the time and I guessed it got to be too much for her. I just felt like although she wasn't physically a part of her son's life that didn't mean that she shouldn't know about it or him. He was just as much a part of her as he was a part of me.

It wasn't lost on me either that Jasmine didn't really care for the boy being around. She wasn't beating the shit out of him, or locking him in closets or no shit like that. Her temperament with him was noticeably different with him from the other kids though. Like, he got in trouble for the same shit that Jordan and Jalil would do, which caused 50 percent of our arguments. *Just because you hate the boy's mom doesn't give you just cause to treat him different. He didn't ask to be here.* What pissed me off now though was that she was doing all this crazy shit and acting all crazy with Junior, and here we were four years in and come to find out there are two children who ain't even mine. Two! Like, for real? I swore if she wasn't already down for the count I'd have put her ass there for this scandalous shit.

Lord, I can't wait until she wakes up. Oh, I'll make sure she's cool in the gang first, but then it's her ass. Ain't no way to worm out of this one. The only thing I ever did wrong was bring another woman and a kid home. Shit, I guess that makes us two for two. My shit was up and out in the open though . . . Secrets definitely hold more sting.

When the nurse came in to wheel Jordan up to the surgical unit I broke down in my mother-in-law's arms. Kids are not supposed to go through these types of ordeals. Yeah, the occasional bruised knee or broken arm from climbing a tree, but near-death experiences? Naw, that wasn't natural. If I would have just gone and gotten the damn kids from childcare none of this would be going on. On the flip side, we would have still had all of these secrets. The entire thing was a mess, but it's always been said that what goes on in the dark comes to light, and right now the light was shining bright as hell.

The doctor said things wouldn't take long; they just had to operate on one of his lungs to get everything moving and he would be good to go. The rejection rate wouldn't be high because the blood was coming right from Jazz, who shared the same blood type. Regardless of the betrayal I just wanted him to come out okay, and was on pins and needles waiting. I paced back and forth in the waiting area of the surgery suite, waiting for any word about my boy. It was like I couldn't get a break. Every time I turned around some crazy shit was happening in my life. I must have been a crazy ass in a former life, because this was just ridiculous.

About an hour and a half into the surgery the doctor came out to talk to us. As soon as I saw him I sprinted over to him, wanting to be the first to hear the news. Jasmine's mom had long ago taken the kids home, and the only one left here with me was Jasmine's dad. I guessed to ensure I wasn't a flight risk. I was past that feeling of wanting to leave though. Now, I just wanted to be sure that everything was going smooth with my wife and son. I wanted to crack Jazz's skull most of all, but there was a time and place for everything. I just needed everyone to come out of this alive.

"Mr. Cinque, everything is looking good, but we are not out of the danger zone yet," the doctor began with a straight face.

"What do you mean, Doc? I don't think I can take much more of this."

"Well, the lung issue is fixed, and the blood transfusion went well. He's just being closed up as we speak. We just need to ensure that there will be no setbacks with the blood transfusion after the fact. Although the blood came from your wife, and everything looks good now, we just want to make sure everything stays good."

"Okay, that's understandable. When will I be able to see him?"

"In about a half hour or so. Once we have him stabilized and in recovery I'll have one of the nurses come to get you and your family. Don't worry, Mr. Cinque, everything will be fine," he answered in a reassuring tone.

"And if it's not?" I questioned back, feeling uncertain.

"Then I will do everything in my power to make it right. I know you want your son home, and he will be soon."

My son. Not the dumb-ass man Jazz was foolish enough to have unprotected sex with, but *my* son. The doctor reached over and gave me a hug, and I had to gather myself before I broke down again. As he walked away, I went and took a seat next to my father-in-law. I wanted to have a heart-to-heart with the man, maybe get some words of wisdom from someone who'd been doing this marriage thing for years. I had questions, and I needed guidance to get through this mess that was my life.

"I know I messed up this time," I began in an apologetic voice. He turned his head to look my way, but didn't say a word. I took that as my cue to continue.

"I just need to know what to do to get back on track. You've been with Jazz's mom since forever. You telling me you never messed up?" I asked him, getting all emotional and shit. I was just so tired of things being the way they were now.

"Of course I've messed up, son. Of course I have," he responded, shaking his head back and forth. "And I know what kind of pain the mess-ups caused to my wife and kids. I promised my wife years ago that I would never do anything else to disrupt our unit. My kids will never see us go through anything damaging again," he said in a sad voice.

"What do I need to do to get back on track?" I asked him in a desperate voice. I needed help . . . I needed answers.

"You get out what you need to discuss and you let it go. Move forward and don't look back. I know you're hurting, son. I know you feel confused because a huge lie was brought to light. Both of y'all did some crazy shit to each other. Discuss it and let it go. Move forward, and create a better atmosphere for your children. All you and Jazz have in the world are each other, outside of family of course, but we can't be or stay married for y'all. It's all on you."

I understood exactly what he meant, and no more words were needed. I had to stand up, and bring us all back together. It was time for me to step my game up, and get everything back on track. Jazz and I needed to discuss how we were going to move forward, whether it was with each other or solo. However it was going down, it needed to be discussed as soon as possible.

I sat back in the chair and closed my eyes, thankful for Jazz's father. Even her brothers. I didn't even have any hard feelings about what they did to me because if I had a sister I would have done the same, if not worse, for her. At the end of the day all we had was family, and we had to stick together through the thick and the thin, no matter how thin shit got.

Lord, I just wanted it to be over. I knew my son would be coming out of surgery soon, and we would be able to meet him in recovery. I wanted to be ready, so I told my father-in-law that I was going to use the restroom right quick so that I could be ready to go down to recovery when it was time.

It didn't take long to relieve myself, and as I stood in the bathroom mirror, I could see the toll the last few days were taking written all over my face. Cupping my hands under the faucet, I took some water and splashed it on my face in order to wake up. That helped a little, but what I really needed was a soft bed. After drying my hands, I dug into my pockets for a piece of gum to get this stale taste out of my mouth.

I felt the piece of paper, and when I unfolded it I recognized the handwriting before I even saw the name. *Monica . . . that bitch! I swear, she always found a way to worm her ass in where she's not wanted.* Jazz's mom didn't know about all the nonsense we went through with her, and I was sure when she approached her she played it innocent. And if she saw Jazz's mom that meant she saw her son. Once again, this was all too much! I simply folded the paper and stuck it in my wallet. I wasn't sure if I was going to contact her or let her find me. Monica always got what she wanted, but what, in fact, that thing was I was unsure about at the moment.

This woman was going to drive me crazy, but I didn't have time to think about that at the moment. Tucking my wallet back in my pocket, I went out and sat down next to Jazz's dad. He gave me a comforting smile, letting me know he understood and he was there for me. I felt a little better knowing that things could get better if we worked on it. The kind of love that Jazz's parents had was undeniable, and I felt like me and Jazz could have the same happiness if we worked hard enough for it.

I remembered on our wedding day Jazz's father told me that marriage wasn't easy, but worth fighting for. There would be plenty of ups and downs over the years, and sometimes it would feel like we would never make it through.

"Son, just hang in there," he said to me over a glass of champagne. "It's a rough road, and when you think you can't take it, look back on what you've already made it through. Those are the times that will remind you that it's worthwhile."

That statement never meant much to me before, but as I sat here and reminisced about how things used to be, I couldn't help but wonder how much work it would take to get it back. Was getting it back even the way to go? *Will Jazz even want to? I'm angry about a lot of shit, and I know she is to, but for the moment we'll just have to see where this road takes us. For better or worse, through sickness and health was what we vowed to one another*. There was no turning back now, and I was ready to fight for mine . . . whatever that is.

Chapter 17

Carlos: Tailgating

"Was it her?" I asked the person on the other end of the phone. I thought Sheneka was lying when she said she saw Monica at the airport. Was the bitch serious? It'd been years since she stepped foot back in Philly, and I wondered for a second what she was doing back here. I still had an unsettled beef with her regarding Rico, and Sheneka had some shit to get off her chest as well.

I had one of my top lieutenants follow her just to make sure. Sheneka had an undying vendetta against Monica, and I had to make sure she wasn't sending me on a wild goose chase like she'd done in the past. Every dark chocolate woman she saw with curves reminded her of Monica, and at one point over the years I had to check her into a mental facility so that she could get her head on right. Hell, she was in one now, and they allowed her to hold a little part-time job during the week, so she worked at a coffee cart at Philadelphia International. I knew she loved the hell out of Rico, in her own way, but was it cause for her to go crazy? She was cool for a while, but it seemed like old crazy and deranged was showing back up, and before any moves were made I had to be sure.

"It was definitely her," the voice responded. "I wasn't too sure myself, but when I saw her getting out of a car at her old crib and talking to some people who lived there I snapped a few pics just to be sure."

"Send them over, and I'll check them out. Who was she talking to?"

"I don't know. Some bitch was outside with her kid. I wasn't sure if she knew the chick, but she went into the house so she had to. I followed her after she came out, and got flicks of the car she's pushing also. Sheneka might actually be on point this time."

"Okay. We won't make any moves yet, just be ready when I give the word."

"No problem."

And the call was disconnected. A minute or so later my phone buzzed, indicating I had a picture message, and sure enough Monica's ass was back in Philly. She was still fine as hell, too. Even better than I last remembered. Wherever she went to must have been a good move because she was on point. I scrolled through the shots of her and the car, quickly realizing that she had a rental. She definitely wasn't here to stay, so what brought her back?

I also noticed that she was by herself, and last I remembered she had just pushed out a kid. Where was the baby? And where was that fine-ass sister of hers? I had plenty of questions, and I knew Sheneka would have plenty more, so I held off on hitting her up right now. I didn't feel like the bullshit with her today.

Rolling over, I signaled for the young buck I had lying next to me to handle her business. Without having to say a word, she gave up the best head service ever. I almost couldn't concentrate, but ol' girl was handling her business. I knew I had to get some answers from Monica, because I was still not convinced that Rico killed himself. He definitely wouldn't have gone out like that, but who did it and why? Questions, and more confusion . . . First thing I needed to do was find out where she was resting her head, and then I would find out why she was here.

Monica had Rico's nose wide open. It didn't take long either. One day he told me he was hitting it, and next thing I knew she had the combination to the safes and everything. I didn't know how it went from her contacting him about a gun to them being all hugged up and in love, but no one was happy about it. Especially Sheneka. Hell, the day before Monica popped up on the scene, Rico and Sheneka were together. They were mad at each other as always, but they were still a unit.

Homegirl swooped through and ceased all of that, and the next thing we knew Rico was calling us from the bing because he was caught with his dick out, literally. They basically snatched him out the pussy, and hauled him off to jail. He was suspicious about the way the entire lockup went down from the gate, and so were we, so I was on it. By the time we got to the spot to clean up, Monica had already cleaned us out. Drugs, diamonds, cash . . . all gone. She was smart enough to make it look like a robbery, but we all knew better.

Rico wasn't even in lockup for that long before we found out that he got knocked, and had some simple-ass prison guard pregnant. That just caused all kinds of confusion because Monica was also pregnant. I was ready to blast her and the baby in her gut, but Sheneka had a heart every so often, and didn't want us to touch her until the baby arrived. She didn't even wait until the baby was here good before she ran up in Monica's crib and trashed it, but that's a story for another time. If it was left up to me she would've been got years ago. Sheneka went crazy, and Monica left town so there wasn't much I could do to get revenge. I wasn't about to jeopardize my shit by looking for her in another city, but her simple ass came back and she wouldn't be leaving without seeing me. That was a fact. I didn't really feel like dealing with the shit right now though, but my head was definitely spinning, and she was going to get hers. For right now . . . I'd just enjoy this blessing, and as I gripped the back of the young girl's head I let my mind relax and my body surrender to the feeling of excellent head service.

Chapter 18

Sheneka: Don't Take It Personal

I told that fool that I saw Monica's trick ass. I was pissed that I even had to go through all the hoops to get Carlos's dumb ass on board. Okay, so a few times I was off the mark, but I was sure this time. I was just waiting on him to call me back to confirm. I wished for a second I was allowed to carry a cell phone because I could have taken a picture of her. The program I was in didn't allow us to have phones, and we had a curfew on top of that! I didn't want to get fired for abandoning my job, so I couldn't follow her out of the building. It's cool though, because I straight used the job phone to hit Carlos on his jack. I wanted Monica's head, and I wasn't stopping until I had it.

Yeah, after all this time I was still upset about Rico's death. Who are you to judge me? I really loved him, in spite of what everyone chose to believe. Yeah, I let Carlos and a few of his other homeboys sample the goods a few times, but that was just revenge when Rico pissed me off. It wasn't that serious for me. I thought we were good, me and Rico. We had a really bad argument and I told that fool to step, but I didn't know Monica was going to swoop in like she did. Put me on ten every time I thought about it!

What pissed me off the most was how fast she had this fool open! *Like, for real, Rico?* I knew that bitch pussy wasn't better than mine, and he was out here acting like he just hit the fucking jackpot! Holding hands in public and everything! Oooohhhh, I was pissed! This dizzy bitch had the stash spot on lock and everything. By the time we got there it wasn't a damn dime or jewel left, and since it was all drug money it wasn't like we could report the shit stolen. Oh, how I hate a bitch more scandalous than me.

Before I could even visit him word on the street was somebody got the drop on Rico. The word was that he was found dangling from the top bunk with a broken neck or some shit like that, but Rico would have never just killed himself. That wasn't how he got down, and I wasn't even believing that shit. That bitch got him murked . . . That's my story and I'm sticking to it.

I wanted to kick that bastard of a child out her gut through her damn nose, but I could never catch up with her slick ass. Besides, regardless of how crazy my ass was, the baby had nothing to do with it. I just wanted her. Before I could get a hold of her she had jumped ship, and I didn't know where to find her. I was patient though, and I knew she would show her face eventually. A few false alarms had me ready to get shit poppin' on complete strangers, and that's when I knew I needed to lay my ass down on a couch somewhere and talk to a shrink. Yeah, they tried to convince me that what I was feeling was connected to some random childhood incident, but I wasn't buying that bullshit with the last dollar to my name. She fucked up my life, I wanted revenge, and no matter how long it took I was going to be on her ass like a fly on an African child with a cracker in his mouth as soon as I saw her. *Oh, it took about four years, but lo and behold the bitch is back . . . and I'm ready for her ass!*

Chapter 19

James: A Brighter Side of Darkness

My boy made it through safe. I was so relieved when I got down to the recovery room and saw him breathing. He was out like a light, and had tubes coming out of his body, but he was alive. I'd take that over dead any day of the week. Jazz's father looked relieved as well. I wanted to ask him how he felt about the news of the second set of twins not being mine, but I figured I'd already asked enough questions for the day, and I would ask once the coast was clear.

The doctor said that Jordan would have to stay for observation, but should be able to go home in a few days. The injuries that he sustained from the accident were healing well and it was just a matter of time before he was back to his normal self. He would still be on bed rest, and it may take a few more days before he was up and moving around, but each day would get better.

That was music to my ears. The doctor was also talking about waking Jazz from her medically induced coma, depending on how the swelling around her brain was looking. It could be a few more days or a few more weeks; they would just have to chart the progress and keep an eye on her. Hell, it'd only been a few days since all this dumb shit went down, it just felt like we'd been here forever.

I stayed with my son overnight, and after putting in for a short family medical leave at work the next morning, I was up at the hospital visiting both my wife and son, waiting for them to wake up. He was really tired, but when Jordan finally opened his eyes and saw me sitting next to him a small smile spread across his face. I called the nurse immediately because he was strapped into the bed. They did this as a precaution so that he wouldn't wake up and yank all of the tubes out. My eyes welled up with tears instantly, and for the first time in about a week things were starting to look up.

He was on pain meds from the rib injury, and he was out instantly when the nurse gave him another dose. I wanted to hold him, but he seemed so fragile. I didn't want to cause him more pain than he was already in, but I did kiss him gently on his cheek and I held his little hand in mine, keeping him close. I was informed that his lung injury was doing great as well and that definitely helped me breathe easier.

I spent a little time with Jazz as well, but the atmosphere in her room was different. I spent most of my time just staring at her, wondering when shit got this bad. We both did things that I was sure we regretted now, and I wondered how she would be once she was finally allowed to wake up. Periodically I would reach over and touch her, but she felt so cold and clammy. I wondered where the love was that I had for her when we first met. Where did that feeling go? I mean, I loved my wife, but it wasn't the same kind of love that we had pre-children. Did she still love me? All of these thoughts swam around in an angry sea of emotions in my head that I just couldn't shake, and to be totally honest . . . it made me nervous.

On my way out of Jazz's room to go grab a bite from the café I was thankful to finally have some time to myself. I guessed Jazz's family didn't feel like I was a flight risk anymore, and I was allowed to visit without bodyguards. As I was passing the rooms I saw transport bringing out the judge's body and everything clicked instantly. *That's why Monica was at the hospital.* He didn't appear to be dead, but he did have machines hooked up to him. I assumed he was going up for some type of testing, but what brought him in here in the first place was the main question. I remembered what he looked like from the court-issued papers we got for Junior.

"Monica probably gave that man a heart attack," I said more to myself as I kept stride right past him and made my way to the elevator. I knew I shouldn't call her crazy ass, but I knew I had to. I reasoned in my head that she probably just wanted to see her son.

I made my trip quick to the café, and by the time I got back up to Jordan's room, Jazz's mom was there. I stood outside the door to let her have her moment. I could see the tears glistening in her eyes and running down her cheeks. At the moment she reminded me so much of Jazz, and I knew that's exactly how Jazz would look when she reached her mom's age. After a few more minutes I walked into the room and gave her a hug. She leaned into my shoulder and accepted it, and I knew in that moment that regardless of how raggedy this situation was between me and her daughter, she still loved me like her son.

"James, you're doing a good job with these children," she began in a sad voice. "I know you were caught off guard by the discovery, but these are your kids. Just promise me you will continue to do right by them."

"I will . . . I definitely will," I reassured her as I held her tight. Didn't she know that these kids were my everything? I'd been beating myself up every day about this horrible accident, and I promised myself that I would be more active in their lives and help Jazz out more.

"That's your son, James, that test doesn't mean a thing."

I didn't even bother to respond because I already felt that in my heart. We were a unit, and nothing would break us. I was just ready to get my family back together so that we could have a clean slate and start fresh.

"Mr. Cinque, glad I was able to catch up with you." The doctor greeted us both as he walked into the room. "Your son is doing well, and I'm thinking he may be released early next week. He hasn't shown any sign of rejection, and his vitals are looking good. Right now he is doing pretty good sleeping on his own, and as you can see, he's just on a drip to keep him hydrated and asleep for now. This will keep him down during the night, and once he wakes up in the morning he should be okay."

"Wow, that's great, Doc! I wasn't expecting it to be that quickly," I responded as I looked from the doctor to my son's sleeping form in the bed.

"Well, the transfusion portion only takes about an hour or so, and his ribs are positioned and bonded. He will definitely be sore, and we will give you pain medication to manage that. Expect him to sleep a lot the first few days home, which is probably better for him to deal with the pain. As long as he isn't developing any fever or hives he should be okay. The tenderness in his ribs will subside over time as well."

During the accident Jordan lost a lot of blood due to the fractured rib that punctured his lung on impact. The transfusion was needed to replenish his blood supply because by the time he was removed from the wreck he bled out a lot and was unconscious. Little Jordan definitely had it bad, and thank God the medics were able to get them out quickly once they did arrive.

I was elated to hear this news, and so was Jazz's mom. She was just telling me how much the kids missed their brother, so I knew they would be hype that he was finally coming home. I knew I would put him in the bed with me where I could keep an eye on him just in case he needed to go the bathroom, or needed more medicine. This was going to be a journey, but I was more than ready to take on the challenge.

"And what about Jasmine?" my mother-in-law asked. I was wondering the same thing.

"We are going to keep her under for a little while longer just to be sure that the pressure in her skull is going down the way it's supposed to. That way it would hopefully lessen any brain damage that may have occurred. With the drilling we performed on her skull, the pressure will subside fairly quickly if everything continues to go as planned."

"Brain damage?" she said more in disbelief than shock. We were informed of the possibility of such things on the night of the accident, and I guessed we were all just hoping for the best.

"How would we know the severity of it?" she asked again, fear creeping up in her voice.

"We won't know until she wakes up. She may be perfectly fine, or it may be severe. As of right now she's having normal brain activity, but it's hard to tell."

"Okay, thank you for everything you are doing," I finally intervened to keep her from getting even more upset. This entire situation was depressing, and I just wanted it to be over.

"No problem. If you have any other questions I'm on call."

After he left the room, we both sort of breathed a sigh of relief. We had one out of the woods, and if Jazz would pull through soon everything would be on track.

Later in the evening Jazz's mom followed me over to the house so that we could prepare for Jordan and the rest of the kids coming home. I had about twelve weeks home with my kids, and hopefully my wife would join us before I went back to work. When we pulled up, I was glad to see that my blood was covered with a new coating of snow so that she wouldn't have to see it. That scenario was just embarrassing, and I just wanted to forget it even happened.

When we went inside we got to work with changing the linen on all the beds, and picking up around the house. Jazz's parents were staying at her brother's house not too far from here, so once we were done she called Jazz's father to let him know she was on her way. I sat by the window with the phone in my hand and waited until she was safely pulled off, and I didn't move until she called to let me know she had arrived safely. It wasn't until then that I was able to kick back and grab me a beer. I needed to get my head on right, and I knew once the kids got back I would have to focus on them. I reminisced about my life over the last four years, and I knew I would do whatever I had to do to get us back.

All of it wasn't a total bust. There were those times over the years when Jazz and I were able to come together as a unit and operate like a normal family. Especially when it came to supporting the kids with school. Even when a morning was hectic, we always showed up to any function, parent-teacher conference, school play, or whatever else was going on the way we were supposed to. I must say, when things were good with me and Jazz, it was amazing. When things got bad though, oh my goodness it was the worst ever.

Rising early the next morning, I made my way up to the hospital to check on my family. Monica had been on my mind all night, but I was able to refrain from calling the number that I got from Jazz's mom. I didn't feel like that kind of drama in my life with her, and I dismissed the thought almost as soon as it popped in my head. I didn't feel like playing with fire.

When I got to my son's room, he was up being fed breakfast by the nurse in between talk about *SpongeBob SquarePants*. I was so happy to see him up. He still looked tired, but he was alive. At that moment that was all that mattered in the world.

"Daddy!" he yelped out in a weak, scratchy voice that almost brought me to tears. There was no way in the world I was going to be able to tell this boy that he wasn't my flesh and blood.

"I'm here, son. How are you feeling?" I asked as I kept my tears in check, and resisted the urge to scoop him up into my arms.

"Everything hurts, Daddy," he spoke in a tiny voice that pulled at my heart.

"We had just gave him some pain medicine, Mr. Cinque, and it should be kicking in soon."

I thanked her, and told her that I would feed him the rest of his breakfast. Switching places, I sat close to the bed after kissing him on the forehead. Studying his slightly swollen face, I couldn't help but try to place it. Whose face did he have? Banishing the thought immediately, I smiled as I fed him a little more food. The medicine was starting to take effect, and I could see him trying to fight to keep his eyes open.

"Daddy, will you be here when I wake up?" he asked right before drifting off.

"I sure will, son," I responded as I laid the back of the bed down, and positioned the pillows so that he could be comfortable. He would be going home pretty soon, and I couldn't wait.

Chapter 20

Monica: All's Fair in War and War

I waited a little while longer before backing out of the driveway just to make sure my little follower wasn't creeping back up on me. Well, that and I saw the shades move in the old Cinque house, and I didn't want the resident to think I was lost or crazy. It puzzled me what all of that was about, and I didn't have a clue as to who would want me trailed. Yeah, I had tons of enemies in Philly, but there were too many to pinpoint at the moment. Besides, I still had to figure out where I was going to stay.

It had been a few hours since I'd been back to the hospital, and I had yet to make it to the mall. I didn't even feel like going at this point. Turning the car onto the street, I decided to just go back to the hospital, and figure it all out from there. The streets were still a mess from a fresh snowfall on top of all the bullshit that we already had, so it took me a little while to maneuver back through the city. By the time I found a parking space across the street from the hospital, my mind was racing a mile a minute and I knew I would need to find a warm bed soon. I needed to recharge so that I could be on point. It was like my enemies could smell my blood in the air, and were trying to box me in. As long as it was understood that I would put up one hell of a fight, that's all that mattered. *I can't be bagged that easily, folks better recognize!*

When I entered the building, the cute little receptionist was back at the desk with her sunny disposition, but I didn't even feel like trying to figure her out today. I did wave hello on the walk by though, and hopped in the first elevator available going up to the room. As I was walking down the hall, I was relieved that none of the Cinques were out and about. Their son was on a different floor, so I was sure someone was there, just not down here right now.

As I strolled the hall, I could see into the patients' rooms. The rooms in the intensive care unit were different, and a shaded window was there as opposed to a solid wall. The doctor said that the judge would only be down there until he was stabilized, and then he would be moved to a bed on the telemetry unit. Nosey by nature, I peeked into the rooms, seeing nothing but sadness and despair. This entire floor was depressing, and gave me goose bumps.

Making my way down the hall I almost tripped over my own feet when I came across Jasmine's room. Now, when the judge was admitted to ICU I didn't think the possibility of running into Jasmine was high because the ICU was huge and there were a ton of rooms on this floor, and when we got here everything was a blur so I wasn't really thinking about it. To see her now was crazy. My goodness, she looked horrible! I mean, her car was wrapped around a utility pole just a few days ago, but I wasn't prepared for what I saw. Her entire face was black and blue, and she had all kinds of tubes coming from her body. I couldn't believe my damn eyes, and had to get a closer look.

Checking my surroundings to make sure the coast was clear, I dipped into her room and stood beside her bed. She had tight, angry-looking stitches across her left eyebrow, wrapping around her jaw, and stopping just at her perfect lips. Dark purple to almost black bruises covered her swollen face, making her look like an alien. A small patch of hair near her ear was shaved off, and I assumed it was from having to have her jaw wired shut. I found myself having to get wired down once years ago, but that's a story for another time.

The dull beep of the machines that she was hooked to in combination with a slight swooshing sound let me know that she was still alive, but the machines were probably what was keeping her here. I reached out hesitantly to touch her hand, and it felt cold and clammy. Snatching my hand back, I was shocked to find a lone tear traveling down the side of my face. I knew the accident was bad, but I didn't know it was this serious.

"Jazz, what were you doing out in a storm?" I asked the dead air, not really expecting a response. I stood there for a little while longer just taking it all in, deciding to leave before I was caught. Just as I was turning around, I could hear someone clearing his throat. Spinning around completely I was greeted by a handsome doctor who held an amused yet puzzled look on his face.

"She's been down for a few days now, but I don't remember meeting you. Are you a friend of the family?" the doctor asked in a deep voice as he entered the room. Taking a second to wipe the tear from my face, I got myself together before answering.

"Yes, Jasmine and James are . . ." I trailed off, not sure of how much to reveal. He didn't need to know that I was a home wrecker who left my baby because I was selfish, and just now decided to pop up and check on him. I also didn't want to say too much because I was sure the doctor would mention it to James whenever he came back up to visit. "They are good friends of mine. I'm here visiting another friend, and I just happened to see Jasmine in here."

"Oh okay, well Mrs. Cinque is unresponsive at the moment, and since there isn't a visitor restriction list I guess it's okay, but I want you to make this visit quick so that she can rest peacefully, Mrs. . . . " He trailed off, waiting for a name.

"Stone . . . Sheila Stone," I replied, giving him the judge's secretary's name instead of my own. In fact, I needed to see what was going on with old Sheila anyway. *It's been years, and I'm sure she misses me. Not!*

"Okay, Mrs. Stone. Wrap this visit up quick, and have a great night."

"Okay, I will."

Once the doctor was gone I turned and stared at Jazz for a few more minutes. What was going on in the Cinque household that shit got this bad between them? This was how I was able to get back in before, and something told me I needed to use this down time between them to get next to my son while I still could. James, I was sure, wouldn't have a problem, but if Jazz was anything like I remembered, she would definitely make this shit an issue beyond what it really was.

Pulling out my cell phone, I focused in on her bruised face and snapped a few pictures of her. Securing my phone back in my bag, I walked off to find the judge, contemplating if I would sell the pictures, and to what news station. I was sure they were worth some type of money, but for now I would sit on them. Just in case I had to use them to my advantage. *You just never know these days.*

Making my way down the hall, I was stopped by two bodyguards who were blocking the judge's door. Before I could go clean off, I was given an envelope and a menacing look as I was instructed to leave the premises. One of the guards took the liberty of escorting me to the elevator, and warned me not to spazz out and to just read the letter. I saw a woman sitting next to the judge's bed, but I couldn't really make out her face from the door. It was probably his miserable-ass wife. I saw her at the airport, so she knew I was here. I was just wondering if she knew we were hooking up while I was here. Still shocked, I got into the elevator, and stepped back as he pushed the button for the ground floor and stepped back out, giving me one last evil look as the doors closed.

I was numb as I walked through the hospital and out to my car, seemingly not breathing until I was safely inside with the doors locked. I sat in silence for a long while before realizing I still had not opened the envelope. Inside was a set of keys that fell into my lap, and a note. Apparently, the judge's wife came up to the hospital while I was gone because she couldn't find him for about a day or so. Calling around to all of the area hospitals, she found out that he was at HUP, and came over to see what happened. That just answered my question about the mystery woman in the room. The butler made up some crazy story about them shoveling the grounds near City Hall and him complaining of chest pain, which led to him being in the ICU as a heart attack patient. She obviously didn't believe the shit, or her ass wouldn't have locked everything down.

When the hell did he find time to write all of this? was all I could think as I continued to read. To cover the judge's ass, he set up a visitors list so that none of the women the judge was sleeping with would be able to just pop up. That satisfied my second curiosity of the night. Inside was the key to the hideaway, which his wife knew nothing about, and the address with directions on how to get back there. The butler was instructed to have me stay there until the judge was able to communicate. What kind of backyard barnigan's bullshit was this?

Feeling like I didn't really have a choice—after all, all of my shit was at the judge's spot—I started the car and got myself together so that I could take the drive out. This was some bullshit if I'd never been involved in any before, and I knew I needed to make my stay in Philly short and sweet. This was already getting to be too damn much for TV!

The directions were precise, citing landmarks and all as I carefully drove out to the outskirts of the city. A dusting of snow fell as I drove, and I took my sweet old time, not wanting to end up wrapped around a pole like Jazz had been just days ago. The only difference between us two was that she had family who cared enough to visit and rush up there to make sure she was okay. If my car skidded out of control and crashed who did I have to call? My sister? If anything she would only care long enough to get a hold of my money and any policy info that I had to collect on. My brother had been MIA for as long as I could remember, and most of the time I forgot that he even existed.

These thoughts made me sad as I drove, knowing that I was really in the world all by myself. Pulling the car to the side of the road to avoid a potential collision, I put my head on the steering wheel once I was safely in park and cried my little eyes out. One would think that I would be immune to these feelings by now, but every so often they crept up on me and broke me down. For a second I thought about calling Jaydah up for company and comfort, but she worked my nerves so bad in Atlanta that I couldn't even be bothered.

Shaking off the sad feelings as best as I could, I eased the car back on the road and kept moving toward the judge's spot. When I finally got there, the butler greeted me at the door, and came to help me inside. Once the door was locked for the night, I barricaded myself in the room, and hopped in the shower to wash the day off. I made sure the door was locked because I didn't want the butler's creepy ass to be masturbating to my naked body while I was in the shower. I mean, he didn't look creepy as far as description, but there was a quiet creepiness about him that I just couldn't put my finger on at the moment. On top of all of this, I was horny as hell, and I didn't want him to catch me at a weak moment. I saw the way he looked at me, and if he kept it up my pussy would be sitting on his lips before he could hum a tune.

Taking the time to dry off and moisturize, I slipped into some boring pajamas, afterward popping out my laptop to download the pictures of Jasmine onto my flash drive. Looking at the pictures, the scarring looked even more brutal as I studied her face up close. Shaking my head, I couldn't believe what had happened to her. It made me rethink selling the pictures, but I knew I would keep them just in case shit got crazy when it came to my son. It was a shame, but it wasn't my fault so I wasn't about to feel guilty.

I downloaded the pictures quick, then made myself comfortable on the bed. My stomach was growling something serious, reminding me that I hadn't eaten all day. I wanted to call the butler, but I didn't want him to have a reason to come up to the room. Taking the chance, I slipped on my Ugg slippers and crept through the house. When I made my way to the kitchen, I found a tray of food set up for me. Creep factor number five! How could he just assume I was hungry? Dismissing the fact, I looked to see what he made me. I had a thing about eating in the room and I already did it once, so I opted to eat at the kitchen bar instead. Searching through my phone, I looked at some e-mails from potential buyers from my art gallery listing as I noshed.

Out of the corner of my eye I saw movement, and I turned to find the butler preparing a sandwich for himself. Damn, he was light on his feet. I stared at the man as he moved about in the massive kitchen like I wasn't even there. Sizing him up I concluded that he had to be gay. Okay, so it wasn't like I was sitting here in lingerie, but I still looked damn good in my Victoria's Secret pajama pants and wife beater. No bra or panties underneath by the way, and I smelled delicious! A sultry mix of pineapple and coconut radiated from my skin in tantalizing waves that even turned me on, so I knew he had to be on it. This man would be a fool and gay, both at the same time, not to want this.

Deciding to test the waters just to see what he would do, I sauntered over to start some shit. He was busy spreading mustard on his bread and pretending like he didn't notice my sexy ass in this room. Stepping out of my clothes, I kindly slid the platter he was working on to the side, and hopped up on the counter, him still standing there holding the knife and the bread. Spreading my legs wide, I leaned back on my elbows, giving him full access to my pierced clit and juicy hole. My nipples were standing at attention, and I had an "I dare you" look on my face. He looked like he was contemplating taking the risk, and I counted down from ten in my head giving him even less time than that to make up his mind. As I approached "six" and prepared to close my legs, he leaned in and swirled his tongue around my clit.

Good boy, I thought as I took the liberty of placing my legs on his shoulders and scooting to the edge so that he could have full access. After this stressful ass day I needed some release, even if it was from the damn butler.

Chapter 21

James: Welcome Back, Jordan

My son was coming home today. After about two weeks, and a major setback, he was finally getting out of the hospital. The puncture in his lung was giving him more trouble than the doctors anticipated and he had to go back into surgery because there was a small leak near the inside suture site, but he pulled through just fine. The kids were so glad he was coming to the house, but it was a bittersweet moment because their mom was still down for the count. Splitting my time between home and the hospital was draining, but I didn't have a choice. Yes, Jazz's family was there to help, but I had to step up to the plate and take care of my business. The doctor said that the swelling in her brain was making progress and going down as scheduled, and they didn't want to chance waking her up too early and making matters worse. She responded to the touching of her feet, and hands, and displayed normal brain activity for someone in a dream state. I was relieved to hear that, and was happy to know that there was still a chance.

The kids and I spent the entire morning decorating the house for Jordan's welcome home party. After baking cupcakes and hanging streamers and balloons, we cleaned up and were ready to go. I warned the kids before I left that Jordan wouldn't be able to run around with them because of the type of surgery he had, and he might be asleep well before the party was over, and they appeared to understand. Janice was super excited because her other half was finally back. She was lost without him, and I could see it all in her actions. She wasn't as energetic as the other kids, and was sad all the time. When I told her that he was coming home, her entire mood changed. *Thank you, Jesus!* There were other family members there as well to great him, and everything was going as planned for the first time in never.

Jasmine's mom and dad stayed with the kids at home and her brother rode with me up to the hospital to help me with Jordan. I didn't want Jordan to see his mom in the ICU, so we stopped there first to see Jasmine before going up. I knew I would have to bring the kids up eventually, but not in her current state. They would have tons of questions that the younger ones wouldn't comprehend and it was just too much at once.

When we got to the room, the doctor was there charting observations, and instructing one of the nurses on doses of medication for Jasmine. We stood back to let him conduct business, waiting patiently for him to finish. I knew he would fill me in on everything afterward. It didn't take him long to finish up, and pretty soon he was ready for us.

"Mr. Cinque, it's home-going day for young Jordan, right?" he asked as he shook my and my brother-in-law's hands.

"Yes, sir, it is." I smiled at him. "The kids and I are excited."

"That's good. He's been waiting for you guys since early this morning," he responded as he scribbled something else in Jasmine's chart. "As for your wife, I pushed up her dosage of pain medication due to her response to the pain overnight. She hasn't woken up yet, but her blood pressure did shoot up a little, and the nurse charted some incoherent moans, indicating discomfort. She was taken off of the drugs that put her in the coma-like state so that she could wake up slowly."

I nodded as he talked, not really sure on how to respond. I had so many mixed emotions, and I wasn't really sure how I was going to be able to deal with Jasmine once she was finally allowed to wake up. How would she respond to her scars? So many emotions and questions were swirling around in my head, and I had to take a seat to digest it all.

"So, for now, I want you to enjoy your time with your son. The hard part hasn't begun yet, James. Once Jasmine comes through, it's going to take a lot of work and determination. There's a possibility that she will be angry at first, and maybe for a long while. We have therapy and everything here to help you through. For now, concentrate on your son, and everything else will fall into place."

I nodded my head as he talked, going into my own thoughts. Were we going to need therapy? I was certain that she was going to be angry because it was my fault that she was in here in the first place. Shit just got real, and I would be the first to admit that I wasn't handling it too well. It just sunk in that it was going to be a long time before there would be some kind of normalcy in our family. *Lord, just help me get through it.*

"So, take a few minutes to let your wife know that you are here. She can hear you, she just can't respond right now. The nurses are here if you need anything, and I know Jordan is excited, so enjoy your ride home," the doctor concluded, shaking our hands and giving the nurse further instructions before leaving.

I was stuck on stupid for a minute just standing there staring at Jazz. Her brother excused himself to give me a little privacy, letting me know that he would be waiting outside the room. There was an awkward silence in the room. It was funny how since she'd been here I never bothered to say too many words to her. The majority of the time I just sat and stared at her and wished that things were different. What was I supposed to say? I was sorry that things turned out like this? I'd already said that a million times. I guessed she would want to know if the kids were okay, but after telling her that what else was there to talk about? It was too early to talk about the "who's your daddy" issue with the twins, and we would just have to cross that road when we get there.

Taking a seat next to her bed, I took her hand into mine and just stared at her. At that moment I didn't see the banged and bruised Jasmine lying in a hospital bed. At this moment it was our wedding night, and we had just finished making love for the third time. Even on that night I couldn't believe I lucked up, and got to marry her. Tracing a finger along her bruise, I saw her at a time when she was taking a quick nap and exhausted from carrying our first set of twins, and not in a medically induced coma. We were so excited and cautious at the same time because she had already miscarried twice before. She had made it to almost seven months, and the twins were doing good.

"Jazz . . ." I began in a hesitant voice, trying to unscramble my words and my thoughts. "Jazz . . . I'm sorry this happened to you. I know I've already apologized a million times, and if I need to I'll do it a million more. I love you, and I'll be here for you when they wake you up."

Her fingers tightened a little around my hand, and a tear slipped from my eyes. She heard me, and that's all that mattered. I sat there a moment longer, taking her in and remembering the times we had. Even the dumb shit that happened over the years, and I knew for certain I wasn't meant to spend my life with anyone else but her. As I prepared to leave, the doctor stepped back into the room.

"James, I'm glad I was able to catch you before I left for the day," the doctor began as he walked closer to us. "A young lady stopped by earlier to see your wife. I believe her name was Sheila. She said she didn't know your wife was here and that you guys are good friends. Just wanted to tell you that just in case she called."

"Oh okay, thanks a lot," I responded. Monica was a slick bitch indeed, and I knew I needed to stop her in her tracks before she started some shit. That was clever of her to give the doctor a different name, but I knew the game and was already five steps ahead of her conniving ass.

"No problem, I'm on call if you need me."

After giving Jazz a kiss on her forehead, I met up with her brother in the hallway, and we made our way up to Jordan's room. I felt for my wallet, remembering that was where I stuck Monica's number, and I decided that I would call her once I got settled later in the day and all of the kids were asleep. This bitch always showed up at the most inopportune times, and I had to get her straight before Jazz came back into the picture. My wife didn't need to be stressed out with her antics; we already had enough drama going on.

When we approached Jordan's room I could hear his laughter before I even got to the door. He sounded stronger today, and that just warmed my heart to know he was recovering in a timely fashion. I hated to see my son all strapped up and taped up with tubes coming out of everywhere, and I was glad to see them removed. It was just too damn emotional. He was cracking up watching a cartoon, and his little voice spoke volumes of how he was feeling.

When I and his uncle walked into the room, his face lit up, and my heart broke when he tried to move in the bed and realized he couldn't. Quickly moving to his bedside, I took him into my arms as gently as I could, and gave him a hug. He looked so happy to see us, and I was definitely glad that he was well on his way to getting better. Just thinking that he could have easily died in that car crash brought me to tears every time, but I had to be strong for him.

"I'm going home today!" my son shouted as he jumped around a little too much for my liking. The pain medicine that they had him on must have really been on point because he was acting like he didn't feel a thing.

"Yes, you are. Are you ready to see your brothers and sisters?" I asked him as I helped his uncle change him into an outfit to go home in. The streets were a little better today, but it was still really cold outside, so we made sure to bundle him up as best we could with keeping him comfortable at the same time.

"Yes, I miss everybody," he said in an excited voice. I swear, they learned so fast from their older siblings, and oftentimes people would be amazed that the twins were so young.

"That's good. They all missed you too," I spoke to him as I blinked back tears. "We have a surprise for you when you get home."

"You do?" he asked with that bright smile on his face that almost made me forget that he was conceived by someone else. "Will Mommy be there?"

The room went silent, and I looked to Jazz's brother for help. He busied himself with the packing of Jordan's stuff, but I could see the nervousness in him. How did I answer the question without causing alarm in my young son? He was still fragile from his own shit, so I didn't need him to worry about something that he couldn't fix.

"Mommy won't be home for a while because she's not feeling well," I began, hoping that he understood. "Your grand-mom and your brothers and sisters are waiting for you though. Are you ready to get out of here?"

"Yes, Daddy," he said as his little eyes began to close. The medicine that they had him on was making him sleepy, and at the right time. Lord knows I didn't feel like answering a bunch of questions that I really didn't have the answer to. Jazz's brother looked relieved as well that Jordan was falling asleep, and once I signed the discharge papers, and got the medicine from the pharmacy, we were ready to go.

As I drove back through the city to take my son home, I just hoped that I could do this by myself. Although I had plenty of help from the family, everyone couldn't stay forever, and would have to get back to their own lives pretty soon. I also had to get at Monica before she started acting crazy. It'd been a few years, but I wasn't sure about her mental state. For all I knew she might just try to take her son from us, and that in itself was a whole, entirely different headache that I didn't feel like dealing with. Jazz probably wouldn't mind seeing him go since she never really got attached to him in the first place and he was such a problem child in her eyes, but the kids would be devastated and I wasn't about to let that happen. This was too much going on at one time, but it was happening for a reason. It was just time for me to embrace it, and try to move forward.

Chapter 22

Monica: Stirring the Pot

I was getting bored sitting around this house. The judge was still locked down in the hospital surrounded by security, and I wasn't permitted to leave the house without a guard as well. This was some bullshit, and I swore as soon as I checked on my seed I was out of this joint. *Philly can kiss my black ass.* Shit with the butler got real old real quick as well. He had the tools to get things popping; he just didn't know how to use them. That was a shame, too, because his head game was off the hook! I ended up beating off in my room because this fool just wasn't hitting the mark.

So, I found myself not wanting to do shit, and the only time I called the butler was when I wanted something to eat. The streets were clearing up, and the storm had moved on, so it was safe to go outside now. I just didn't have anywhere to go. I wasn't even amused by the Cinque updates on the news anymore, and I was getting pissed because James had yet to call me. What was this fool waiting on? The one time I snuck up to the hospital I found out that their son had been discharged by cutie behind the desk, but Jazz was still there. I attempted to visit Jazz, but as soon as I stepped off the elevator, the judge's bodyguards rushed me and had me escorted back out. They weren't even trying to hear that I was there to see someone else, and that time I was actually threatened not to show my face up there again. That was like a week ago, and I was ready to bounce.

The plan was to dip into Philly, check on my seed, and slide back out undetected, but shit never worked out the way I wanted it to. I had a damn lunatic following me around in a car I didn't recognize, but it had me nervous about going back out on the street alone. The Cinques were experiencing their own bullshit, and I was stuck in this gorgeous-ass house with nothing to do but play with my pussy all day. For some that may have been the bomb, but for me this was not the move. I wanted out now!

I just couldn't bring myself to leave for some reason. There was no one or nothing keeping me from driving to the Philadelphia International

Airport, turning in my rental, checking my bags, and getting the hell out of dodge. Not one thing that I could think of really. My assistant kept me abreast on business, and everything was running smoothly. She even checked the condo while I was away, and there was nothing to report, so what was really keeping me here?

Even though I gave up my son it was my responsibility to make sure that he was safe and being taken care of properly. This feeling I was getting in my gut wasn't merely a case of bad gas; my son needed me. Or so I led myself to believe. From what I'd seen so far he didn't seem to be in harm's way. His hair was cut and his clothes were clean, he was gathered with the family and not set off by himself, and he looked like he was being fed and not undernourished. There was just something that I couldn't see right now, and I knew if I left before finding out what it was I would regret it, so for now I was staying until I felt like I could go in peace and not have to worry about him.

Deciding to make contact with the outside world, I thumbed through the Rolodex in the judge's office to see who I could get to help me with this kid situation that I was having. I knew there had to be someone out there who could help me, and I didn't want to have to wait on the judge to get better to get to work on this. I was not staying in Philly any longer than necessary. I had businesses to run back in Atlanta, and being here wasn't working in my favor.

A lot of the names I didn't recognize, but from the listing of the Rolodex they appeared to hold prestigious positions so I took the liberty of storing the info in my phone of the ones that I could utilize later on. I made my visit to the office quick, after snagging Sheila's number, because I didn't want to get caught by the butler. After all, Stenton was just asking for someone to be in his business. My office would never just be left open for anyone to walk in and browse around. I had too much at stake.

Once back in my room, I blocked my number and called Sheila to see if she would answer. She was probably at work and wouldn't answer right away, and I decided against leaving a message because I knew she would never call back. Allowing the phone to ring until the voice mail picked up, I hung up and called the courthouse instead. That was a phone she had to answer.

"District Court, how may I direct your call?" Sheila answered the phone in a very professional voice that held a lot more confidence than I remembered. I guessed once I left Philly she was able to do her.

"Sheila, it's Monica. I need your help," I began, ready to run down a list of errands for her. As I was talking I noticed the phone was awfully quiet on the other end. Taking the phone from my ear, my screen read that the call was disconnected. *Did this bitch just hang up on me?* Going to my call log, I hit the number again, waiting for her to answer.

"District Court–"

"Did you hang up on me?" I spat into the phone, ready to get rowdy if necessary.

"Monica, now is not the time–"

"Then when is the time? This is about my son," I said, cutting her off midsentence.

"Look, I get out of here at five. Get a pen and pad to take down my number and we can discuss it then. Right now, I'm working and don't have time for this."

Seems like we got a backbone while I was gone, I thought as I got a piece of paper ready. I already had a number for her, but the judge's Rolodex may not have been up to date, or she may have been operating from a different phone. The number she gave me was the same number I had, and after confirming that I would call her at five-fifteen, I hung up. I needed to get in touch with James, but I wasn't really sure how to go about it.

Falling back on the bed, I just stared at the ceiling, trying to sort everything out. My phone ringing scared the shit out of me, and I jumped up to see who it was. The screen read Jaydah's name above the number, and I was not beat for her today. I was surprised that it took her this long to call me. Maybe she had book signings or something that kept her busy because surprisingly she hadn't called me since we touched down in Philly three weeks ago. I wondered to what I owed the pleasure of her call today. I was almost tempted to let her go to voice mail, but I was bored out of my mind and could use some form of entertainment for the time being.

"Hello?" I spoke into the phone in a sleepy voice like I had been awoken from a nap or something. Hopefully she would take that as a hint and not want to talk my head off.

"Monica, how have you been?" She spoke in what I assumed, by the huskiness in her tone, was supposed to be a sexy voice, but I was not moved by it at all. As good as the sex was with her, I didn't need to give this chick any ideas. She was too damn clingy for me, and I just didn't feel like the shenanigans.

"I've been good," I responded, not bothering to give up any detail. She knew what I was here for, but I wasn't about to give up details. We were just fucking, ain't like we were buddies.

"Okay . . ." she said, becoming silent for a while. I just sat on the phone, listening to her breathe. "Well, did you find your son?"

"I never had to look for him. I know who he's with."

"Yeah, but you said they had moved, and—"

"So, what exactly is the purpose of this call? I know you didn't call to get in my business," I responded, rudely cutting her off. This bitch was acting like we knew each other forever.

"Well, I was in fact calling to see if you made progress, but you've made that clear that it's not my business," she answered in a measured tone that indicated I might have struck a nerve and was working her nerves. Ask me if I cared.

"I'm doing okay."

"Cool. So . . . ummm . . . when are you going to let me eat your pussy again?"

Speechless. Direct and right to the point was usually how I liked it, but this one definitely caught me off guard. I must say she had me intrigued. Taking a second to think, I knew I had to meet up with Sheila later in the day, but it was still early. Maybe I did have time to fool around with Jaydah for a second. I could definitely give her something to write about in one of her freaky novels. The butler was out getting food and paying bills for the judge, and I didn't see security anywhere so maybe I could sneak out undetected for a while. He wouldn't even know I was gone.

"Okay, what's your address? I can't stay long, but I guess I can come and play for a little while."

"Or I can come to you if that would make it easier," she offered, sounding suddenly happier that I agreed.

"No, I'll come to you," I said, looking for a pen to write down her address. I couldn't be that disrespectful and invite her here because I didn't know how the judge would feel about it. I had a feeling that I might be able to talk the butler into a threesome, but Jaydah didn't like to go home when it was time. I found that out the hard way when she came to my house. Basically, the safest bet was to just meet up with her.

Writing her info down, I took a few minutes to refresh and get myself together because if I knew her, she would be on me the moment I walked in the door. The streets looked pretty clear from here, so I made sure I was by myself before jetting out. I didn't feel like being surrounded by bodyguards today, especially since I didn't really need it. Unless the judge had a hit out on me or some shit.

I got down to Jaydah's house in no time, keeping an eye on the rearview mirror to make sure I wasn't being followed. I didn't know who was trying to set me up, and my motto was always to trust no one. When I pulled up to her condo I could hear my phone ringing, and became instantly annoyed. *Is this bitch eyeballing me from the parking lot?* I never told her what kind of car I was driving, so how did she know it was me? Searching my bag for the phone, I pulled it out, ready to go in on her ass, only to see a strange number on my screen. I didn't think nothing of answering, figuring maybe she was calling from a house phone.

"I'm on my way up now," I spoke into the phone as I gathered up my stuff. She must have been extra horny to be stalking me, but it was cool. I was one hell of a catch.

"Monica?" A male voice came across, and I had to pause for a second. Was this who I thought it was?

"James? Is this you?"

Chapter 23

James: Moving Forward Looking Back

"Monica, I'm sorry if I caught you at a bad time," I stuttered into the phone nervously. I didn't know if she was going to ram on me and start cursing me out or what, and I just wanted to brace myself for it.

"Oh no, it's not a bad time," she responded, just as nervous. "What's going on?"

I had to pull the phone back and look at it. Was she serious? Not sure what kind of games Monica was playing, but I just wasn't beat for it. *She gave my mother-in-law the number to contact her for a reason, and if it ain't about her son then we ain't got shit to talk about.*

"Well, you took extreme measures for me to contact you. Is this about your son?"

Again the phone went quiet on the other end. I was starting to lose my cool with her, and this was about to be a wrap before it got started.

This was the first time in weeks that I got a moment to myself, outside of Jordan being upstairs sleep, and I needed to get this with Monica—whatever *this* was—done and over with. I just didn't have the energy to go through the motions with her at this point in my life.

"Ummm, yeah. Is there a way I can meet him . . . I mean, meet up with you to discuss the situation?" she asked in a still-nervous voice. I decided to be a little nicer to Monica. I was sure this had to be hard for her, and it took a lot for her to even step foot back in Philly in the first place.

"Well, we definitely need to talk. When can we hook up?"

"Right now."

Now it was my turn to be quiet. I didn't want to get caught up in her web again, so I didn't want to bring her to the house. I also didn't want being seen out with her in public to be misconstrued, so I knew I had to be discreet. We definitely couldn't meet in Philly, but I couldn't leave my son alone. The kids were at school, and the adults were at work. I was curious about what brought her back here, although I had an idea. We hadn't received a check from her since we moved, partly because Jazz never set up the post office box, so I was sure that the return mail was cause for alarm. Maybe getting her to the house real quick was the best move. At least there she could state her purpose and keep it moving.

"Hello?" she spoke into the phone, probably thinking that I hung up.

"Yeah, I'm here. Do you have a pen? I'll give you my address so that you can come by the house."

I regretted it as soon as I spit the numbers out, but it had to be done. Hopefully we could just get this done and over with, and her seeing a few pictures of her son would be enough. My luck was never that good, so I just braced myself for the worst.

What I needed Monica to understand was that she couldn't just pop back up into this boy's life like everything was cool. As crazy as shit was, Junior thought Jasmine was his mom. Plain and simple. Yeah, she was extra hard on him, but she was all he knew. He grew up with the other kids, and knew us as a family. What if she wanted to take him away? How would the kids react? So many thoughts went through my head, and I could feel myself starting to panic. Monica could act crazy if she wanted to, but if she tried some slick shit it would be on. I needed to restore some type of order before Jazz came home, and getting her out of the way was one of the top things on the list to do.

"How long will it take you to get here?" I asked as I looked around to double check that the house was neat. I didn't want her to think that we weren't on point around these parts.

"Give me thirty minutes."

"Don't be late."

Not even waiting for a response, I just hung up on her. I hated to admit it, but I was nervous. Monica made me weak, and I really hoped that she would be strictly business today. She still looked damn good, and I had to adjust my growing erection in my pants. Just thinking about what those lips and hips were capable of had me ready to get it popping. Shaking my head, I went to check on Jordan. He would definitely get my mind straight for that devil that was about to show up at my front door.

I thought to maybe at least call Jazz's mom to see if she could stop by after her workday was over; that way if things got heated she could possibly show up just in time to stop it. Monica was irresistible, and I knew I would want her. I just had to try my best to stick to the matter at hand.

The clock seemed to be moving in slow motion, being as though only about ten minutes had gone by. A part of me was hoping that she would show up early so that we could get this over with. I already decided that if she showed up even a minute late then she would have to reschedule. I didn't want her to be here when the kids got home from school because there would be too many questions. They would want to know who she was, and I would have to lie because they weren't ready. This was already becoming too much.

At the twenty-three-minute mark I heard a car pulling up to the door. My heart was pounding in my chest, and my palms were sweaty as I walked toward the door. Who was I kidding? I was not ready for this meeting, and I should have just told her that now wasn't a good time. Hell, it was too late now because she was already here.

Approaching the door, I took a deep breath before opening it, only to be greeted by Jazz's mom. Damn, she showed up too early! I thought she had to work, but she either had the day off or only worked a half day. I should have called her when I thought of it. At least I would have known she was on her way and I could have stalled her to show up after Monica got here. Well, it was too late now, and I would just have to wing it. After all, Monica only had about five more minutes to show up, and then it would be her loss.

Of course my luck wasn't that good, and as soon as I took the bags from my mother-in-law's hands to take in the kitchen I heard another car pull up. I kept walking like I didn't hear it, and decided to let her answer the door so that I could feign surprise that Monica actually showed up.

From the kitchen I heard a muted conversation between Monica and Jazz's mom, so I busied myself with putting the groceries away to buy more time before I went into the living room. Just as I was putting the eggs and milk into the fridge, the two women appeared in the kitchen doorway. I was speechless because Monica looked even sexier up close, and once again I had to control a growing erection.

"James," Jazz's mom began, "this is the young lady I saw at the hospital who gave me the number. I didn't know you called her."

"I just got around to calling her today," I responded as my eyes bounced around the room, trying not to make eye contact. It appeared that she was almost wallowing in my discomfort, but she wouldn't win today. "She's an old friend of Jazz's and mine."

"Yes, she told me that at the hospital. I'm going to be heading out soon. I just came to check on Jordan and to make sure the kids had food for breakfast. I have to get home to start dinner for that spoiled husband of mine," she said with laughter in her voice and love in her eyes. I wondered briefly if Jazz would feel that way about me one day.

"He should still be sleeping. I just gave him some pain medicine not too long ago."

"Okay, I'll go check," she said to me before turning away. "Go ahead and catch up with your friend. I'll stop back in before I go. It was nice to meet you again, Monica."

"Nice to meet you as well," she said, extending a sweet smile. She was so damn conniving and came off as sweet and innocent. I had to keep that in mind as I talked to her fine ass.

"Well, have a seat," I offered as I sat down on the opposite side of the kitchen table. This entire experience was just too soon, and I knew I was making a mistake. When was it going to bite me in the ass was my biggest concern. Jasmine would not be happy about Monica being here in this house, around these kids, or anywhere in Philly for that matter. I knew that would be another hurdle to cross, but I couldn't tell this woman she couldn't see her son. I mean, I could, but all that would do was cause problems in the long run, and it was better to just avoid the shit now. Jasmine would be angry but she would just have to get over it. It was a decision that both her mother and I thought was a good move, and as the man of the house the decision was final. I gave her mom bits and pieces surrounding Monica's involvement regarding the kids, and I knew I would have to fill her in once it was time for them to actually meet.

Staring at her for a moment too long, the first thing I noticed was that she still looked exactly the way she did the last time I saw her. She didn't appear to have aged at all; she just looked more mature. Everything was definitely still on point.

"So what brings you to my neck of the woods?"

"James, you already know what it is. I came to see about my son."

Before I could respond, Jazz's mom came back into the kitchen to let me know she was leaving. I excused myself to lock the door behind her, and to get myself together. I commended her for getting straight to the point, and for the first time since our initial conversation I felt like I could get through this. I just hoped she didn't flip the script on me and try to seduce me . . . She might just end up getting some head out of the deal. Yeah, I was sure her main reason for the visit was to see about her son, but Monica used sex to get results for everything. That wasn't to say that she hadn't changed over the years, but that's the Monica I remembered and it made me nervous.

Chapter 24

Monica: Any Way the Wind Blows

The moment James said that I could come to talk about my son, I hopped back in the car and was on the road. I was driving so fast that I forgot to call Jaydah and tell her that I had to make a detour. I left my phone in the car, so I couldn't even call her once I got inside, but it didn't matter. At this moment she was a nonfactor, and I had to handle my business.

We sat quietly at first once he returned to the kitchen. I smelled his cologne before I saw him. I had to squeeze my thighs together to keep my clit from jumping, and to control the splash that would soak my panties. I couldn't believe that this man still turned me on. He looked less bruised and beat up now, and I could tell that a lot of the scars would heal nicely, and not be a permanent fixture on his fine features. He looked more . . . mature. Like he got older, but not necessarily looked like an old man. A shy smile crept up on my face as a thought of one of the times we hooked up popped into my head, and I had to make myself stay focused. I was here to get the dibs on my son, and that was it, but if he made a pass I couldn't guarantee that I would resist.

"How is your wife?" I asked, my voice sounding foreign to my own ears, and I didn't recognize the sound coming out. I did a quick scan of the room, taking notice that it was just as laid out as the living area of the house. I wondered briefly what the bedroom looked like, but I knew I could never go anywhere near it. The things that would happen on that bed would be a sin and a shame, and that wasn't the purpose of my visit this time around.

"You're not here to talk about her."

Stung. James was playing hardball, and I knew I needed to bring my A game with him. It was apparent that this wasn't going to be a pleasant meeting, so I might as well get down to business. Now wasn't the time to pull punches.

"Okay, well I'm here because the checks were being returned and I couldn't get in contact with you. What's up with that? Then I get here, and this horrible-ass accident is going on, and I just needed to make sure my son is okay." I came at his neck with way more attitude than needed, but

I felt the conversation warranted it. No, I didn't come to talk about his damn wife, but asking about her was the polite thing to do. *Damn, I see I can't even be nice to this fool. Every time I think I can get out of "bitch mode," somebody shows me that I can't.*

"Okay, first off, he hasn't been your son since the day you dropped him off on my kitchen table. A check doesn't make him yours."

Boom! And there it is. I guess he told me, huh? I almost didn't have a comeback, but I wasn't about to let this fool chump me. He had the wrong chick for that. I took a second to gather myself, because James's simple ass was about to catch a bad break. I knew he may be angry about some shit, but he really didn't want it with me, and I guessed I needed to remind him of how ignorant I could get.

"James, you're about to take me to a place that I haven't been to in a long time. I did what I had to do at the time for me, and what was best for my son. You think that was easy for me?"

"I'm not saying—"

"And I'm not done," I cut his ass dead off. He was about to put me in my bag, and I had to rein it in before it got ugly in this joint.

"I did what was best for my son because I

knew I wasn't going to be able to provide a loving home for him. That shit was not easy, and I knew with you he would get the love he deserved. Who are you to judge me? What did you want me to do with him? Put him in foster care?"

"No, I wanted you to get a damn abortion. I told you that from jump."

Pow! It was like we were in a boxing ring and he kept giving me gut shots. I don't know what made me think that this was going to be a pleasant meeting, but I didn't think it was going to get this real this fast. It was obvious that there was some resentment toward me for jetting out, and it wasn't like I gave him a choice. I got that. I dumped my son on the Cinques and left. It was as simple as that. Maybe I should have at least kept in contact, but in all actuality I was really trying to get past this portion of my life.

I guessed sending the checks was my way of keeping an attachment, and keeping the guilt at bay. Hell, I needed some peace. I couldn't even get a real good sleep in the first year I moved to Atlanta because of the guilt. Rethinking my position, and the position I put him and his family in, I decided to go with a different approach. After all, I wasn't here to start trouble. I just wanted to make sure everything was cool.

"James, listen, I'm not here to disrupt your

life. I had a gut feeling that I needed to be here for whatever reason and I followed that instinct and came back. Not because I want to fuck up your marriage, or sleep with you, or take my son away. I just want to be sure that he is okay," I said with a straight face, partially telling the truth. My motive definitely wasn't to bed this man, and if my son was living in safe conditions that would solve my next issue and I could leave peacefully. He just needed to know that I was ready to do whatever it took to ease my mind, and if taking my son back to Atlanta was it, then that's where we would be headed.

The look on his face changed to one of a little less aggression, but the aggravation was still very evident. There were so many things that I could have done differently, because even though Jasmine probably didn't want any dealing with me, James still sent the pictures and the video clips and all of that to me so that I could still watch my son grow up. I owed him at least the courtesy of respecting his feelings.

"Listen, the kids will be getting home from school soon, and I don't want the first meeting to be this abrupt. I will call you in a few days once I've prepped the children for your arrival, and we will further discuss this situation then," he said, wiping his hand down his face. I could see the confusion and questions in his eyes, but I decided against pressing the issue. At this point I was just grateful that he was cooperating, so I would just leave it at that.

Thanking him again for his time, we shared an awkward hug at the front door that we both might have enjoyed a little too much. I almost melted in his arms as he held me close, and it was like we both didn't want to let go. I could feel his growing erection pressing against my stomach, but I gave him a pass because I knew if I pressed the issue it could have easily popped off. That and his son was upstairs. In combination of his kids coming home soon, and not knowing when one of his in-laws would pop their head in, I gave him a break and rolled out. He was definitely still weak for me, and I felt the same way.

Finally stepping back from his embrace, I did a light sprint to the car, making sure the coast was clear before pulling out. It wasn't until I got down about four blocks that I remembered I forgot to call Jaydah when I got back in the car. Of course I had 60 million missed calls and about 8,600 texts from her, but I didn't even care. I was definitely in a good mood, so whatever bad mood she had would change once I got there. I was gonna wear that ass out in more ways than one . . . if she didn't give me too much trouble that was.

Following the GPS directions, I made it to her house quickly and it didn't take long to find a parking spot that was closer to the door. As I was going up to her building she was ringing my phone again, but I sent her straight to voice mail, opting to deal with her face to face. When I approached her floor the phone started ringing again, and I could hear her getting an attitude as I walked up to her door. Oh, she was pissed, but she wouldn't be for long.

She didn't even bother to ask who it was as the door swung open and the attitude that showed in her face changed to a look of concern. I pushed past her, inviting myself into her place. Looking around, I could see she had the potential for good taste. She just needed a few of my paintings in here to seal the deal and she would be in there. Everything had its own neat space, and it didn't look as if she tried to clean up real quick because I was coming. It looked like it naturally stayed in order. Taking a seat on the couch without asking, I called her over to me. She was pouting, and it was too cute, but she came and straddled my lap anyway.

"I had an emergency," I began as I rubbed my hand across the exposed skin of her shoulders. She melted instantly, and I knew I had her exactly where I wanted her. "I got a call about my kid, and I needed to go handle it."

"It's okay, you don't have to explain anything to me. I was just worried," she responded, followed by a moan as I gently took her erect nipple into my mouth through her sheer night top. Homegirl was definitely ready to get it in, and I was about to definitely get in it.

"So, you're not mad at me?" I questioned as I ran a finger over her slit, through the matching thong that barely covered her pussy. My finger smeared the juice that seeped out of the side, up to her covered clit, soaking it a little. This was going to be fun.

"No . . ." She moaned out again. "I'm not mad at you."

"Good. Are you going to show me what I've been missing?" I asked as a finger slipped in between her folds, and was sucked in by her tunnel. Her walls clenched around my finger like she was milking a dick, and that shit had me turned all the way on.

Instead of responding, she lay down on the couch, lifting her legs to remove her thong, and spread her legs wide so that I could see her glistening pearl clearly. My mouth began to water immediately. Scooting down, I positioned myself between her legs, and ran my tongue across her swollen clit, making her jump. Taking my time, I slurped and sucked her into a screaming orgasm that I was sure made the earth move. Homegirl wasn't ready, and we wouldn't be stopping anytime soon. I'd been needing to get one off since I got here, and now was the perfect time. Replacing her face with Jasmine's, I gave her a session that she would never forget.

Chapter 25

James: Beautiful Liar

It took me awhile to unglue my feet from the door after Monica left. Just the smell of her had me open again, and I was almost tempted to peek into my checking account to see how much I had available for a night with her. Yeah, I knew now wasn't the time to be thinking about sex, but I was a man after all. Shit, I couldn't remember the last time I got laid properly, and I didn't even know when the next time would be. *Lord, let me just go check on my son, and get a snack ready for the kids.*

Peeking into my room, I saw that Jordan was still asleep. He shared a room with the boys normally, but with him having to heal, and the boys used to being rough I decided it was better to keep him with me during the night. He was moving around a lot better, and was able to go longer in between doses of pain medication, so that was a good thing. When I took him back for his follow-up visit the doctor said he was right on schedule, and would be back to normal real soon. I couldn't wait, and I knew his brothers and sisters were ready for some real playtime.

Janice was so attentive to her brother when he was around them, making sure he didn't try to run too fast and wasn't in any real pain. I could tell that she was happy to have him back. All of the kids were. I also noticed that Junior seemed a lot more at ease, and less troublesome without Jasmine around. He hadn't gotten in trouble in school since they'd been back, actually earning a gold star every day. The teachers were very impressed with that. He also wasn't as distant and mean to the other kids, and they all got along nicely. What was Jazz doing that I wasn't, and vice versa? The kids seemed at peace, and it was odd that none of them really inquired about her whereabouts. That definitely struck me as odd, and I couldn't point any fingers because I was out doing me most of the time, and Jazz would be stuck with the kids. I was sure she was extra stressed out, and was probably in here snapping on them. Things were definitely going to be different once she got back home so that we could maintain a happy household. It was a must for these kids.

From what the doctor had told me, things were looking good and she was having consistent brain activity for someone in her state. He was taking her out of the sleep-induced coma slowly and giving her a chance to wake up naturally, so it would be determined once she was awake when she would be able to come home. The dosage that he was using was being lessened over time to prevent any further complications. It was explained that bringing her from that type of sleep to fully awake wasn't a good idea. The family and I hoped that it would be soon.

I decided that I would talk to Jazz's mom about the situation with Monica. I didn't have anything to lose, so I was going to just run down the entire sordid affair from the beginning so that she could understand everything. The last thing I wanted to do was keep Monica from her son. I just needed her to know that she couldn't have him back. The kids would be devastated, and that would open up a can of worms that no one was ready for.

By the time the kids got home, I had peanut butter and jelly sandwiches and cold milk waiting for them on the table. They were usually hungry when they got in, and that would hold them over until dinner was done. I must admit that I could never be a *Mr. Mom*–type dude. All this cleaning and cooking, ironing and folding clothes, checking homework and doing projects was all too damn much for one person. Yet, Jazz did this and held down a job. Women are truly amazing.

Jordan was just waking up when the kids pulled up to the house in their uncle's truck. He volunteered to pick the kids up from the afterschool program for me so that I wouldn't have to drag Jordan out of the house every day in his condition. I wanted to talk to him about the situation, but I didn't want to risk getting punched in the mouth again. I even thought about Jazz's dad, but I wasn't sure how he would take it either. Jazz's mom was the safest bet, and I decided I would call her while the kids were enjoying their snack.

I was helping Jordan out of the bed and into the bathroom when the kids came barreling into the house. They were hyped up, talking about whatever happened in school, and I was sure they talked the entire ride home. Jazz's brother was running around as Junior and Jalil chased him around the living room in a never-ending game of freeze tag. Their laughter reminded me that sticking all of this out was worthwhile.

"Jordan!" the kids screamed in unison as we approached the steps to come downstairs. He smiled as he held on to the railing and took the steps down slowly. He was so excited to see the kids every day, and I knew that he couldn't wait to get back to school. The doctor said that he would only need a few more weeks. Hopefully Jazz would be home by then.

"Kids, there are snacks in the kitchen for you to eat until dinner is done. Everybody wash their hands first!" I yelled after them as they ran toward the kitchen. I couldn't help but smile at my children. Jazz's brother had the same look on his face.

"Thanks a lot for helping me out. Can I please at least give you gas money?" I asked him as I gave him a quick handshake. He refused every time, so I knew this time wouldn't be any different.

"No thanks, James. This is what family does for each other."

"I really appreciate this, man. Thanks for everything."

"No thanks necessary. See you tomorrow," he replied, giving me one last pound. "Bye, kids!" he called out toward the kitchen.

"Bye, Uncle Ronnie!" the kids sang in unison, sounding like their mouths were full. All we could do was smile.

I went to use the phone while the kids chatted about their day, and caught Jordan up on what was going on in school. I had a nagging thought on my mind, and as much as I was trying to get past it I couldn't. Deciding to first call Jazz's mom, I dialed the number that I had dialed what seemed like over a million times since this incident has happened. I needed some understanding and clarity, and I knew she would have the answer for me.

"Hi, Mom," I spoke into the phone the minute she answered.

"James, how are you and the kids?" she responded, and I could hear the smile in her voice.

"Everything is good. Are you busy? I just needed to talk to you about something real quick."

"Sure, just got to my son's house, about to start dinner. What's troubling you?"

"Mom, I'ma need you to grab a seat. This is about to be heavy."

It took me about forty-five minutes to run down the idea of the threesome turning into an actual act, and all that happened before that. I'd spent years blaming Monica solely for the demise of my marriage, when in reality had I not sought her out in the first place it wouldn't have even gotten to this point. Yeah, Monica had an agenda, but so did I. I just wanted a threesome. Who knew that it would turn into all of this?

"And the last time we saw Monica she was driving away from my house after leaving my son on the dining room table," I concluded with a sigh. After revealing to her who exactly the girl was who gave her the number at the hospital, it all clicked for her and she was extra quiet on the phone.

"Well, James . . ." she began, becoming quiet for a second again. "This is a tough decision. The things that you did in the past are just that: the past. Every mother wants to have a connection with her kid. I don't see it being a problem because she appears to come in peace. Let's make it a day over the weekend so that all of the kids can meet her at once, and we can all be there."

"I like that suggestion. Is this weekend too soon?" I asked, not sure if I would go through with it if I waited too long.

"Better now than never. Go ahead and give her a call. I'll come on Friday to help you break the news to the kids."

"Thanks, Mom. I appreciate everything you're doing."

After we hung up I sat for a minute to think about my next move. Something was telling me to just let it go, but I couldn't. Since we were all reconnecting and getting closure from past events, there was just one little matter that needed to be handled. Scrolling through my call log, I hit the number I had used to call Monica earlier, hoping she would answer. Three rings later she picked up, sounding like she was out of breath.

"Monica, I'm sorry to bother you. I just had a question to ask you."

"It's not a problem, James. Can you hold on for one second?"

"Sure."

It took her about a minute or so to return to the line, and she sounded a little clearer. I might have caught her in the middle of something, and the visual in my head caused my dick to jump in my pants. Shaking my head to clear the image, I attempted to focus on the situation at hand.

"Sorry about that. Is everything okay?" she asked in a concerned voice. She probably thought I was calling to tell her she couldn't see her son, but I squashed that immediately.

"Everything is fine. I just wanted to see if we could meet up on Friday to discuss the kid situation. My wife's mother will be here."

"Oh, sure, that's not a problem. Just give me a time and I'll be there."

"Be here by two, so that way we can talk before the kids arrive. It hasn't been decided yet how we will introduce you to the kids, but it will definitely be done," I informed her as my mind raced. I wanted this experience to be as smooth as possible without any backlash if I could help it. The way I figured it, if I gave Monica what she wanted, and that was to see her son, then we could be done with this and move on with our lives.

"James, I'll be there, and I really appreciate this."

"No problem. I'm just doing what I can. Just know that the kids may not be as receptive as you could be expecting them to be. You are a stranger to them, Monica."

"I totally understand that, and once again I appreciate everything you are doing."

After running down the discussion we would have, and how she would be introduced, she sounded a lot more relieved. That nagging thought in my head wouldn't go away, and I just needed to get it out and over with. It was like a now-or-never type of situation. I yelled her name out before she hung up and I lost the courage to dig for more information.

"Monica, I have a question to ask you, and I just need you to be honest with me."

“Sure, James, what do you need to know?”

“Well . . .” I paused before continuing. I was about to open a can of worms that I knew I probably wouldn’t be able to close, but I just couldn’t help it. “A few years ago when you left that letter on the table you said that Jasmine had an affair with some twins at the gym. How true is that statement, and can you help me find them?”

The line sounded like it went dead, until I heard her breathe on the other end. I needed to know the truth, and she was the only other person who could help me. I left that part out when I talked to Jazz’s mom. Although she found out when I did that the twins weren’t mine, she didn’t know that I had this suspicion for years. I needed to know the truth, by any means necessary.

Chapter 26

Monica: No Turning Back

Speechless. Who knew that James would bring that up after all this time? I mean, from what I saw, all of the kids looked like him. Why would he have a reason to believe that they weren't? Unless of course something went down with that twin who was in the hospital, and he found out that way. Either way, we already spent too much time keeping secrets, so I told him what I knew about his wife's baby father. Whichever one of the twins it was. Besides, I didn't want anything to compromise me seeing my son.

"Well, James, I can't promise you anything. I'll have to make a few calls because I haven't seen the twins in years. I overheard them at the gym talking about the threesome they had with Jasmine, and I felt you needed to know. That's why I included it in the letter I left you before I moved out of the city," I responded, referring to my good-bye letter that I left with my son, along with the adoption paperwork on their dining room table. I called myself tying up all the loose ends before I rolled out of here, and years later all of this mess was still an issue that was obviously never dealt with.

"They were bragging about my wife in public?" he asked, sounding angry and surprised.

Shit, that's what men do: lie and brag about their sexual trysts in public. Why was he so surprised? "Basically. You know how guys are at the gym. They all want to brag about who slept with who, who has the biggest dicks, et cetera. You know the drill. From what I heard, when you guys split up Jazz was going to them for personal training. I guess it got more personal than just working on the machines."

He got quiet for a minute, and I allowed him that time to digest what I just told him. Even though men cheat, it's different somehow when a woman does it. It's like, they can dick down a dog and it be cool, but as soon as we let someone else besides our mate dip in the cookie jar we are tainted, damaged goods. Women obviously do it better. Cheating, that is. Hell, not only did she step out, but she pushed out two babies and still held the secret for years. Jazz was a bad bitch, if I could say so myself. I guessed James had no reason to suspect her of being pregnant by someone else because they already had a set a twins, and twins probably ran in either or both of their families. I never cared enough to find out either way.

"Hello?" I spoke into the receiver to make sure he was still there since I didn't even hear him breathing.

"I'm still here. Could you just do me that solid and get the information for me? I would really appreciate it," he said, sounding weary and defeated.

"Sure, no problem. I'll get the info you need to contact them by Friday. I'll have it when I come over."

"Monica, thanks for everything. I really appreciate this."

"Thank you as well. I'll see you then."

I had to get my head together for a second. From what I gathered, it appeared that everything was really a mess over at the Cinques! It's always been said that what you do in the dark comes to light, but damn. I couldn't say that I blamed him though. If I had been in his situation I would have done the same thing. It's not like Jazz would keep it real with him about it anyway. Knowing her, she probably wouldn't even want to discuss it, and when you got something like that bugging at you, it's hard to let it go.

Looking to my left, I found a pissed-off Jaydah staring back at me. I apologized because we were in the middle of handling business, but I needed to take all calls, and I couldn't afford to miss any. I saw that it was almost five, and I needed to get at Sheila when she got off work. Rolling over I jumped right back into action, knocking that attitude clear off her face. I really didn't feel like any beef with this chick, so I needed to at least let her get a nut before I bounced out, and thankfully it didn't take long.

The minute she was done convulsing and hanging on for dear life, I peeled her naked body from mine and hopped in the shower. I needed to call Sheila, and I didn't want her to have any excuses not to help me. Oh, Jaydah was pissed that I was rolling out and I had to promise her I would come back just to get out of her place. She was still just too damn clingy, so I knew I would have to watch out for her ass. Taking the steps two at a time, I got down to my car as quickly as I could, locking the door before pulling my phone out. It was five-thirty, and I was supposed to have called Sheila fifteen minutes ago. *God, please let her answer the phone.*

"You're late," she answered the phone, not even bothering to say hello. I wasn't in the position to snap back because I needed her, so I took a deep breath before responding.

"Sheila, I apologize. I was caught up and—"

"What do you want, Monica?"

For real? I had to pull the phone back and look at the screen to make sure I dialed the right number. The times had definitely changed, because the Sheila I remembered would have never talked to me like that.

"Well, can we meet up somewhere to talk?" I asked hesitantly, not sure of what to expect. I couldn't believe this chick had me nervous.

"Talk about what? I have to pick up my son, and I have things to do before then. I don't have a lot of time right now for your shit."

"Sheila, you might want to bring it down some. I'm not calling to start anything up. I just need your help, and I thought since we were friends—"

"Friends? With who?" She cut me off with even more anger in her voice. "Bitch, you tried to ruin my life, or did you forget that part?"

Speechless once again. Between her and James I didn't know who was worse. You leave your beloved city for a few years, and come back to totally different people. Yeah, it was time for me to get back on my game because it was obvious folks done forgot how I got down. Playing it cool, I put the phone back to my ear, feeling totally in control. *Sheila had better recognize real quick who she is dealing with.*

"Sheila, first of all I don't know who pissed in your coffee today, but you might want to tone that shit down. I just need some info from you, and I was going to pay you for your time, but since you want to be a dizzy bitch—"

"Hold up—"

"No, you hold up. All of this attitude you giving me is really unnecessary. I ain't calling you for your raggedy pussy. I need your help. Now, do you want to make this money or not?"

"Meet me at Ms. Tootsie's in an hour," she said in a defeated tone. I was going to apologize to her, but I changed my mind. Apparently she liked being checked . . . Simple ass.

"I'll see you in forty-five minutes," I responded before hanging up. Starting the car, I backed out of my space and pointed my rental toward Center City. I swear I didn't feel like all of the aggravation that I was experiencing in my hometown, and best believe when all of this was over Philly would never see this face again. It was too much damn work.

As I was driving I noticed a few cars back that same black car that was following me before. But then, I wasn't sure if it was the exact car or just someone with a car like it. Turning off a few blocks down, I noticed the car did the same as before and turned off with me. This went on for like ten minutes. Deciding to drive slow, the cars that were in between us went around me, leaving the car that was following me no choice but to catch up. Stopping at the red light, I put the car in park and prepared to get out. I couldn't see who the other driver was because the windows were covered with dark tinting. My plan was to go tap on the window and see who was inside. This shit was getting ridiculous.

I hoped for a second that maybe they had the wrong person, and maybe they needed to see who I was. Everyone knew that my fellow Philadelphians hated me. That wasn't lost on anyone, but after all this time folks still wanted my head on the chopping block? Really? I hadn't stirred up anything in years, and totally left Philly alone when I rolled out of here. This time, I just needed some information, then I would be gone. No harm, no foul.

Putting my hazards on, I got out of the car, leaving the car running and the door open just in case I had to get back inside and get ghost. I did not feel like dying today, but someone was gunning for me and I wasn't in the mood to run. I popped the trunk like I had to get something out of it, just in case my plan to approach the car didn't work too well and I lost the heart to do it. I wasn't even five steps out of my car before the car behind me rolled back a little and then slammed into the back of the rental. I barely had time to jump out of the way. Landing on the ground near the curb, I saw the car back up once again, and the driver turned toward me. I hopped up off the ground and dodged in between two cars just as he got up on me, and whipped the car the other way. Yep, someone definitely wanted me dead.

Other pedestrians and drivers stopped to gawk at the scene, and a few even came over to help me. I could already hear someone speaking to the police on the phone, repeating the license plate number of the other vehicle to the cops. It was a good thing I did get out of the car because I could have been seriously hurt.

"Ma'am, are you okay?" one of the pedestrians asked me as I stumbled toward the car to get my phone and pocketbook.

"Yes, I'm okay. I just need to call my friend to tell her I will be late," I responded in a daze as I searched under the seat for my phone. I could not believe this shit was happening, but it's cool. I knew I had to call in reinforcements for this one. Wasn't nobody in Philly going to chump me.

"Sheila, is there somewhere else I can meet up with you in about two to three hours? I just got into a car accident, and I'll need to handle this so that I can get another rental."

Surprisingly she cooperated, and gave me the address to her house. My next call was to Enterprise, informing them of the damaged vehicle, and that I would need another one. Thankful that I opted to get their insurance as opposed to using my own, I cleared the car of my belongings once the cops took my statement and the statements from a few witnesses. The tow truck didn't take long at all, and pretty soon I was back at Enterprise in a new vehicle with tinted windows, and the deductible paid on the damaged one. I needed to make this visit with Sheila quick and get back to the judge's spot before anything else happened. I must admit that I was a little shook, but I was too cool to let the enemy see me sweat. If they were going to chase me out of here they would have to try harder than that.

On the ride over to Sheila's place I ran through a list of people who could possibly want to take me out. It wasn't a long list, but a list nonetheless. I mean, there was that situation with Rico that never got resolved. After I cleaned out the spot I knew for sure that his team would want me dead. I didn't take everything; the cops did grab a few items "for evidence," or so they said. Those were the very same cops who wrecked my place down the line. I swear, you can't even trust the law to stay clean nowadays.

There was Rico's girlfriend at the time, Sheneka. Now, she was a crazy bitch, and apparently really loved Rico. At the time that Rico and I were kicking it, it was only a setup thing that I helped my fellow boys in blue with. Rico was one of the largest dealers in the city, and the cops had been trying to get him for years and never could. It was nothing personal, and after the setup was complete I was gone. I never thought about Sheneka since she was never spoken of by him.

He told me that they weren't even together at the time, so homegirl had her beef with the wrong person. She more than likely thought I got Rico killed in lockup, but I was just as surprised as everyone else when I found out that he was dead. I had nothing to do with that shit, and even after I questioned the prison guard who was pregnant by Rico I still came up with no answers. I was more than happy to give them that information if they wanted it, but the money and jewels I got from him was long gone, and wasn't no getting it back.

There was Sheila, but I just as quickly dismissed that thought because that wasn't even her type of thing. Yeah, I slept with her brother-in-law, but I didn't know he was her family at the time. I also got her involved with James, which caused her to get let go from the job she worked at Jasmine's law firm, but I hooked her up with the ultimate gig working for the judge, so she was cool.

The Cinques were a thought as well, but I dismissed that notion too. They had my son, and my money. Why would they want to kill me? There was the judge's wife, and the mayor's wife and daughter, and even that cop I slept with to avoid getting a ticket that time, but none of them seemed like logical candidates. Sheneka didn't even know I was in the city, or did she? I was confused, but out of all of those people someone wanted me dead. The question was who, and I would try to figure that out before I left the city. That was, if I made it out of here in one piece.

I arrived to Sheila's apartment about two hours later, and I could see that she was definitely making more money now. Instead of the little apartment she used to have, she now lived in a split-level layout in Presidential City right off of City Avenue. It made me smile to see that she had come up the way she did. When I got into the building I had to sign in at the desk, and wait for a call to be placed to her apartment to let her know I was there. They had this thing on lock, so I knew there was no way I could come kicking and banging on her door like I did back in the day. After all of the technicalities, and damn near being strip searched, I was granted access to the elevator that led me to her floor. When I got off I could see her door cracked open, waiting for me to come inside. I was a little irritated that I even had to go through all of that, but I didn't even feel like getting into it with her.

Once inside, I was very impressed by the layout. Cherry wood accented dark-chocolate furniture, which played off of hunter greens and maroons. African art, and surprisingly a few of my paintings, added to the décor and everything looked really nice. Her furniture looked imported, and not like it came from Ashley or Raymour & Flanigan. I took my shoes off because I didn't want to risk scratching the hardwood floors, and as I crossed the room my feet sunk into the area rug, which showcased a beautiful carved coffee table, which looked like a family tree minus the names. Yes, I was truly impressed.

Sheila looked amazing. When she walked out from what I assumed was the kitchen, holding a steaming cup of something, I checked my smile as I took her in. The last few years had been good to her. From the top of her neatly curled head to the tips of her cranberry toes and all the curves in between, homegirl looked good. She sat down on the chaise across from me, tucking her shapely legs under her body. Making eye contact before speaking, she sipped from her cup and set it down on an onyx coaster. Damn, I wanted to kiss her.

"Why are you back here?"

"I just told you over the phone—"

"No, why are you here in Philly? The city was at peace without you."

Taking a deep breath, I ran down the entire story concerning the Cinques and the returned checks and how I was being followed since I arrived. I skipped telling her that I was staying with the judge, but I did remind her of the reason for my visit.

"Although I don't think he will use it against me, or keep me from seeing my son, I know this is important to him and I really need that information."

She sat and stared at me for a long moment, and I thought for a second that maybe she didn't hear what I said. I wasn't in the mood for anything extra, but if I had to I would throw in some extra cash, or whatever it was that she wanted. I just needed to get this over with.

"It appears that today is your lucky day. The twins work out at the same gym I do, and one of them is my personal trainer. I have their number, but you didn't get it from me. I don't want no part of this bullshit." Sheila spoke with venom as she looked at me through slits because her face was in such a scowl. I guess she had a reason to hate me. I mean, I did bully her for months, and I guess I might have forced her to have a few threesomes with James that almost got our asses killed in the Cinques kitchen.

Going through her phone she scribbled down some information for the twin who was training her, and the location of the gym that she used close to the job. It was an awkward moment because I didn't know that Sheila could be this strong without me, but I was grateful. She was so quiet and mousy years ago, and so easy to control. I had her wrapped around my finger, and she pretty much did whatever I told her to. She wasn't as sexy four years ago either, and she looked like she was slimmed down and toned up nicely. This was definitely a new Sheila I was looking at, and I was happy that she came into herself and took control of her life. She had to once I left because we both knew, had I stayed, she would have still been a damn puppet for me to play with.

I didn't want to waste any more time, and since it was getting late I needed to get back to the judge's house. I was sure by now his butler/bodyguard knew I was gone and I didn't want any shit. Getting up, I headed toward the door, slipping back into my shoes when I got there. When I turned back around to thank her she was still on the chaise, sipping from her cup. She was definitely a totally different person than I remembered, and I was happy that she had gotten stronger.

"Monica, do me a favor," she said to me as I slipped into my coat.

"Anything for you," I responded, waiting for her request.

"Make sure you never contact me again, and feel free to lock the door behind you."

Damn, was it like that? It caught me off guard, but I wasn't about to give her the satisfaction. Taking my cue, I exited stage left and went on about my business, leaving her to her thoughts. When I got outside I made sure to lock the car doors, and I searched the lot for suspicious activity before pulling out. I paid close attention to the road and the rearview as I made my way back to the judge's spot. A million thoughts swam through my head as I drove, mainly on who was trying to off me, and I knew I would need me a good stiff drink once I got inside. I wondered briefly how different my life would be if I had stayed, but I knew going was the best move I could've made in my entire life. If my own child couldn't keep me here, there was nothing else here for me.

I was greeted by the butler when I pulled up, and that shit creeped me out a little because I didn't know how he knew I was even pulling up at the time. I got out of the car and tiptoed through the door, ignoring the scowl on his face. I needed to get my thoughts together before Friday got here. I had something to bring to the table to level the playing field and I was ready to go to war if needed. I was all hype about meeting my son, but what if he wasn't ready to meet me?

Chapter 27

Carlos: Let the Games Begin

"You did what?" I barked into the phone. I swear, whenever you want something done right you have to do it yourself. I told this fool to just keep tabs on Monica. How hard was it to follow someone around without being seen?

"It was an accident. She got out of the car like she was about to pull a hammer from the trunk, so I stepped on the gas. I didn't think I was going to hit the bitch."

"Yo, you are so fuckin' stupid. She ain't carrying no hammer, fool!" I yelled into the phone, steaming. Monica with a hammer? She ain't never been that kind of chick. Yeah, she needed to have her ass served for the shit she did to my homie, but she wasn't a known criminal. Damn!

"Dude, I didn't know. I was just trying to—"

"Where did you put the whip?" I cut him off, mad as fuck that he wrecked my damn ride. *That*

Infinity set me back a nice amount, and this fool goes and bangs it up. Irked!

"I took it to the garage."

Click! I had to get my head on straight before I blasted this fool. I had a plan set up, and people just didn't know how to follow directions. Simple-ass directions that a toddler could get with ease. I owned several auto body shops and convenience stores in the area, so I wasn't worried about getting it fixed, but the cost was coming out of his cut. Damn that.

Rolling out of the bed, I took a quick second to roll an el before popping a squat on the toilet. Sheneka was on my damn top, and I knew that she was ready to get shit poppin'. Sometimes you just have to slow down, and let things play out the way they are supposed to. Monica was very smart, and at this point I was certain that she knew someone was gunning for her, even if she couldn't put a name to the face. Now we'd have to wait it out, because no doubt she would go into hiding. *I swear a boss's job is never done.*

After smoking the entire blunt to the head, I did my hygiene thing, and got myself together for the day. The young buck I kept on deck put up a little fuss about getting out of the bed because she was tired, but she already knew that when I left everyone in the house left. *You won't be snooping around in my shit while I'm gone.* I didn't doubt that she was tired because I was up in them guts all night, but she could catch up on sleep when she got home. After tossing her a couple stacks, we parted ways as we got into separate vehicles. She gave me some shit about needing her hair and nails done, and a new outfit, and I didn't feel like the bullshit so it was easier to just toss off.

I made a few rounds, making sure that business, both legal and otherwise, was on point. I had to keep the legal business to wash the money I was making on the street, but I had to admit that once Rico got knocked it took awhile to get my game back up. Niggas was acting crazy now that the top dog was down, and I had to make a few examples of some folks to put the word back out on who was in charge. I hated to even take it there, but some folks need hands-on experiences to get the picture.

Pulling up to one of the warehouses that we kept merchandise in for the body shops and convenience stores, I made sure the coast was clear before entering the building, and locking the door behind me. As I made my way to the back, I took notice of the inventory in stock, and what I might need to order more of soon. Heading straight to the back I took the steps down to the basement toward another door. It was dark and cold down here, but it served its purpose. When I opened the door I was greeted by one of my soldiers tied up in a chair, bloody from head to toe. Several of my other men were seated around him with menacing looks on their faces. I just shook my head as I looked at him. He was one of the best I had; too bad he had to die.

"So, did you get all that you wanted?" I asked him as I leaned against the wall and stared into his swollen eyes. He had been caught skimping off the top awhile back, and today was pay day.

"Yo, C, you gotta believe me. I wouldn't do this to you, man," he pleaded through bruised and swollen lips. All of that bullshit fell on deaf ears. We had solid proof and too many witnesses to even believe the bullshit he was spitting at the time. As he droned on and on I checked my Myspace account, bored by what he was saying and needing a distraction. Looking through my updates, I saw a post from this fool, posted a few hours before he was snatched off the street, bragging about stealing my shit and me not finding out that. Shaking my head, I turned the phone so that he could read the screen through his one good eye. *People are so stupid.* If you ever want to know the truth about someone, or any of their fabrication, just look on their

Myspace page. Folks are forever telling all of their business in public forums.

His eye stretched open wide as he read what he typed. Immediately he started stuttering and blabbing, swearing that it was all a lie and had he known I had an account he would have never talked bad about me. I was tired of hearing it, and apparently so were my other soldiers. Before I could react, my lieutenant came from the sideline and busted him in the mouth again. Shards of teeth hit the floor as he fell over in the chair, cracking his dome on the concrete. I just shook my head and looked at him as the guys sat him back up in the chair.

"Didn't I make sure your family was well fed?" I asked him in a calm voice that countered what I was really feeling. I was heated, and ready to blow, but I kept it cool. He was about to meet his Maker at any moment. I waited for the birds to stop flying around his head because he was no doubt feeling dizzy from the fall.

"Carlos, my dude, I will never play you like that. All of that was just talk because of the beef I had with those dudes up on Fifty-fourth Street. It was their safe house that we robbed, and their boss Carlos that I stole packs from."

"Wow," I said with a look of disbelief on my face. "You must really think I'm stupid, huh? So there's another Carlos selling the same product as me on the other side of town, huh? I guess our storage houses got broken into around the same time, too, right?"

"Carlos, I respect you too much to think that, man! I would never bite the hand that's feeding me. I got kids, man. My baby moms is pregnant right now. I'll get off the block. Just please let me ride," he pleaded for his life. None of that shit fazed me, and I was already over it. The team knew the consequences of stealing, so off with his head it was.

"Wrap this up, guys. You know what to do," I instructed as I turned to walk out. I thought he suffered long enough. By the time they cleaned up the body and the mess it would be ready for Monica's simple ass. I hated to even have to drag her fine ass through the warehouse, but when you crossed the crew those were the consequences. I didn't make the rules, I just reinforced them. Besides, Rico would have wanted it this way.

Leaving the warehouse, I dropped by a few more spots before going to check on Sheneka. This entire Monica situation had pushed her over the edge, and had her tripping. The facility had to put her in isolation, and they had her on meds to calm her down. I knew the sooner this ordeal was over the better, and maybe she could get back to her old self. Either way, it was going down . . . just as I planned it.

Chapter 28

James: More Secrets More Lies

I was nervous. I couldn't wait for Friday to get here, and now that it had arrived I was stuck. What if this thing didn't work out the way we all planned it? Jazz's mom came back to the house with me after we visited Jazz, and I was kind of relieved that she was still under. The doctor said that her brain activity was still stable, so I was happy that things were going as planned. I could only deal with one thing at a time, and I needed to get this Monica business out of the way first.

I decided to let her meet the kids, but under certain circumstances. I just hoped she would understand that Junior could not know she was his mom. That would confuse all of the damn kids, and I wasn't even in the mood for it right now. I wasn't a hundred percent sure if the older twins knew the deal on Junior, and after all this time they might have forgotten about it since it was never really brought up again and he came into the picture when they were both really young. I had Jazz's mom there, hoping that Monica would have enough respect for her to not flip out in front of her, but you never knew with Monica. She would lose her mind without warning, and there was no stopping her at that point. We decided that she would be introduced as their aunt, and that's how we would roll with it. After all, she just wanted to be sure that he was in good hands. I couldn't knock her for that.

I had her scheduled to arrive before the kids got home, so that way we could just ease into it. I wasn't too sure what the kids' reactions would be, but hopefully everything would go smooth. I was a nervous wreck, and Jazz's mom tried to calm me down by telling me I was doing the right thing, but I wasn't so sure about that. *What would Jazz do in this situation?*

The ringing of the doorbell startled me, and I had to grab my chest. It was about to go down and there was no turning back. I was inviting Monica into my world again, but this time we would be following my rules. I could not invite her to my bed again, and I kept that in mind as I answered the door.

"Hey, Monica, glad you could make it. Please come in." I greeted her at the door with a smile on my face.

She was dressed nice in a pair of fitted jeans that cupped her plump ass just right, and were tucked inside of a pair of riding boots that I knew Jazz would die to have. Her Coach peacoat fit nicely on top of a cowl-neck sweater in a burnt orange that went nicely with her highlights. She had a touch of lip gloss on kissable lips that I had to avert my eyes from. I took her coat to place in the closet, and took a quick whiff of her perfume before hanging it up. Thoughts of her legs wrapped around me tried to invade my mindset, but I pushed them to the side and kept it strictly professional.

"Thanks for having me, James. I really appreciate this," she responded nervously, and I could understand why. She was meeting her son for the first time today officially, and I was sure she was on pins and needles. What if he didn't respond to her the way she thought he would? I wasn't sure what she was expecting to get from the meeting, but if I were in her shoes I would think that she was hoping the situation went smoothly. This entire situation could turn out to be a total mess.

We settled around the kitchen table, and Jasmine's mom joined us after giving her a hug. That made me smile because that's just how Jazz's mom was. She always welcomed everybody regardless of the situation. I offered her a drink, which she declined, so I decided to just get down to business.

"Okay, so after talking this over with Jazz's mom, we decided that you can meet your son under the guise of being introduced as his aunt," I began, being sure to keep eye contact.

"His aunt?" she repeated more so than questioned. I knew she was hurt by the revelation, but I figured once I explained it she would better understand.

"The way we figured it, if we told Junior you were his mom it would undo everything we already have set in place. He only knows Jazz as his mom, and although the older twins know the deal, it would just confuse everyone. Do you understand what I'm saying?"

"I totally understand."

Both Jazz's mom and I were shocked. I warned Jazz's mom that Monica had a temper, and might spazz out, so we were prepared. Although I was surprised that she didn't go clean off then, I still needed to stay on guard because you never knew with her.

"Okay," I continued, trying to move this thing along. "The kids will be arriving home soon, so do you want to help us get the snacks ready?"

"Ummm . . . sure. What do you need me to do?"

After setting the table and getting cookies and juice out, I pulled Monica to the side while Jazz's mom was in the restroom. I didn't want her to feel funny about the situation, and I guess I needed her to know that there were no hard feelings.

"Monica, everything is going to work out just fine. The kids are going to love you."

She gave me a nervous smile as she finished up with the snacks. I could see her tense up as we heard the kids burst into the house, followed by their uncle in a never-ending game of freeze tag. I could hear Jazz's mom yelling for the kids to wash their hands and get ready for their snacks. As the kids barreled into the kitchen, they all came to a halt as they entered the kitchen and came face to face with Monica.

She looked frozen as well as they all made eye contact. I stood back to see how the situation would play itself out. Like I warned Monica during our talk, the kids may have clung to you or just the opposite. She was a stranger, and although the kids were pretty easy to get along with, you just never knew.

"Hi, I'm Janice. What's your name?" came a small voice from the crowd of onlookers. I wasn't surprised that she was the first one to speak up. She had always been very inquisitive, and curious about everyone we came across.

"I'm your Aunt Monica. It's nice to meet you, Janice," Monica replied as she got down to eye level with her. She looked a little nervous, but once Janice came rushing toward her and wrapped her little arms around Monica's neck in a loving embrace, the tension left the air immediately. All of the kids followed, and it was just one big hug fest. I certainly felt relieved, and the relief was on Jazz's mom's face as well.

"Okay, kids, wash your hands. We got snacks!" I hollered out. The kids crowded around the sink as I pumped out foam soap into their little hands. The kids engaged the adults about their days as we ate cookies and drank milk. I stepped away from the table to prepare dinner as the conversation went on. They didn't even put up a fight when their grand-mom left because they were all so intrigued by their new aunt.

As they were having fun at the table, I could see Monica staring at her son periodically. It was crazy how much he looked like her. They had the same smile that accentuated deep dimples, and were almost the same complexion, with Junior being a half shade lighter than Monica. It was a great moment, and I was glad that she came by. At least if she never came back, she could say that she got to meet him face to face. Unraveling this white lie would be a mess, I was sure, but for now this was how it had to be.

"So, where do you live?" Jaden asked as she stuffed her face with Oreos. She looked so much like her mom at that moment it was scary.

"I live in Atlanta," Monica replied with a polite smile. I watched just to make sure I didn't have to intervene, because the kids would question you to death. I didn't want her first and possibly only visit to be overwhelming for her.

"Where is that?"

"It's far away," Jalil answered before Monica could. It brought out the prettiest smile on her already gorgeous face, and drew a quick laugh from the crowd. Of course Jaden didn't think that it was funny, and it showed on her frowned-up face.

"Dad." Jaden turned around, ignoring her brother. "How come Mom-mom didn't say who Aunt Monica was when we were at the hospital?"

It got quiet and all eyes were on me, ready for an answer. Monica looked horrified, and ready to jet. I knew this meet and greet was going too smoothly. I came from around the island, and took a seat at the table, ready to tell my trusting children more lies. The only reason I knew I would get away with it was because I was not that close with my family, and once Jazz and I got married I didn't keep in contact with them. The kids spent the majority of the time with

Jazz's family, and that's just how it'd always been. I hated to even go there with them, but like the old saying goes, "you tell one lie and end up telling another, and you tell two lies to cover each other" . . . You know the song.

"Well, that is because Grand-mom had never met Monica because I don't see that side of my family a lot. Aren't you glad she's here now?"

"Yes," came tiny voices in unison.

"And what do we do when we're happy about something?"

"Hug fest!" all of the children yelled as they embraced me and Monica.

We barely dodged the bullet on that one, but I was happy I was able to skate through. As the kids continued to chat, I went back to preparing dinner. I couldn't help but wonder, as I watched Monica with the kids, if I was doing the right thing. I mean, things with me and Jazz were on the brink of being over, and I briefly wondered if I could do the family thing with Monica. Just as quickly the thought left my head. My place was with my wife . . . or was it?

Everything just seemed so easy with Monica here today. Normally Jazz and I would be fussing with the kids to get their hands washed and get seated for dinner. Junior would no doubt be fighting with one of the older twins, and the tension between Jazz and me was always thick because we never ever resolved any previous arguments. The shit just piled on from one drawn-out disagreement to the next, to the point where we didn't even know for sure why we were upset with each other at the current moment. Was it some recent shit, were we beefing about something from the past, or a combination of both? It was just a mess, and we didn't hide as many arguments from the kids anymore. It didn't get downright ignorant like it did in the privacy of our bedroom, but the side comments and snide remarks weren't missed, and luckily the kids didn't get it. They knew something was wrong, but exactly what remained to be determined.

There was a sense of calm in the kitchen, and fascination on the kids' behalf. The girls were in awe and wanted to play in her long hair, and the boys just smiled at her openly. The flow of conversation just . . . well, flowed! It was a great night all the way up to dessert, and it just seemed to happen so naturally. Just the way it should have been all the time.

Dinner was amazing, and I marveled at how my and Monica's moves in the kitchen were nearly synchronized. Even during the meal, she served all of us before fixing her own plate, and her interaction with the kids was great. Jazz would fix the kids' plates and hers, cooking just enough for them and maybe some scraps for me, leaving the rest of the food, if any at all, for me to scrape from the bottom of the pans. Even after dinner, we had a good family night as we played Twister and Scrabble with the kids, and even tucked them in at the end of the night. All of the kids went to sleep with smiles on their faces, and Jordan even insisted on sleeping in his own bed. I was hesitant at first because of his injuries, but Monica reassured me that it would be okay. I even stayed back as she kissed each kid good night, and made sure that they were all tucked in. All Jazz ever did was holler at the kids during bath time, threatening them to hurry up and get in bed. There were no bedtime stories, or tucking them in, and if it weren't for me going back to their rooms after they were all done to say good night, and make sure they were okay, the kids would probably think we didn't love them at all. Monica handled this all very differently. *A girl after my own heart.*

After rinsing the dishes and stacking the dishwasher, we sat down to catch our breath from the busy afternoon and evening. Monica still had that bewildered look on her face, and I knew she was probably just taking it all in. I was happy that she got to see and spend time with her son, but at the same time I wondered if that would be enough.

"So, what do you think?" I asked her, directing my question about the evening we just spent as a family.

"It's . . . I don't know. A lot, I guess. I could see myself doing this."

It got quiet again. Those roaming thoughts popped in my head again, but I knew I couldn't go there with her. There was no way I was going to walk out on Jazz and leave her ass out to go live it up with *our* jump off. I gave her a gentle smile, indicating that I understood.

"How long are you in Philly for?" I asked in an attempt to change the subject.

"I'm not sure. Had some things on my to-do list that I needed to get squared away, so once I'm done with that I guess I'll be heading out."

"I hear that," I said, followed by an awkward silence. "Well, let's be sure to get together again before you go so that the kids can get to see you before you head back to the ATL. You know they will ask about you."

"I'll be sure to do that."

We sat there staring at each other, and I could feel the connection. I had to divert my eyes and think about baseball because my boxers were getting tight. Getting up, I went and grabbed her coat out of the closet and walked her to the door. I was afraid that if she didn't leave right then it would definitely go down. Planting a kiss on her cheek, I waited until she was securely in the car and pulling off before I closed the door and locked the house down for the night. I didn't go upstairs until she called to let me know she was home, and once we were done with our brief conversation wishing each other a good night, I was able to get my head on straight.

Later in the shower I couldn't help but fantasize about the things I would have done to her pressed against the shower wall. I had a firm hold on my manhood as I leisurely stroked one out, pretending my hand was her mouth. Lord, that woman still had me open. After toweling dry, and slipping into my PJs, I doubled back to check on the kids, and was happy that everyone was asleep. Slipping into my bed, I willed myself to do the same thing. Saturday mornings in the Cinque household meant fixing breakfast for five hungry bellies, and the kids never let me sleep late.

As I rolled over and got comfortable I came to terms that I did the right thing by letting Monica come by, even though we had to formulate a lie that I was sure would later haunt me. After all,

Jazz's mom agreed to it as well so it had to be cool. Hopefully she would just leave because I wasn't too sure that I would be able to stay off of her the next time she came around smelling delicious like she always did. Closing my eyes, I dozed off with a smile on my face as my mind drifted to her chocolate thighs resting on my shoulders while I used my tongue to scoop out her creamy middle. I knew I couldn't have her in real life, but in my dreams anything went.

Chapter 29

Monica: On a Brighter Note

I got to see my son. That made me smile from ear to ear. I'd never thought I would see the day, and I couldn't believe how much he looked liked me. I changed my number a little over two years ago, and the pictures I had of him in my phone were erased so that I could attempt to move on. Kids change so much when they are growing and he looked the same but different than the past photo I saw of him. He definitely belonged to me though. Same dimples and everything. I gave all of the kids equal attention, but it took all that I had not to grab him in my arms and just hold him. I wanted to memorize the feel of his hands, and that smile, and his scent so that it would be etched in my mind forever. I caught myself a few times staring at him, and I got choked up, almost busting out in tears in front of everyone. But I held it down, and I felt good about this entire situation. He was obviously loved at the Cinques, and I came to the decision that I wouldn't interrupt their flow. That wouldn't be fair to them. I did decide that I would make more trips to Philly to keep in touch though . . . that was, if I survived this one.

That whole thing with the weirdo who banged into my car earlier was still on my mind. Who sent this fool, and why was he trying to kill me? It wasn't lost on me that people wanted my head in Philly, but was it really that deep? I mean, damn! It'd been years since I'd been here, and stayed longer than it took to handle business, and not too many people knew I had even touched down when I did. I did see the judge's wife when I first arrived in the hotel lobby, but it wasn't that deep. Did she have that kind of pull all of a sudden? This was all too much at one time, and I just needed to think.

Being mindful of my surroundings, I kept watch on the rearview mirror as I drove back to the judge's spot. I was not in the mood for any more surprises, and I really just wanted to think about my day before going to sleep. I noticed that Jaydah had called me a few times while I was in with the Cinques, but I didn't feel like being bothered with her tonight. She served her purpose and it was time to move on. I might hit her up before I rolled out, but I would just have to play it by ear.

When I got to the judge's spot, of course the annoying-ass butler was waiting by the door. This man was wearing me out, and as I stormed past him into the house I felt like I was a teenager being scolded for missing curfew. I mean, damn. I was grown the last time I checked. Making a beeline to my room I was greeted with flowers and a card from the judge. I didn't even bother to read it, and skipped past the flowers as well. This was getting to be a headache, and suddenly I felt like I would be better off in a hotel. At least that way I could come and go as I pleased. I thought I needed the judge to help me, and I guessed in some ways he did. If he would have never had that heart attack I wouldn't have run into the Cinques at the hospital. He didn't help me the way I thought, but I would take it any way it came.

At the same time, there was that little issue with my stalker I didn't really feel safe from, so maybe it was best to stay here. I didn't even feel like thinking about it, and decided to just call it a night. I took a little longer in the shower to sort my thoughts, and I wished for a second that I was more of a family type of girl. I would do great with those kids and Jasmine wouldn't need to be there. She was probably pissed at what happened anyway and wouldn't want to be there. We would be a happy family, and the kids would love their Aunt Monica.

Shaking the thought from my head, I decided I would go up to the hospital to check on Jazz's progress, if it was at all possible, just to be nosy. Maybe she had woken up, and since James made it painfully clear that his wife's well-being wasn't any of my business I had to find out on my own. The judge still had the floor on lock, and I wasn't sure how close I would get. The doctor did what I needed him to do by telling James I was there, so I didn't anticipate it being an issue if I was caught in there again. I just needed to know what was really good with her. I never really got into the particulars with James, and maybe he would be more open to talk about it. I did well with the kids, so I was sure he didn't see me as a threat anymore. I honestly didn't want any trouble; I just wanted to be up to date.

When I got out of the shower I took out my laptop and sat on the bed naked. Who wanted me dead? That question kept running around in my head like crazy. No one had tried to kill me per se, but that's always how it ended up in the movies so I was sure it wouldn't be different now. The car incident was on purpose, and I just barely missed that. What would be next?

Pulling up some files in my computer I looked at Rico's crew. They definitely had a number on my head, and it was probably them behind the car crash incident. Out of all the people who hated me, they lost the most so it was just the logical guess. I just couldn't picture the rest of my enemies gunning for me that way. The thing that got me was they weren't normally that sloppy. I tried to get a look at the driver. But between the dark, tinted windows and having to dodge the collision, I didn't really have a clue. I knew people in the city, so that would just be a call in the morning to look at the red light tapes. Even if I couldn't see directly in the car, they would have the license plate. At least with that I could find out who owned the car. I didn't even think about getting that info at the time because I was so busy rushing to see Sheila.

This entire situation had me exhausted, so after securing the door and getting comfortable, I took my little bullet from the drawer and tested the battery to make sure there was still some juice left. Being wrapped around James was still on my mind, and I couldn't help but wonder if he was thinking about me too. I thought about calling him for a quick phone sex session. But that would just fuck up everything I worked hard for. Closing my eyes, I let my mind work wonders as I pressed the vibrating bullet to my clit.

Pretending it was James's tongue and fingers, I explored my slippery folds with my toy, pulling my knees back and pushing my legs out as far as they would go for maximum pleasure. A small puddle formed at my opening as I took the tip of the bullet and swirled it around in there before sliding it up to my firm clit. Taking a nipple into my mouth, I drove myself crazy as I fantasized about me and James.

The thoughts quickly turned to me and Jazz, and I could almost feel her soft body pressed against mine, and her mouth greedily slurping and sucking on my body. I could feel her chocolate nipples on my tongue as I kissed and fondled my body. It quickly turned into a threesome as Sheila joined us on the bed, and shit got wild. My imagination was on overload as tongues and fingertips were stuck in every possible pleasurable hole, and the buildup in my body finally erupted in a creamy volcano that created a huge puddle on the sheets under me. The tingling in my body from the tips of my nipples down to my toes caused mini spasms throughout my body, and the moan that escaped my mouth surely woke up the entire neighborhood.

I had to brush my hair from my damp forehead before rolling to my side. That shit was intense, and I was almost embarrassed because I was sure the butler heard me. I didn't really care though, and once I found the strength to pull the covers up over my shoulders, I settled down in my wet spot and went to sleep. I had a lot on my plate for the morning, and I needed to be ready to work. I could see the old Monica had to come back out, and Philly was about to get what it'd been asking for. Revenge.

Chapter 30

Jaydah B: Picking Sides

"She's not answering the phone, Sheneka. I told you she was visiting her son today. I may have to try in the morning."

Out of all the women I'd met, of course Monica had to be the bitch who got my sister's boyfriend killed, or so they said. I mean, out of all the women in Philly she had to be the one I met and fell in love with. Can you say *irked?* I just wasn't convinced that how the streets were saying it went down was really the way it happened. Rico was the man . . . with plenty of enemies . . . anyone on the joint could have murked him. He had a price on his head, and for years had been untouchable. It was just his time when he got locked up. He got caught slipping, and I could see how. Monica was that bitch. Period. Everyone she came across probably got lost on the same spell. Even my simple ass.

I didn't think it was going to be that deep. When I met her at the demonstration it was supposed to be just a quick bang thing, but I didn't know home girl was going to put it down the way she did. When I got to Atlanta she had me in feen mode, and I couldn't get enough. It was almost like every moment that I had free she was in me or wrapped around me, and I found myself falling head over heels for her. Shit, I would have easily picked up my stuff and made the move if she had asked me to. I wasn't sure exactly what happened, but a letter came one day and my trip was cut short. It was cool because I needed to get back on my grind anyway, but she kinda got ghost when we got here so I gave her room to breathe.

Now, when I had the conversation with Sheneka about her I didn't know that *my* Monica was the same chick who had turned her world upside down. When I got back from my trip I checked on my sister's crazy ass to make sure she hadn't possibly committed suicide while I was gone. We weren't as close as our mother would have liked us to be, but we were at least cordial and would check in every so often. I knew that she was hurt by what happened to Rico and was hell bent on getting revenge on the person who did it. I just never put one and one together, and

I didn't discuss my business with her like that for her to have done the same. I really didn't pay much attention to her ramblings during phone conversations because she just repeated the same things over and over again. It was very frustrating, and I just didn't have the energy for it.

Sheneka was in *love* with Rico, you hear me? It was like this dude could do no wrong. Never mind the fact that he had dicked down a few of her girlfriends, and had the tendency to smack her around from time to time. She was doing her thing as well, so I guessed that was the nature of their relationship. Maybe the Gucci and Chanel were enough to forget all of those little mishaps. A pure mess if you ask me, but since you're not I'll just keep it moving.

So now Sheneka wanted me to help set Monica up, but I wasn't really sure that I could. I mean, I really liked her . . . loved her even! Why would I do a crazy thing like that? I was even thinking of exploring the possibility of us being together, on her terms of course. I figured she liked me too, judging by the way she beat my pussy down when she was here a few days ago. She had a lot on her plate though, and I didn't want to crowd her with my shit when she was handling business with her son. It was only right to give her the space she needed.

"Call her again," my overly aggressive sister demanded as she paced back and forth, wearing the carpet down behind my couch. I rolled my eyes in my head as I pretended to call Monica's phone, and actually dialed the number for information. I wasn't about to be blowing this chick's phone up again because that was clearly one of the issues she had with me, and she would jet off because I was on her heels. I loved my sister and all that, but I wasn't about to let her fuck up a good thing again. Now ain't even the time to get into what happened with Nevaeh, but I learned from that lesson. I wanted to hook up with Monica again before she left, possibly to seal the deal. That way, once she went back home I could spend more time in the "A," and we could work on us.

"Sheneka, she's not answering the phone, and it's getting late. What time do you have to be back at the program?" I asked her as I held the phone to my face. I made a mental note to talk to our mother about possibly switching Sheneka's facility to one that was more controlled. I understood that they were all grown people there, but allowing her to come and go as she pleased wasn't a good idea in her mental state. Unless she dipped out again like she did the last time. I knew they at least let her out to work, and she probably lied just to get out this evening. A damn mess if I'd ever seen one.

"In an hour," she answered as she continued to pace the floor. "What's her number? I'll just call her myself."

"You tripping if you think I'm passing off that kind of info. Just come back in the morning and I'll call her then. I have a book to finish up that I need to get to, and it's getting late," I responded as I stretched and yawned like I was tired. In reality I was a little irked that Monica was back to ignoring me, but I wouldn't spazz right now. She had until tomorrow though; then it would be on. I envisioned that she was probably sitting right there staring at the phone seeing my call come up. The smirk she probably had on her lips made my blood boil, and I had to shake my head to come up out of my daze before I snapped out. If she thought she was sneaking out on me she had another think coming. I didn't just give me heart to anybody, and she was going to love me whether she was ready or not.

"Listen, I'll be here early—"

"Don't ring my phone before eleven—"

"I'll be here by eight," she cut me off as she gathered up her coat to bundle up in the cold weather. I could see that crazy and deranged look in her eyes that she got when she was about to go off, and tonight her ass would be 302'ed because I was not in the mood. I slipped on a jacket to walk her outside, and I noticed that the car we approached was banged up in the front.

"What happened to this car, and who does it belong to?" I asked as I inspected the damages.

"I borrowed it real quick, don't worry about it. Just go in, and I'll see you in the morning."

I decided to mind my business because you just never knew with Sheneka. She ran with some unsavory characters, and I didn't want any part of the shit. Whoever she got the car from did something dumb to it, no doubt, and her simple ass was probably caught up in it. Shaking my head, I raced back to my building, out of the cold, and into the house. Monica still hadn't called back, but it was cool. It had gotten a little late, and she was probably asleep. I would just call her in the morning.

Busting out my laptop, I worked on my story, incorporating the wild sex I had just had with Monica into my story. Just thinking about it had my walls clenching, and I knew I wouldn't get through the night without stroking one out. As I lay back on my bed, I replayed my time with her like a never-ending porn movie as I satisfied myself. I knew I would have to get back with her because as satisfying as masturbating was, I needed the real thing. Savoring the last moments, I allowed my body to release on my toy as if it were Monica's tongue, willing her to call me back the entire time. As I drifted off to sleep I wondered where Monica was staying, and how I could send her a bouquet letting her know I was thinking about her. I simply couldn't wait to have her all to myself.

I couldn't help but think of the ugly picture that my sister tried to paint of Monica, and I dismissed the thought immediately. There was no way one woman could have that much power over so many people. Somebody had to be on to her game by now, right? As I snuggled up under my covers I thought about my story line, and how I would make Monica the main character.

I was sure she would love the idea, and I couldn't wait to run it past her. After all, I wrote *New York Times* bestsellers. There was no way she wouldn't be down with that. With a smile spread across my face, I dug down a little deeper into the pillow and allowed sleep to take over. I had to be rested to deal with my crazy-ass sister come the morning, and I knew she would come with full force.

Just as I anticipated the morning came too soon, and it was exactly eight on the dot when I heard the banging on my front door. I knew it was my simple-ass sister, but it was really too early for this bullshit. I rolled over, and dug down deeper into the covers, hoping she would get the hint and come back later. Of course she didn't, and when she started hollering my name out and banging on the door like a crazy woman I knew I needed to get up before one of my neighbors called the cops. Haphazardly tossing on my robe, I made sure to tuck my toys away in my top drawer before storming into the living room to answer the door. I didn't need her all in my personal business, and I planned to make this visit quick.

"Sheneka, are you serious?" I forced out as I swung the door open and glared at my sister. I swear I didn't like being up early unless I had to be. That's why I wrote books for a living, and didn't work a nine-to-five like most people I knew.

"Oh, did I wake you up?" she nonchalantly tossed over her shoulder as she glided past me into my space, and made her crazy ass comfortable on the couch. Sighing, I closed the door and locked it, afterward grabbing my phone. I knew she wouldn't leave until I at least tried, and I promise you I just wasn't beat for the bullshit with her today.

"What time do you have to be to work, Sheneka?" I asked with all kinds of attitude in my voice. Her lunatic ass would be late today if she wasn't driving because I was not about to get dressed to drive her anywhere and she worked clear across town.

"I have time. Call up the chick."

Sighing out loud, I dialed Monica's number just for it to go straight to voice mail. My face frowned a little as I hung up and tried it again only to get the same result. It briefly popped in my head that she might have stayed the night with her kid's father, but I quickly dismissed the thought. There was no way she was giving my pussy to someone else.

"Her phone is going to voice mail, Sheneka."

"Well if you just give me her number I could check back later."

"And I already told you I wasn't doing that."

"Then get ready to keep seeing this face because I'll keep popping up until she does."

I didn't even bother to respond. Grabbing her jacket, I watched as she marched out of my condo, slamming the door extra hard behind her. Locking the door, I hurried back to the room and got in the bed, hoping I could fall right back into my sleep. Monica was starting to burn me out as well, but I wasn't about to even take it there.

I dialed her phone once more and still got the voice mail, but I kept my cool. I would just catch up with her later in the day. *If Monica knows what is best for her she had better answer the phone soon. She really doesn't want me to get on my bag, and for her sake she better hope that I remain calm.* Her trip to Philly would not be a good one, if you get my drift.

Chapter 31

James: Caught Mid Stride

I wasn't surprised that Monica called a few days later wanting to see the kids again. I kind of figured as much. I told her she could come over, and as a surprise I sent the other kids with my mom so that she could have some one-on-one time with her son. I was certain that she understood that he couldn't know the truth, but I knew she needed that time or she would never feel complete.

Her perfume arrived before she did, tickling my nose as the winter wind carried it across the driveway and wrapped it around me in a soft cloud. She looked scrumptious as always, but I kept it in check. I could easily get it poppin' with her, but we were not going there this time. *That's how we ended up in this shit in the first place.* I allowed her scent to linger around my head a little longer before attempting to shut it down.

I moved my eyes from watching her hips sway back and forth, and traveled up to delectable breasts that were begging to be held and kissed. It was like she was moving in slow motion like how it's slowed down when an old love approaches in the movies. The only thing was we were definitely never in love, but she could get it.

I hugged her when she got close enough to step into my embrace, and she felt soft like she could just melt into me. We had to stop doing this. I stepped back reluctantly to invite her into the house, and she looked like I had moved away just in time. Yeah, I would be making this a short trip because I didn't trust myself around her.

"Thanks for letting me come back," she responded while removing her coat. I didn't even bother to hang it up, instead draping it over the back of the chair because she wouldn't be here long.

"No problem. Junior is here. I sent the other kids with their grand-mom so that y'all can have some one-on-one time," I told her as I kept a good distance from her. She had a puzzled look on her face that I could clearly read. "She knows the situation involving the kids."

"Oh okay."

Without saying a word I took to the steps with her following close behind me. Junior was taking a nap, and I decided that I would let her wake him up. I reasoned in my head that it was okay for them to form a bond, as long as it didn't interfere with the other kids, but a nagging little part of me still had doubts. When we got to the room he was knocked out with his mouth open wide, snoring softly. That boy didn't play any games when it was time to sleep.

She hesitated at the door, and I moved to the side, letting her know that it was okay for her to go in. I could see her get a little teary-eyed when she approached him, and she quickly wiped them away as she took a seat on the side of the bed. They looked so much alike it was scary, and she was probably having regrets. Hesitantly, she reached out and rubbed his back, waking him gently. He stirred a little bit, but Junior did not like to be disturbed from his sleep. I smiled a little as I watched them connect, and I knew that I had made the right decision. Giving them some privacy, I went to prepare a light lunch for all of us. I knew Junior would be hungry after his nap, and he would want to play. Monica was definitely in for a treat.

They entered the kitchen right on time as I was putting the food out on the table. I wasn't sure what Monica had planned for the day, but they entered the kitchen laughing about something, and that put me at ease. They were getting along, and I was happy about it. We chatted over soup and sandwiches, and Monica caught us up on her goings-on in Atlanta. Junior had so many questions about why they had never met her before, and I let her take the reins as I watched them interact. They even ate and chewed the same.

"I moved out of the city when you were born, but your dad always sent me pictures and videos when you were a baby," she answered honestly. I was glad she did and didn't make up an entire story that I would have to remember later. I already had too many lies to remember and keep going as it was.

The questions came back to back, but Monica handled it all pretty well. I was hoping that he didn't bring Jasmine up, and he never did. She didn't really like him, and I didn't need Monica acting up. We made it through lunch unscathed, and ended up in the den playing *Michael Jackson: The Experience* on the Wii. I called to check on the kids throughout the day, and they arrived in time to play with us as well.

The kids were hype, and I wasn't surprised that Monica was able to keep up with the moves required to get points on the game. I even got in there a few times to show them how "Smooth Criminal" was really supposed to be done. We were having a ball, and it actually felt like family. Only this time the kids had a female figure, and didn't have to hear their mom yelling from the other side of the house to be quiet. The girls loved Monica, and were elated that she let them play in her hair. They wanted to bust out their mother's nail polish, but she told them that the next time she came they could all go to get it done professionally.

She tired the kids out, and once again got the opportunity to tuck them all in after bath time and kiss them all good night. When the last door was closed, we took a seat on the couch, exhausted from the day as well. She had her head leaned back on the sofa with her eyes closed. I smiled at the cute little makeshift hairstyle that the girls gave her, and I was so glad to see that she had a human side. Why couldn't Jazz be this chill?

"Want a glass of wine?" I offered as I got up to get myself one.

"Sure, but just half of a glass. I still need to drive home."

Nodding in understanding, I went and got us refreshments. I knew I should have sent her home right the hell now, but I wasn't exactly ready for her to go yet for some reason. I'd been surrounded by nothing but kids and family for weeks, and I needed someone on my level to relate to. When I came back with her glass, our fingers touched as she took hers, and it felt like a spark passed between us. I paused as I resisted the urge, and I sat down all the way on the other end of the couch, adjusting myself in the process. I could feel myself growing and throbbing next to my thigh and I needed to get a grip.

She took notice, but played it cool as a sly grin spread out across her face. I was uncomfortable and it showed on my face as well. We both took a sip of our wine and breathed a sigh. My wife was in the hospital in a coma, but even that thought didn't keep my dick from jumping in my pants. I moved to adjust myself and I swear I somehow ended up on the middle cushion closer to Monica. I needed to release and lie between some warm thighs, but I knew it was the wrong thing to do. Still, the body wants what it wants.

"I'm going to use the restroom," Monica said, setting her glass down on the table. There was a bathroom in the hallway, but she went upstairs. *Lord, why does she have to go near my bedroom?* Downing the rest of my drink for some liquid coverage, I crept up the stairs and checked on the kids. They were all sound asleep, but a part me was hoping that at least one of them would be up. I started to nudge Jordan awake, but it would be hell trying to get them back to sleep.

Walking past the bathroom, I was making my way to my bedroom when Monica opened the door. She had brushed her hair back down to the way it was when she first got here, and her lips looked moisturized with a fresh coat of gloss. I knew I was wrong, but I entered the bedroom anyway hoping that she would follow. She did.

No words were needed as she entered and closed the door behind her, being sure to lock it. I sat down on the edge of the bed and watched as she came out of her clothes one piece at a time. The stripper at the joint I went to was damn close to being Monica, but the real thing was out of this world. She walked . . . no, more like strutted toward me like a lioness ready to eat its prey. My entire body shook as she seemingly slinked over to me, reminiscent of a cobra ready to strike. From her cranberry-colored toes to the honey-blond-streaked tresses that covered her shoulders, she was gorgeous. And that was putting it mildly. She was a bag of dimes all balled up into one. I licked my lips in anticipation of what was coming next.

Her body wrapped around me, and I could smell her essence when she spread her legs and straddled me. I took the liberty of spreading her lower lips and dipping my finger into her honey pot, giving it a slow stir before I brought it to my lips and sucked it clean. My eyes closed as her sweetness coated my tongue, and I felt like I had died and gone to heaven.

Lying back on the bed I rolled her off of me, and stood to come out of my clothes. My rigidness sprung free from my boxers immediately, and I ripped away at my clothes in wild abandonment, ready to dive in. First placing my wedding picture face down on the nightstand, I rolled back to get in between her thighs. Pre-cum stained the comforter as I made contact with the bed, and the pulse that flowed through my midsection had me about to lose my damn mind, but I had to taste her. I had been waiting, fantasizing, and dreaming about this moment for way too long to just let it slip away.

Monica was still nasty just like I liked her, and I loved that she was ready to go. Opening her legs even wider, she took the liberty of spreading her lips for me causing her clit to pop out. I slurped it up greedily, plunging into her tight hole with my tongue. I dug my fingers into her juicy ass cheeks, loving the firmness of it. I had been feening for her since her last visit, and I was in too deep to stop now.

Our bodies were on fire as she pushed me out of the way, and placed her body over mine in the sixty-nine position. It felt like I'd submerged my dick in lava when her mouth covered me, and I almost coated her tonsils on contact. She placed her neatly trimmed pussy on my mouth, and I ate up like it was the *Last Supper*. It was like we were in a damn sauna it was so hot in here, and the heat radiating from our bodies had us melting together like candle wax. Damn, she had me open again, and that was never a good thing.

"Monica," I moaned out in between licks, "I'm gonna bust, baby. You have to stop."

She ignored me as her mouth and tongue worked the underside of my length down to that little space beneath my balls, her small hands massaging my sac in the process. I didn't know how long I was going to be able to hold on, but I knew I wanted to get up in her guts before I lost it.

I couldn't take it anymore, and with what felt like superhuman strength I lifted her naked body up and positioned her over me in a backward riding position. She took the cue immediately and slid down on my pole, milking me with her tight walls. It was agonizingly delicious as she worked me, and I held tight to her hips just above her plump ass as I met her thrust.

Leaning up a little, I wrapped my arm around her hips and found her clit. Using the pads of my fingers, I stroked her slowly at first, building up a rhythm as it stiffened under my touch, indicating that she was about to blow. We moaned in unison as my cream began to rise to the top as well. I knew I should probably pull out, but it felt so good I just couldn't do it. In fact, I dug in deeper attempting to knock the bottom out of her pussy. It was so juicy and tight, and her warm body felt so good pressed against me that I felt a tear slide down the side of my face. I was glad it was dark in the room because I was in straight-up bitch mode.

She dug her nails into my thighs as my fingertips played a wicked song across her clit and I could feel her pulsate as her walls clinched and unclenched around me. We both went into convulsions as she bore down on me and we both shot off at the same time. That shit took the life from me, and I wondered immediately if the kids had heard us. That was confirmed when a tiny knock was heard on the door. Guilt spread across both of our faces, and as we unwrapped ourselves from around one another. I slipped into my boxers and a T-shirt to answer the door.

"Daddy, are you okay? I heard you crying," my little Janice said as she looked up at me from the door. That definitely made me feel like shit. My baby girl mistook my moans of passion for cries of sorrow. A hot damn mess.

"Yes, baby, Daddy is fine," was my response as I picked up her little body and carried her back to her bed. All of the other kids were asleep, thank God.

"Is Aunt Monica gone?" she asked as she rubbed her sleepy little eyes. This made me rethink for the hundredth time today if it was a good idea bringing her around the kids. Jasmine would have had a fit if she knew Monica was here like that around the kids. The only leg I had to stand on was that Jazz's mom thought it was a good idea also.

"Yes, she's gone."

"Will she be back to visit before she goes to Atlanta?" she quizzed in her little tiny voice.

"I think she will. She likes you and your brothers and sister."

"I like her too, Daddy."

Kissing her on the forehead, I tucked her back in, and before long she was asleep. When I crept out and closed the door Monica was standing at the front door in her coat with her car keys in her hand. Meeting her at the door I opened my mouth to say something, but she placed her finger up to my lips, silencing me. Leaning in, she kissed me once more then left. I locked the door behind her, this time not waiting to see if she pulled off. *What did I do? Again?*

Hopping in the shower, I did my best to wash her scent off of me, but my hardness betrayed me until I stroked one last one out. This shit was dead wrong, and I felt guilty as hell. Yet, I wanted some more. This was exactly how she got me in the beginning. For now on I knew I could not have her here without another adult being around, or I would be right back to where I was back in 2004.

Finally out of the shower, I laid my moist body across the bed, lost in her smell, which was still lingering in the air and on the bedding.

I had a wife.

In the hospital.

Possibly on her deathbed.

What did I do?

Rolling over, I jumped a little when the phone rang. I was going to ignore it because I thought it was Monica letting me know she had gotten home. When I looked at the screen I saw that the number was from the University of Penn Hospital.

"Hello?" I answered the phone hoping not to hear any bad news. Hell, I already felt like shit for what I did.

"Mr. Cinque, this is Nurse Samuels calling from U of P. I just wanted you to know that your wife is awake. The doctor is on his way here."

"Really? When?" I asked in astonishment.

"About an hour ago. When can you be on your way?"

"I'll be there within the hour."

Disconnecting the call, I immediately dialed up my mother-in-law to give her the news. After deciding that she would come here so that I wouldn't have to wake the kids, I got myself dressed, and waited downstairs for her arrival. Jazz's father was in the car, and he drove us over to the hospital. I was quiet the entire time. My wife was awake, and my mistress was back in town. What was I going to do?

The doctor did inform me that he would be bringing her up out of her sleep and had stopped giving her the meds that were keeping her under. I was so caught up in this Monica business that it must have skipped my mind for a second. At any rate, she was up and it was show time. Whatever was going to happen from here on out determined the tone that our lives would be revolved around. I was scared, nervous, excited, feeling crazy . . . Like a million emotions flooded my senses all at once. There was no turning back, and no time to second-guess anything. My wife was awake. I had no idea what was coming next.

Chapter 32

Jasmine: A Rude Awakening

Damn my head hurts.

Bad.

Like I got hit in my dome with a sledgehammer.

I started to panic at first because I didn't know where I was. The last thing I remembered I was careening out of control on an icy street before hitting a utility pole. I was glad that I made it because as tight as that steering wheel was pressed against my chest I knew I was a goner.

And the kids . . . *Oh my God! What happened to the kids? Did any of them get hurt or, even worse, die?* I wouldn't be able to live with myself because I knew I had no business trying to drive and text under those conditions. Lord, I just wanted to go back to sleep and rewind my life to the day before all of this mess happened. *Things must be horrible because from the looks of things I'm in the hospital, and that can't be good. I've probably only been out for a day or so, so I'm not going to panic, but I need answers.*

I tried to open my mouth, but an excruciating pain kept me from doing so as I grabbed my face in reflex. My jaw appeared to be wired shut. *Wow. Shit must be worse than I thought.* Reaching up I felt that a patch of my hair was missing from the side near my temple, and I almost couldn't breathe. *What happened?* The tubes coming out of my mouth and nose, and the swishing sound from one of the machines near my bed put me on edge. *Did I die?*

My moving around caused an alarm to go off and I lay as still as possible waiting for a nurse to show up. It's not like I had that much mobility anyway considering that every inch of my body hurt like hell, and I had a million tubes running in and out of me. I tried to control my emotions, but by the time the nurse got to me I was in tears. *How long was I out for, and has my family been here? What's going on? Did anyone get in contact with James?* My head was spinning and I wanted it to stop.

"Mrs. Cinque, I'm glad you are awake," the nurse began as she stopped the machines from beeping and began to check my vitals. "I'll get you something to manage your pain as soon as

I get all of your vital signs. You won't be able to talk due to the wiring of your jaw, but if you need to say something I can provide you with a pen and a pad. Not sure how much you will be able to write, but I'll do my best to help you."

I simply nodded as I felt her run an ink pen up the bottom of my foot, making my toes curl because I was ticklish there. The blood pressure cuff began to squeeze my arm, and the compressions on my legs began to squeeze me as well. I had so many questions, but I was so sleepy I couldn't keep my eyes open. The nurse must have given me something good because my body began to feel more relaxed, and I felt less anxious. As my eyelids got heavier I made a mental note to curse James out the first chance I got because if he wasn't out acting a fool we wouldn't even be here right now. I had a bone to pick with Mr. Cinque, but right now all I could do was sleep. . . .

Chapter 33

Monica: Let the Games Begin

Wow. I can't believe we took it there. My trip to Philly was not to disrupt anything if I didn't have to. I came to check on my son, and things were cool with him. *Why can't I just leave? James just had to be nice to me, didn't he?* Making my way back through the city I took the time to get my thoughts together. It was definitely time for me to leave. I would see what was up with the judge, and in the meantime I would be looking for a flight out. I would just see the kids once more the day before it was time for me to go or something like that. I felt like if I didn't roll now I would miss my opportunity, and I just didn't feel safe here anymore.

I paid attention to my surroundings as I drove because I didn't know when Rico's team would strike again. It was obvious that Carlos had a hit out on me just going by the stuff that had happened thus far, and with these goons you just never knew when one of them would run up on you. I had the information for the judge to handle whenever he got better, but I was hoping to be gone before anything serious popped off. This was just too much, and sleeping with James threw my entire thought process off. That was definitely not a good thing, and I knew it, but why was my body aching to feel him inside of me again? Shaking my head back and forth in an effort to clear the naughty visions of us from my head, I gripped the steering wheel and focused on the road ahead. I just needed to make it back to the judge's house in one piece, and then I could lie down and think.

Jaydah was an entirely different issue. She called me a few times the other day when I had visited the Cinque household, but I just didn't feel like being bothered. Maybe I would call her before I pulled out as well. I mean at the airport right before takeoff.

Thinking twice about it I decided to just call her and get it over with. That way when it was time to jet out I wouldn't have to even deal with her. Peeping at the rearview for followers first, once I determined the coast was clear I dialed her number. I knew once I got back "butler security" would be on my heels. To my surprise she answered on the first ring.

"I called you days ago, Monica," she answered with a ton of attitude, not even bothering to say hello. I was still zoning and pulsating from the feeling of James being inside of me so I wasn't fazed in the least.

"I know . . . ummm . . . sorry about that. Where are you now? We need to talk."

"We sure do. I'm at home. How fast can you get here?"

"I'll be there in like fifteen."

She was saying something afterward but I had already hung up. I planned to just dip in right quick, and then I would be on my way. I needed a good night's sleep, and that wine I had back at the Cinques' had my head feeling a little fuzzy. Stepping on the gas, I zoomed across the city to get this done and over with. By the time I arrived she had the door cracked open for me to come in. I left the door cracked and didn't even bother to take a seat. It ain't like I was staying long anyway.

"So, what did you want to talk about?" I asked, really not even interested. This girl was surely a pain in my ass.

She sat down on the couch across from me after closing the door, and she looked like she was about to get into something I didn't even feel like exploring. I was so not in the mood for the nonsense this evening, so I gave her the game face right back. I was not easily intimidated, and I thought she was going to find out the hard way.

"We need to talk about us," she spat out like she meant business, and I knew instantly that I should have taken my ass home. Figuring I should just go end it, I let her make her point so that she could be done with it. That way I could just wrap up the situation with her as well as the mess with James and the kids, and once I left here that would be the end of it. *Philly has seen the last of me around these parts, and I just can't get out of here fast enough.*

Chapter 34

Jaydah B: The Lion's Den

"What about us?" she replied like she was already bored. I swear I could tell that Monica was a bitch. She was wearing me out because she acted like she was a gift to all women or something. I was slowly beginning to see what my sister was talking about regarding her nonchalant attitude, and it was beginning to piss me off.

"We're going to be together so I need you to decide what we're going to do about your living situation. Am I moving to Atlanta with you, or are you coming back here to live with me?" I gave it to her straight, no chaser.

She sat there motionless for a second, just staring at me. I was confused because she was still like a mannequin almost. I looked at her, puzzled, waiting for a response. She blinked a few times like she was thinking, and then the next thing I knew she busted out laughing. I mean, homegirl was holding her gut and cracking up like she was about to pass out. That just pissed me the hell off, but I kept my cool. *Never let them see you sweat.* This entire scenario played out differently in my head for some odd reason. It definitely wasn't supposed to be going like this. She was supposed to be happy about us being together, and offer me a spot in her house for a while. We would commute back and forth until the commitment was made, and within a few months we would make it official. *What's happening right now is the exact opposite. Irked!*

"What's so funny?"

"You . . . This! We're not in a relationship, Jaydah. I mean, you're cool and all that, but this is just a fun thing. You know . . . no strings attached and all that."

Heart hurt and crushed at the same damn time. Was she telling me that we had nothing? At all? Like the time we shared in Atlanta and the love we made just days before was a "fun thing"? It didn't mean anything to her? I closed my eyes and counted to ten as I thought about my next move. Sheneka said that she was known for fucking over people's feelings, and she got the right one this time. Monica didn't know who she was dealing with, and I was just the right one to show her.

I reached into my pocket, pulling the phone out a little so that I could see, and sent a simple message with two words: she's here! I had the message already typed so when I slid my thumb to unlock the screen all I had to do was hit the send button. That way I wouldn't have to pull the phone all the way out of my shirt pocket right in front of her. Once the message was sent I then pulled the phone all the way out, and pretended like there was something interesting going on.

My damn blood was boiling, and at this point I didn't give a damn if Sheneka and Carlos strung her simple ass up like a Christmas tree. I hated bitches like her, and I wasn't about to let her keep doing me or anyone else this way. I flipped over to my Myspace page and pretended that I was reading posts as we talked. I was just wasting time because my mind was already made up. The bitch had to go.

"Jaydah, listen, I'm sorry if I led you on in any way. I'm almost certain that I made it clear what this was. To be totally honest with you, if I didn't have to come to Philly to check on my son we probably would have never seen each other again."

My head snapped up from looking at the phone screen, and my eyes bore into her like looks could really kill. Was this chick serious? It took everything in me not to run across the room and drop kick her in the chest. She couldn't be serious. Could she? I mean, I didn't think we were head over heels in love, but I thought we at least connected in Atlanta. The way she was all up on me and sweating me all hard . . . I had to take a breather.

My sister texted me back to tell me she was on her way here with a crew and it would only take about ten minutes. I needed a damn drink in the meantime, but I didn't want her to try to leave just yet. I was busy counting backward from one hundred, trying to keep my composure. Tears were threatening to spill from my eyes, and I just wasn't having that. Not at least until I was by myself again. She was not about to see me weak and upset.

"Jaydah, I'm really sorry. It's just that this thing with my son and my having to run a business is a lot on my plate right now. Besides, you live here, and I live in Atlanta. It could get costly commuting back and forth you know."

"Would you like a drink?" I asked as I finally got up to get something. I couldn't take another minute of just staring at her, and listening to this bullshit she was trying to feed me. I really needed my sister to hurry up.

"No, I'm okay. I had a little wine earlier, and I'm already feeling a little fuzzy."

I didn't bother to respond, and simply poured myself a full glass of Moscato. I usually only did half, but I would need all of it tonight. I was itching to get at my laptop because that Monica character would be going in an entirely different direction now. I might just kill her off just because. I was so pissed I could spit nails! She just had this stupid-ass look on her face that I wanted to knock clean off, but it was cool. She was about to get what was coming to her simple ass.

There was an uncomfortable silence between us, and I couldn't help but feel like she played me. Okay, so we never actually talked about being in a relationship, and she never really said that she was interested in me. All we really had was amazing sex . . . over and over and over again. Maybe I should have given it more time to build. I was sure that if we spent a little more time together she would have been on board with my plan. *Damn, I think I just fucked up again.*

"Okay, this entire night just got kind of weird so I'm going to head out. Once again, sorry I misled you, and if you'd like I'll contact you before I head back down south."

As she was getting up to leave a knock came from the door and the knob turned. I didn't even have a chance to hide her, and was pissed that I forgot to lock the door. Before I could do anything, Sheneka and Carlos walked in along with two other people. I wanted to protect Monica, but I knew I couldn't do a damn thing. This was about to be a mess and a half, and I couldn't blame anyone but myself.

The look on Monica's face went from confusion to rage as she recognized the visitors to my house. I knew she and Sheneka had beef, but I wasn't sure I believed all of the stories that my sister told me, and how often they saw each other. I didn't know if she had ever seen Carlos at all. She looked from them, and back to me, and I could tell that she was trying to figure out her next move.

"I told you I would catch you slipping, bitch. You got my man killed; now it's your turn." Sheneka spat venom as she approached Monica. Not an ounce of fear showed in Monica's eyes though, and I wondered briefly who would win the battle.

"You set me up?" Monica asked me, but she kept her eyes trained on Sheneka and her crew. I could see her balling up her car keys in her fist with the key poking out between her fingers. She definitely wasn't going down without a fight, and that just made me love her even more.

I didn't get a word in edgewise before Sheneka charged across the room. The two women collided with such force, and before I could react they were both on the floor throwing wild blows that thudded upon connection. Sheneka was going HAM, but Monica wasn't a chump, to say the least. The two women went at it, and my feet felt like they were stuck in dried cement so I couldn't even move to stop it.

In a desperate attempt to gain control, Sheneka reached up and grabbed my lamp from the end table, busting Monica in her head and face with it over and over. When a gush of blood flew from Monica's mouth, I knew I had to step in. My feet felt heavy, but I managed to get over to the women, and grab Sheneka off of her, afterward grabbing the lamp. She put up a hell of a fight, but finally let it go. Carlos pulled Sheneka up from the floor, and still had to hold her back. When I looked down, there was blood everywhere, and Monica's eyes were swollen shut. *Did she kill this bitch?* I stood there holding my breath, wondering what to do next, and suddenly Monica began to breathe.

The men who were with Carlos and Sheneka pushed me out of the way and began to bind

Monica's feet and hands together with duct tape. A painful moan slipped from her bloody lips as the biggest guy scooped her up and threw her bruised body over his shoulder like a rag doll. A dark crimson circle was left on the floor where she was just lying, and I thought I might have seen a tooth in the midst of the carnage. *What have I done?*

Taking the car keys from the floor, Carlos tossed them to the smaller guy, and said something to him in Spanish that I didn't understand. I was sure he told him to get rid of the car, and the guy would probably be taking it to one of Carlos's garages. Sheneka was nursing her bruised hand and busted lip, but I didn't feel sorry for her. I just wanted them all to go.

"Good looking out, sis," she replied as she walked toward the door. Carlos didn't bother to say a word, and the ignorant bastard left the door open on his way out. After locking the door I ran to the bathroom and vomited for what felt like forever. How could I get her out of this situation before it was too late? I paced back and forth from the kitchen to the bedroom, past the blood on the floor. I was racking my brains for what felt like a lifetime when an idea hit me.

Sprinting into the bathroom, I grabbed a bucket and some peroxide, and got the blood up so that it wouldn't stain my hardwood floors. Afterward, I looked through Monica's pocketbook that was left here for a picture. I found her phone, but I didn't know who exactly I would call in it so I just tucked it away. I was hesitant at first, but I knew I was doing the right thing. As I pulled my cell phone from my pocket I dialed 911, and prepared myself for the ride that was sure to come.

"Nine-one-one emergency, how may I help you?"

"I would like to report a missing person," I spoke tearfully into the phone as my tears ran down my face and soaked the collar of my top. I needed them to act fast before it was too late. Sheneka would be mad, but I would just have to deal with that when the time came. For right now, I had to save my baby.

Chapter 35

James: Back at Scratch

My wife was fully out of her coma. I didn't know if I was happy or sad about it, to be honest with you. Monica had my head boggled, and I was so pissed at myself for letting her get to me like that again. On the way to the hospital I found it weird that she didn't call me to let me know that she was home, but at the same time I was glad she didn't because I didn't feel like having to explain to my father-in-law why my phone was ringing this time of night and the woman on the other line wasn't a family member. I wasn't sure how much Jazz's mom had filled him in on the Monica situation, and I wasn't about to bring it up to find out. I didn't feel like being busted in my face about some bullshit again, so it was best to just let it go.

I was in a fog the entire ride, and I could not get Monica off my mind. I could still smell her, and feel her body pressed up against mine. I had to adjust myself because I was getting an erection just thinking about how good it felt when her body was twisted around me. She had her claws in me again, and it was so much easier this time around than it was the last she got in. Only this time it wouldn't get as far as it did, and she would not get her hands on my wife! I wasn't about to let that happen. My feelings were all over the place, and then it hit me. *We didn't use any protection!* I just put my head down into my hands and tried to breathe. What the heck was I doing? What if she got pregnant again?

So many thoughts were going through my head I was starting to feel sick. I could not afford for Monica to be pregnant again. We already had three kids outside of the marriage, and a whole ton of other bullshit that we needed to work through. Another kid would be a damn mess. I was forever putting my dick somewhere it shouldn't be. All I was trying to do was let her see her son, and I just opened up a whole other can of worms that I wasn't ready to deal with.

When we got to the hospital, I was a mess. I was so nervous about seeing Jazz up and alert. Every time I'd been in her presence she was down for the count, and not able to talk. Her mouth was wired shut so she still wouldn't be able to say much, but I was sure that her attitude would do all of the talking if she could remember anything. Lagging behind a little, I followed her dad through the hospital and up to the intensive care unit where Jazz was being held. My palms were sweaty, and my heart was pounding in my chest. I was not ready for this, and I didn't know what to expect or how I would react.

When we got up to the room I could see the doctor attending to her. She shook her head either yes or no to whatever the doctor was asking her, and when he ran an ink pen up the bottom of her foot and her toes curled, I was suddenly relieved. *She might just be okay.* I entered the room hesitantly, and when we made eye contact I busted into tears. My wife was alive. This all could have turned out so differently.

I sat in the chair next to her, and placed my head in her lap. The tears flowed like a faucet, and when her hand caressed the back of my head I completely lost it. Would my kids have been able to keep going without her? Yes, Monica was a nice distraction for them, but she wasn't their mother. I was crazy to ever think another woman could raise our kids.

I looked up into her face, and she had tears in her eyes as well. I could tell she wanted to say something, but the wire was preventing her from talking. I started to get her a pen or something to write with, but I decided that we would have plenty of time to catch up. For now, she just needed to rest, and I would take advantage of her being quiet while I had the chance.

"Jazz, I'm so glad you made it through. The kids missed you so much, and we were all hoping that you would make it out okay."

She looked at me with a puzzled look, and I knew that I had to at least fill her in on the basics. So much happened since she'd been gone, and I didn't know where to start. Did I let her know that I knew about the twin she got pregnant by? Although Monica gave me the number on her first visit I had yet to use it. I already decided that I would be calling them, but when would the time ever be right? *Do I hit her with the news that Monica is back in town? Do I inform her of Jordan's condition, because I'm sure that she would want to know that the kids are okay?* I just needed to say something to clear the air.

"You've been in a coma for about five weeks, but it was medically induced so that your brain would heal. You hit your head on the steering wheel pretty hard," I told her as I held her hand. The tears flowed from her eyes and I could tell she was shocked. I felt bad even telling her, but I knew she would want to hear it.

"You look great though, and the kids are all okay," I told her, trying to clear the air. I could see the relief on her face after hearing that.

I caught her up on the minute stuff that was going on, leaving out the incriminating details about Monica being back in the picture, and the sex we slipped up and had just hours ago. Jazz's father looked misty-eyed as well, and I just hoped that he would not tell her anything that would upset her right now. We still hadn't talked about how much he knew about Monica, but I was certain his wife gave him some details about her and why she was here. There was no doubt on my mind that once it all came down to it she would be pissed, but today we would have some peace.

I stayed up at the hospital well into the morning. Jazz's dad had left hours ago, and I didn't want to leave Jazz by herself. She was sleeping on and off, but I made sure that I didn't budge because I wanted to be there every time she woke up. The nurse gave me coffee and crackers to snack on, and that was pretty much what I survived on for the hours that I was there. All the hours in between I was in my head heavy and sleeping on and off.

What was I going to do if Monica turned up pregnant? I could check her getting rid of it off the list because she wasn't even about to do that. *Who knows? Maybe she changed over the years, and just might be up for an abortion this time around. Or if that isn't an option, at least keep it with her. The responsible thing to do would be for her to just flush it and keep moving.* I didn't even have to know all the details. As long as she wasn't bringing another child into the world at my expense we would be good.

What was I going to do about these kids? They'd already gotten a taste of Monica, especially the girls, and I knew they were going to want to know what happened to her. Kids can't even hold water without pissing the bed, so I knew they would tell their mom that she had been around. My dilemma was, *do I tell her beforehand, or do we discuss it once the cat is out of the bag? Jazz is off the chain, and I just don't feel like the bullshit that's surely going to come with it. Maybe with her mom present at the time of reasoning it will soften the blow.*

Besides, her mom thinks that Monica was just there to see her son, and that part is true. She doesn't know that I got up in her guts and it was the best thing since sliced bread. I'm chalking it up to being a freak accident, because I'm sure that wasn't her motive this time around. It was something that just . . . well, happened! Neither of us was really at fault, we just fucked up and gave into our urges. My heart was definitely heavy, and I had a lot on my plate right now. I just needed to figure out what to do next so that we could be moving along. The sooner Monica got back to Atlanta the better we would all be.

I dozed off sometime around seven in the morning, and the next time I opened my eyes I was looking at the doctor. I wondered how long he had been standing there as he made notations in Jazz's chart. I sat up, wiping the crust out of my eyes, waiting for the verdict.

"Good morning, Mr. Cinque. Glad you could make it over here last night. I'm sure your wife is happy you are here. Sorry we didn't get a chance to really discuss all of the goings-on with your wife when you first arrived."

"I'm glad she's awake."

"Well, she's pretty much right on schedule. We began weaning her off of the drugs that were keeping her asleep a few weeks ago so that she could slowly wake up with the least amount of pain. She may be out of it for a few days because of the dosage of pain medicine she will be given. Her jaw wire is scheduled to be removed by noon, and then we will take it from there. Your wife should be home within a matter of a few days."

That was a lot to take in, but I was ready for whatever came next. Jazz was gone from the kids long enough, and the sooner we got into our new routine the better off we would be. She didn't appear to have any memory issues, and knew who I was. She had yet to talk though, so that would really be the determining factor. Things were looking up for the most part, and I was ready to tackle what was to come in the future. Whatever it was, and with the help of God and family, I was ready for it.

After the doctor finished up his progress report he gave me all the ins and outs of the quick surgery that would allow Jazz to talk again; then he was on his way. I called and gave the family the 411 on Jazz's situation, and I told Jazz's mom that I would take a cab back to the house once Jazz was out of surgery and stable. That way I could be home by the time the kids got in from school, and maybe by then Jazz would be up to seeing them. I knew they were missing her as well.

I was determined to get my life back on track, and move my family forward. I had to get Monica gone, and I had to make this work. It had to because if this didn't work I had no more options.

Chapter 36

Jasmine: Back in the Swing of Things, Kind Of

I lay there like I was asleep, but I heard every word that was said. The pain medicine that was being administered made me sleepy, so I was waking up for intervals, but I so had a bone to pick with him. He probably thought I was crying because I was happy to see him, but I was really just pissed that I couldn't get out of this bed and beat his ass. *He did this shit to us! Now I'm banged and bruised for no damn logical reason. Okay, maybe my texting and driving played a small part in it, but had he been on his game none of this shit would have happened. Point. Blank. Period.*

I was in a coma for five weeks. *Five weeks! Like, for real?* I breathed a sigh of relief when he told me the kids were okay, and I was happy to be alive so I wasn't going to complain. I was, however, going to knock his ass clean out the first chance I got. He thought that my brothers got with his ass back in the day. *He ain't seen nothing yet.* I would make sure of it; he would definitely pay for this.

A few times during the night I woke up briefly, and stared at James while he was sleeping. It was a restless sleep nonetheless, and I wondered what else had this man troubled besides this horrible accident. *What happened while I was lying up in this hospital all this time?* I knew James well enough to know that he was leaving shit out, and he wasn't giving me the full story on what was going on with everybody. I was certain something went down while I was asleep, and I would definitely get to the bottom of it. As for right now, I just needed to get through today so that I could get the heck out of here.

There was a lot on my mind, and I didn't even really know how to bring it up. By the time I dozed off a few times and woke back up I was being wheeled down to surgery. To be honest with you, every time James would wake up I would close my eyes real quick and pretend like I was asleep until I actually fell back to sleep. I wasn't really ready to face him just yet, even though I was so mad I could spit fire. I didn't have the capability to curse his ass out just yet, and if he said something crazy I didn't want to miss out on the opportunity to read him his damn rights. Nope, he wouldn't get off that easy, so I would just wait. Hell, I'd been out all this damn time and didn't even know it, so waiting a few more days or so wouldn't make that much difference.

I had the weirdest dream while I was in surgery, and I was certain that my blood pressure had to have been sky high. It felt like it was so real, and it had me nervous. I was still shaken when I woke up, but I played it cool like it was just from the surgery. I wasn't in recovery for long at all, and pretty soon I was back in my room. It felt like I was asleep for days, but once I heard the voices in my room I was pretty sure that it had only been a few hours. It still hurt to move my facial muscles, and I tried to be as still as possible when I opened my eyes.

Shutting them quickly, I was sure I was maybe still in a dream because there was no way I was seeing what I just saw. Yep, that good old anesthesia still had me in a zone because there was no way this was happening to me so soon. I chanced a peek out of one eye and then the other, trying to focus either way. A sheen of sweat quickly appeared all over my body. I wanted to get out of the bed and run but I couldn't move. I closed my eyes and counted to ten only to open them and still see a nightmare. My husband was conversing with the twins, one of whom was my kids father. I still didn't know which one had actually gotten me pregnant, and had successfully avoided them up until now. What were they doing here, and did James know how we were connected?

I could have gotten run over by a bus at this very moment and wouldn't have cared. This was just too damn much at one time, and Lord knows I wasn't in the mood. I closed my eyes again, and zoned in on their conversation, and sure enough the cat had been let out of the bag. James found out that the twins weren't his. That wasn't even what intrigued me the most though. *Did he just say that Monica was in town and had come by?* Yeah, I had to have been hearing things, because there was no way God would allow both of my pains in the ass to visit all at once.

I chanced a peek again, but this time James saw me and immediately ceased the conversation, walking over to my bed with a straight face. Gone were the relief and the happiness to see me alive. Although he didn't have a look of death on his handsome face, he definitely didn't look happy. I looked him in the eyes with worry on my face, for the first time happy that I couldn't talk just yet because he would undoubtedly want answers that I couldn't give right now. The twins came to the foot of the bed as well, and they all had the same semi-pissed look on their faces. I could clearly see my twins in their identical faces, and it was weird that all three men favored so much, like they could be related. *How did he get in contact with them?*

"Jasmine, I'm certain you know who these gentlemen are," James spoke in a strained voice, like he was trying to control his anger. "We have a lot to discuss, but it won't happen today. We do have each other's contact information and once the time is right we will all sit down and hash things out. Okay?"

I slightly nodded my head up and down as best I could as tears streamed down the side of my face. Things were not good, and more secrets were flying out of the closet. James bid the men farewell, and sat by me on the side of the bed. It wasn't a loving sense of comfort I felt this time around, and all of the shade I planned to throw him was retracted. *Seems like I'll be kissing ass for a while.*

I wanted to talk to my mom and dad, and I knew they would be here eventually. I was scared to stretch my jaw because it was still painful, and I wished I could go back to the day before I met Monica so that we could do things differently.

I should have never agreed to that threesome. Things probably would have been way different and better between me and James now. My head hurt, and I just wanted to ball up under the covers and go to sleep.

Pressing the button to administer more medicine, I allowed the drugs to rock me into a fitful sleep. I was so not ready to deal with all of this, and I hoped by the time I woke up my family would be here. I would just avoid this situation with James for as long as I could, but I did have questions. Lots of them. I needed to know all the details, and, furthermore, where was Monica?

Chapter 37

Monica: Fit to Be Tied

My head was pounding when I came to. I shook my head a few times to clear the fog only to be met by an overwhelming smell of piss. I was lying on my side on something kind of soft like a mattress, and my mouth was covered. My hands and legs were also bound tight, and I could barely move. I saw enough movies in my time to know that this wasn't a good thing. The room was pitch black, and the only sound I could hear were the muffled voices coming from the next room. There were no windows in the room I was in, so I assumed they took me to some location where my body would probably never be found. Laying my head back down on the surface I was lying on, I could only breathe and think. I knew one day it would come to this. Well, maybe not this exactly, but I had done so much dirt to people over the years that it was bound to come back to me eventually.

Jaydah definitely had me fooled! Out of all the people in line to get payback, I never thought that she would be the one smart enough to set me up. It's a small world, and you'd be surprised how many people know each other. *She and Sheneka know each other? Wow, I would have never put that together in a million years.* Shit, they were both crazy as hell, and they always say birds of a feather flock together.

I was trying to ear hustle on the conversation, but I couldn't really make out anything they were saying. I just knew that this might be the last of me that Philly, or anyone for that matter, may see. I wished I had done so many things differently in my life. At the same time so much horrible shit happened to me that revenge and payback was all I really knew. It started with my uncle molesting me when I was young, and from the time I tried to kill his ass up to now I had always been in survival mode. Shit, if family doesn't give a damn about you, you can't expect anyone else to. My mother taught me that early on.

Out of all of the horrible things that happened in my life I couldn't really say that I regretted everything. I managed to open up a refuge for young girls who had been molested just like I was at their age. I remembered feeling like there was no one in the world who could understand the pain I was going through at home, and I had nowhere to turn. At least I made a way to give back to the community and help people. I also got to live out my dream by opening my art gallery. I spent so many nights up painting my pain away, and the pieces that I created and sold helped to fund the Safe Haven that these girls called home. That definitely made me feel good on the inside. These young ladies went from battered and bruised victims of abuse to college students, and other forms of furthering their education. Of course there were a few who got away, and we couldn't undo the damage, but the good outweighed the bad and the refuge helped.

When it came to my little sister, I did all I could do to help her. I figured taking her out of Philly would help, but there were drugs and dealers everywhere, and the girl had a habit she couldn't control. My mom always told me to look out for my siblings, but there wasn't much I could do for someone who wasn't ready for help. All I could do was be there when she needed me, and ready to go when she was willing to get help. I knew once I was dead she would be gone soon after. The money that she would inherit from me would no doubt be used to support her habit until she overdosed. It was a crazy demise, but that was probably how it would all go down if I knew Yolanda like I thought I did.

I got to see my son. The thought brought a huge smile to my face and tears to my eyes. After all of these years I never thought I would step back into Philly for anything. Coming back here put me in the situation I was in now, but I accomplished what I came for, and I was okay with that. At least he got to see me face to face, even though it was a lie how we were introduced. He would forever think I was his aunt, but I felt great knowing he was in good hands. The Cinques were good people, and I was glad that my son would be okay. Maybe they would tell him all about me one day.

As the tears flowed I thought about James. I regretted sleeping with him, but I wished I could do it again once more before these goons killed me. He was so gentle with me, and I briefly wondered how life would have been if I were his wife instead of Jasmine. I would have made sure he never looked outside of the marriage for sex and support. That's what they were lacking, and that's how I was able to get in. That's not to say that he wouldn't have done the same thing to me, because men are never satisfied.

I had been nothing but a huge burden for the Cinque's since I came on the scene, and it was all just pure selfishness. I could have just had the threesome and kept it moving, but I had to be greedy and mess up a good thing. I probably could have kept getting it if I had played my cards right. It was like I fucked up everything and everyone I came in contact with. Maybe it was better that I did go now. My son didn't need me coming back messing up what he had, and no one else really needed me around for that matter. The *Safe Haven* and my art gallery were left to a trusted business partner, so everything would be run as planned. I was at peace with leaving this earth knowing that.

Closing my eyes, I lay there and listened to the incessant muffled conversation on the other side of the door, wishing that they would just come and get it over with. Would they torture me or would it be over before I knew it with a quick shot to the head? All of this was because they thought I got Rico killed. I could tell them until I was blue in the face that I didn't have anything to do with it, but I learned a long time ago that when a person's mind is made up there was no changing it. I wasn't even about to waste my time or breath trying to convince them otherwise.

It felt like I was still clothed, and my body didn't feel sore in any other places but my head, so at least they hadn't raped me. Hell, I probably deserved it after all the shit I'd done. Sheneka looked crazy and deranged when we got into that fight, and I remember the day I met her up at the prison when the guard was giving me a hard way to go. I didn't know that I was there seeing her man at the time, and she even helped me mess up the guard's car afterward. It just goes to show you never know people. Not that I knew her like that before, but came to find out she was more of a lunatic than I was.

The sound of footsteps nearing the door snapped me out of my trip down memory lane. I wished I could wipe my tears from my face before they came into the room, because although I was scared to death, I didn't want these fools to think they had me that easily. This was some fucked-up shit, but everybody had to go somehow, and this was the way it was written for me.

The door opened up and it took a moment for my eyes to adjust to the light that was streaming in from the space behind them. I couldn't make out any faces in the semi-dark room, so they just looked like big black shadows looming in the doorway. I was holding my breath, trying to pretend like I was still out. I didn't know what to expect, and I wanted whatever was going to happen to be done quick so that I could meet my Maker. Wasn't any use in dragging out the inevitable, right? I read in a book once, a Shakespeare play or something, that if you remained in prayer during the last moments of life and asked God for forgiveness you would be granted a place in heaven. Closing my eyes even tighter I started to pray in a low whisper, and that was my plan for up until they shut my lights out.

I heard the footsteps of one of them come closer, and my body tensed up as I forced myself to keep my eyes closed and to stay in prayer. I asked God over and over again—in my mind, because I didn't want them to see my lips moving—to forgive me of my sins. My heart was pounding in my chest so hard that I thought a heart attack would take me out before they could. This was some bullshit, and I just couldn't believe I got caught slipping like this.

"Is she still out?" asked the guy who sounded farthest away. My palms became sweaty instantly, and my head pounded harder than before.

"I don't know, she's not moving still," another answered as he gripped me by my hair and pulled me up on the bed. I wanted to scream, but I managed somehow to stay quiet with a limp body. I knew there was a possibility that they were going to beat the shit out of me, or at least Sheneka would. They were definitely going to let her get her shit off since she had waited so many years for revenge.

"Well, it's time for that bitch to wake up then. Flip the switch and bring a chair in here. We need to get this done and over with." The guy near the door barked out orders. I heard several pairs of feet shuffling to fulfill the command, and when he tossed me back to the bed I blinked my eyes and pretended like I was just waking up. The light was definitely blinding, and my face ached from the earlier attack from Sheneka, but I still played it cool.

I was dead weight as my body was hoisted roughly from the bed and up to a sitting position in a hard chair. My head rocked back on my neck as I performed like I was really out of it. A painful moan escaped my lips as they cut the bind from my hands and secured them roughly with rope to the back of the chair, afterward doing the same to my legs on the sides.

"You sure your sister won't say anything?" I heard one of the men ask.

"If she does we'll just get her ass next. Both them bitches can go as far as I'm concerned."

Just as I was preparing to open my eyes, a hard slap jarred my eyes open, making blood gush from the side of my mouth. A scream rang out only to be quieted by a slap from the other side. I was seeing stars as a blow to my chest knocked the wind out of me, and vomit rushed up my throat, splattering all over my legs and on the floor. I could feel my eyes start to swell as blows rained down on me, and I could no longer hold in the screams. Just as quickly as it began it was over, and I cried as bloody saliva dripped from my busted lips. I wanted God to take me now, but it wasn't going down like that. I would have to suffer this one out until they were ready to take me out of my misery.

"You had my man killed, bitch," I heard Sheneka say close to my ear as she circled my chair. I kept the prayer going in my mind because trying to reason with Sheneka at this point would be useless.

"I knew you would slip up and come back here eventually. When Carlos got the call from Yolanda that you were touching down here I didn't believe that your very own sister was still that scandalous after all these years. I thought she was pulling my leg up until I saw you at the airport. I knew I wasn't letting you leave without an ass whipping. This is for Rico."

The punch that landed on my forehead was so hard it knocked the chair backward, sending me crashing to the ground. It wasn't lost on me that she said my sister set me up. Now it all made sense. No one in Philly knew I was coming here; that's why it was so weird that I was being followed after only being here for a few days. I was hurt, but I wasn't surprised. This wasn't the first time Yolanda put me in harm's way, but I vowed that if I didn't die out here and I made it back home she would definitely get what was coming to her. Keeping up with the prayer, I did my best to brace myself as Sheneka kicked and pounded on my body. There was nothing I could do but stay in prayer and take what was coming to me.

"The Lord is my shepherd . . ." I mouthed Psalm 23. I could feel myself losing consciousness and I hoped that the next time I opened my eyes I would be out of this world and on my way. I had no regrets at this point and was ready to go.

"Cancel this bitch," I heard Sheneka say as she got one last kick in before leaving the room. Her crying could be heard from the hall, and it rocked me to sleep like a lullaby as I slipped away. I felt my body being scooped from the floor as they lifted the chair up, and just as they were cutting me out of the binds and picking my bloodied and battered body up I surrendered to my will.

I was hoping to be out completely by the time we got to wherever they were taking me, and by the time they slammed my body into the trunk of a car and pulled off I just prayed that this was the end of it and I could just go. I had already made my peace with God, so there was nothing left to do but get in line and head toward the Pearly Gates.

Chapter 38

Jaydah: Second Thoughts, Last Regrets

What the fuck did I do? I was pacing the floor as the cops questioned me about Monica's whereabouts, and I felt like shit about what I was getting ready to do. I couldn't let them do my baby like this, and if they acted fast maybe they could catch them before too much damage was done.

"So you're saying that she got into a fight with your sister outside, and some men came and snatched her. Do you know who the men where?" the detective asked, looking at me skeptically. It dawned on me that they might take me down with the rest of them, but I didn't touch her and was at least trying to help her. Maybe that would work in my favor.

"Yes, well only one of the men. His name was Carlos. He runs an auto body shop in the city, and I can give you the address. My sister's name is Sheneka, and she's certifiably crazy. I really hope you act fast because I think they are going to kill her," I responded as I pulled out a pen and pad to write down all of the information I had on both of them. I could feel myself hyperventilating and feeling lightheaded, and I had to take a seat before I hit the floor.

"Ma'am, are you okay?" one of the officers asked.

"Yes, here is the information. Please hurry," I said to them as tears stained my face. *I fucked up royally this time, and I don't know what I will do if they killed Monica. I wouldn't be able to live with myself.*

They took down my contact information as well, and after they left I collapsed on the couch in a heap of tears. Monica was going to die if something wasn't done, and I just couldn't stand by and let it happen. Hopping up from the couch, I grabbed my wallet along with Monica's belongings. I had to get over there and try to stop them. Once I got to my car I called my sister's phone, only for it to ring out to the voice mail. Deciding against leaving her a message, I started my car and typed into the GPS the address I obtained to the auto shop. It was only about a half hour away, from what the screen read, and I figured maybe if I took the back roads I could shave off some minutes.

Once on the road, I called my sister's phone a few more times, and decided I would keep calling until she answered. I was getting angrier as the minutes passed, and I was losing hope. What if I was too late? What if they had already gotten rid of her? I called my sister at least fifty times before she answered and I was pissed. *They better not hurt Monica too bad, or it will be on.*

"Why are you blowing up my damn phone?" Sheneka answered in an angry voice laced with tears. She was still hung up on this Rico shit after all these years, and it irked me that she never got past it at least a little bit.

"Did you hurt her, Sheneka? Tell me she's okay," I pleaded into the phone as I rushed through the streets.

"That bitch is canceled, and if you keep up with the dumb shit you will be next. Don't call my phone no more!"

"Sheneka, wait," I screamed into the phone. I was met by dead air, and when I looked at my phone the call was dismissed. I was so super irked, and couldn't stop crying.

As I pulled up to a stop sign I noticed Carlos and his boys riding past in the opposite direction. After they got past me I made a U-turn and quickly followed them. Reaching for my phone again, I called the cops. They needed to come now.

"You've reached nine-one-one emergency. How may I assist you?"

"There is a body in the trunk of the car I am following. I need someone to come now!" I yelled into the phone, hoping that would get someone to come out quickly. I didn't know where they had Monica at, but at least if they pulled the car over and searched it or something, they may get arrested and tied into Monica's missing person's case.

"Ma'am, how do you know that? Did you see them put the body in there?" the officer questioned. I was getting pissed that there wasn't a squad chasing us down by now. Every minute that went by was wasted time on saving Monica.

"Yes! The license plate number on the car is C-B-O-4-Z! Please hurry!"

I stayed close behind as I waited for the cops to show up after giving them my location on the block that we were driving down, and we went for about a good six blocks before I started to hear sirens from police cars. A part of me hoped Monica was in the trunk so that she could be saved. I was so stupid for setting her up, and once again acting on my emotions. At the next light the cops began to swarm in, and I slowed my car down a little to lag behind. When the cops pulled them over I parked my car a few spaces back to see what would happen.

They were first ordered out of the car, and were lined up against the wall as the car was searched. I was starting to lose hope, and was hoping they would open the trunk up to be sure. The cops began to search the vehicle, and discovered several guns in the back seat. There were at least five of them, and they probably used them to kill Monica if she was already dead. I wanted to scream out the window for them to pop the damn trunk already, but before I could say a word the lid of the trunk went up and a few of the cops rushed over to it. Before I knew it I was out the car and over there too.

"Ma'am, you have to step back." One of the officers grabbed at me. I was still trying to push through to see the inside of the trunk, but the cops had me gripped tight.

When the cops dispersed there was nothing but guns inside of the car. There was no body in the trunk like I had hoped. Just more guns and a suitcase that had yet to be opened. Where was Monica's body, and where was my sister?

"What did y'all do with her? Where is she?" I screamed as I cried and collapsed into the officer who was holding me up.

"Ma'am, you need to calm down."

"These guys killed my friend. Where is the body?" I was feeling delirious, like I was going to faint. It was too late, and there was nothing I could do about it.

I heard one of the cops calling for an ambulance, but all I could do was ball up in a fetal position on the ground and cry. It was too late. My baby was gone, and it was all my fault! All I remembered was the EMT scooping me from the ground as I watched the officers handcuff Carlos and his crew. I couldn't let it end like this. I had to find out what happened to her. As I was stretched out and checked out in the ambulance I began to formulate another plan. I had to make sure that they stayed in jail until I at least figured out where the body could be. They wouldn't get away with this, and for Monica I had to find out what went down.

Chapter 39

Jasmine: Home Sweet Home Going

I was pretty quiet for the days remaining after I came out of surgery to have my jaw wire removed. James ran it all down on how he found out that the kids weren't his because Jordan needed a blood transfusion for his injuries from the car accident. When they ran his blood for a match it came about that he wasn't the dad, and wasn't even the same blood type to be able to donate. I felt like shit when he revealed that information to me. A lot of stuff happened in our past, but that type of secret was unforgivable. I couldn't blame him for being upset, and I allowed him to get his feelings off his chest without interruption. He deserved at least that much.

I was shocked when he told me that my mom knew everything. I mean everything! She was there when the doctor revealed that the kids weren't his, and he even told her Monica's role in all of it. They both knew about the twins, and came to find out my dad was the one who called the twins up to the hospital to talk to James. They had been trying to be included in the kids' lives for years, but I never allowed it. James didn't know that when we moved from our old house I was not only running from Monica, but from them as well. I didn't need them just popping up one random day, especially considering I cheated right in our very bed that James and I shared every night. Everything was a mess, and I deserved whatever happened to us and this marriage.

None of that took away from the fact that the accident happened, and because he wasn't holding up his end of the responsibilities I had to come out of work that day and almost killed all of us. Just thinking about it pissed me off, but I knew arguing the point was pointless. *The main thing is both me and the kids made it through, and hopefully we can pick up the pieces and move on with our lives.*

I was released a few days later from the hospital in a whole lot of pain. It felt like every inch of my body was falling apart, but I was alive at the end of the day, and that was all that mattered. I got a prescription for some painkillers, and was also set up with appointments to manage my back pain because I had developed herniated disks from the accident, and it was hard for me to bend. I would be in therapy a few days a week to get my body back in working order.

On the day that I arrived home I was surprised with a welcome home party. People from my and James's jobs, as well as family and a few friends were there to greet me. I stayed downstairs with them for a while, but the level of pain that I was experiencing made me turn in early, and once James was done with assisting me up the steps and helping me get ready for bed he went back down to the party. I was out quickly, and didn't even realize James was in the room until a sharp pain woke me up. I tapped James, and he jumped up immediately to help me. I wanted to smile but it hurt too bad. Even after all of the mess that had come out and gone on, he still loved me enough to take care of me.

It didn't take long for me to start slowly moving around the house by myself, and I had to tell James to let me be sometimes so that I could do things myself. We had yet to talk, but I knew we had to clear the air. Things were different around the house. I could still feel the tension between us. When, during dinner one night, the kids asked him when their Aunt Monica was coming back to visit, I was surprisingly able to keep my cool. She was here to see her son I was sure. We did just up and move out of the blue, and she had no way to contact us. I wasn't sure what she did to find us, but any mother who loved her child would have gone through the same measures that she did. It was just sad that I didn't get a chance to talk to her about her son, and I wondered how much she knew.

Junior got on my nerves, but lately he seemed like a different child. He was a lot calmer, and got along better with the kids. James even said that the people at his afterschool program said that he was doing a lot better. I was happy to hear that, and I knew my behavior toward him had to change. That was probably the biggest part of the reason why he was acting the way he was in the first place.

"So, the twins want visitation rights. I think it's only right. They are willing to be in the kids' lives under the guise that they are their uncles so as not to mess up the flow of how we have things going. Monica did the same thing when I introduced her to the kids, and I think it's the best thing for everyone," James said to me before bed about a week after I got home.

"I don't have a problem with that. What's up with Monica anyway? Why hasn't she been back?"

"I'm not sure. Her phone has been going straight to voice mail for the last week or so. Maybe she lost the phone, or got caught up in something. I don't think she will just go back home without at least seeing her son one more time. She'll pop up. I'm sure of it."

I didn't say anything more about the twins or Monica, and decided to cuddle up with my husband and enjoy right now. We had so much damage to get through and undo, and work through. Years and years of damage and dumb shit that almost crumbled us. I would have never thought that years down the line this was where we would be. *I'm just glad that we are at a point where we are willing to make it work.*

As I snaked my arm around his back in the bed, my hand got caught a little between the headboard and the mattress. I felt something silky on my fingertips, and yanked at it to see what it was. The looks on both of our faces were of pure shock as I revealed a hot pink thong with a gold "M" monogram sewn into the top part of the thong right where it would sit at the top of her ass if she had them on.

"What the fuck is this? James, was Monica in my room?"

"Babe, let me explain . . ."

I didn't know where I got the energy from, but before I knew it I was up out of the bed and pounding on his chest. This bitch was still causing havoc in my household, and James's simple ass had fallen for her again. He got me back down on the bed, and was trying to restrain me without reinjuring me, and all I saw was red through the tears. I knew I hated her for a reason, and I was so pissed that she was able to sneak back in again. I couldn't do this with her, and she had to go. She could never show her face around here again.

"Jasmine, it's not what you think. She came up here to use the bathroom while she was here with the kids. Your mom was here with us, and so were the kids. She must have snuck them in here then. Baby, I love you. You have to believe me."

The look on his face was one of desperation, and I wanted to believe him so bad. He held me in his arms and we just cried. Every time we thought we had gotten away, Monica found a way to throw a monkey wrench in the program. I knew we had to stay strong, and we had to keep moving forward.

Turning the television up a little louder so that the kids wouldn't hear us, we both were silenced by what flashed across the screen. A split screen with pictures of Monica, one with a made-up face and one of her badly beaten, was shown before the newscaster started her story.

"Early this morning, the woman that was just shown was found badly beaten and raped in Fairmount Park along the joggers' trail. A female jogger saw her crawling from the side of the hill near Lemon Hill, barely able to move her left side. She was naked from the waist down and there was blood everywhere. It is said that when she got to the hospital she could not tell the cops who beat her, and that she was from out of town visiting a family friend.

"It wasn't until this woman, famous erotica writer Jaydah B from right here in Philadelphia, came up to the hospital and identified the guys to the police. Apparently, just over a week ago, the very men she identified were pulled over for supposedly having a body in their trunk, but the cops only found guns and drugs. What was even more interesting is the writer's sister was involved with the beating as well, and all of them are in custody of the police and are being charged with rape and attempted murder. More of the story to come after this commercial break. . . ."

Both James and I were sitting with our mouths wide open. *What the hell is going on in the world?* No wonder James hadn't heard from her in over a week, and she was lucky even to be alive after all this time. I felt horrible about what happened to her, and I wondered how I could find out what hospital she was in. *She must have fucked up someone else's life for that to have happened to her, but damn. Was it that serious?* They flashed the photos of the guys who beat and raped Monica, and of the girl who set her up. This was some crazy shit, and I knew at that moment that we had to get our household and our lives right for these kids. We weren't perfect, but we were all they had. When they say what goes around comes around, it definitely does. Karma is a bitch who isn't playing any games. I was content with not running into her anytime soon.

Later that night after we checked on the kids, James and I decided that we had to make this work. We had a lot of pain and secrets in our lives, but we had to start living for today. We were starting from scratch. As I lay in his arms and inhaled his scent I knew this was where I belonged and there was no looking back. We would get things straight to find out which twin fathered our twins so that visiting rights would be in order, and we would deal with Monica when the time came. All of this was scary for both of us, but we had to make it work. We just had to.

Chapter 40

Monica: On a Wing and a Prayer

Raped and beaten to damn near nothing. Is this what my life is going to be like from here on out? It's like, I know I've done some shit, but why couldn't I have just died? Why did God allow me to live through all of that, and what was I supposed to do now? I wanted to get out of here on the first thing smoking back to the ATL. I had plans to see my son once more before I went, but I just needed to get gone. Philly was not the place for me.

I really thought my time was up though. Those guys raped me for what felt like hours, and the beatings that took place in between were unbearable. My eyes were swollen up to mere slits, and I was missing at least ten teeth. There were patches ripped out of my hair, and everything was so sore. I had cracked ribs, and my clavicle bone was fractured on the left side. Both of my arms were broken, and several of my fingers. My wrist was fractured on my left hand, and my right ankle was sprained something horrible. The doctor said that I was lucky to even have been able to crawl out of the space I was in and up the hill with all of the broken bones I had. I was surprised at the amount of damage as well.

What I did know was that I didn't want to spend any more time here than I had to, and I didn't even get into who did what when the cops came. I told them I was kidnapped and didn't know who did it. Jaydah was the one who ran everything down to the cops, and luckily the guys were already in custody from being caught up earlier in the week. Sheneka was found in a crack house out of her mind, and on the brink of overdosing. Everything was a mess, and I was just glad that they would be served.

I denied all visits to Jaydah, and when she came up here the nurse had to call hospital security to have her escorted out because she went off in the hallway. As far as I was concerned we didn't have anything to talk about. I was grateful that she told the cops what happened, and even more glad that she turned in my pocketbook with all of my stuff in it, but I still didn't have any rap for that simple bitch. She was just as crazy as her sister, and I could do without the drama.

My sister would be cut off as well. The nurse was kind enough to charge my phone for me once I was able to talk, and she even put my earpiece in so that I could make calls. I loved that all I had to do was say a name, and my phone would call it without me having to dial. I spoke with the judge first, and he was hysterical on the phone.

"Why didn't you stay in the house, Monica? They could have killed you! What hospital are you in? I'll have security outside of the door twenty-four/seven. Are you trying to give me another heart attack? What the fuck where you thinking?"

I let him ramble on for a while before cutting him off to give him the information he needed. He was coming up here regardless of the bed rest restriction that he was on. There was no use in trying to stop him. Once he made up his mind there was no changing it. I called the Cinques next, and spoke with James. I wasn't ready to talk with Jasmine yet, and I simply thanked him for the opportunity to meet my son, and I apologized for everything else. I had their address, so I informed him that I would resume the payments as scheduled, and that I would only keep in contact when he reached out to me. I knew that he and Jazz were probably trying to pick up the pieces and put their lives back together, and I didn't want to be a distraction. He offered to escort me to the airport when I was ready to go, but I declined. The judge had me covered.

As I settled into my bed and got as comfortable as I could, I thought about the direction my life was going in, and I knew that it was time for a change. I needed to settle down, and maybe find someone of my own. I thought I was on my way out of here, but since I was given another chance at life I decided to do things right. No more messing with other people's wives or husbands. No more blackmail and conniving situations, and no more holding grudges and lying. I wasn't getting any younger, and it was time for me to start living my life . . . whatever that was.

The doctor told me that I would be here for a while, and he wouldn't recommend me flying back home right away. I decided that I would stay at a hotel even though I was certain the judge would insist that I stay with him. I just wanted to be by myself so that I could put my life in order. A new Monica was emerging, and it was better late than never. My new life was starting now, and as soon as I could I would start by clearing out my phone of numbers that I wouldn't need anymore, and my sister was at the top of the list. She was poison, and I just couldn't do it with her anymore.

I also decided that I needed to move, and I would contact my Realtor in the morning to start looking. I didn't want anyone I didn't want in my life anymore to know where I was. It was time for a new beginning, and I was taking my life back. *Maybe I'll move out of Atlanta, and go to Cali. I always wanted to live among the stars*. The more I thought about it the more I loved the idea. Smiling, I imagined my new life, and the new potential businesses that I could open up out there. Oh yeah, I was ready to go. *Good-bye, Philly and Atlanta . . . Hollywood, here I come!*

Chapter 41

James: Getting Back to the Basics

I was surprised to hear from Monica. Those dudes really did a number on her, and it was the running top story for about a week on the news. Jazz and I still couldn't believe that she got handled like that. *I hope that never happens to any of us, and I hope Monica has learned whatever lesson she was intended to learn from this.* I offered to escort her to the airport when she was ready, but she said that she was cool. She just wanted to let me know that she was okay, and that she would call soon.

As for my family, Jazz and I are in marriage counseling. It was for the best. Although we tried to move past our issues, there were too many to try to push to the side. We had a lot on our plates, but we loved each other and we wanted to make it work. Therapy was hard, but it was necessary if we ever wanted to get over that hump and live life happily. The kids deserved that much.

As I sat in the sunroom and watched the snow fall I took in everything that had gone on in my life for the last few years. The kids were out back building snowmen, and making snow angles. A cute little snowball fight took place, and all of the kids were in their element and getting along. This was how it was supposed to be. I peeked over at my wife curled up on the chaise enjoying a novel as we both took periodic sips of hot chocolate from our mugs. This was what life was really about: meeting your soul mate and building a family, growing old together, and instilling family values in your kids so that they could pass it along to theirs. These were the moments that made it all worthwhile.

Sometimes we think what we have at home isn't enough when in reality it's exactly what we need. It's crazy that it oftentimes takes a tragedy for us to see it. Getting up from my spot, I went out and joined the kids in a quick snowball fight before running back in the house to start dinner, since Jazz still couldn't really stand that long to maneuver around the kitchen without being in a lot of pain. I whipped up their favorite meal: spaghetti.

I called out for Jazz to have the kids get ready for dinner, and they all showed up just as I was putting out the place settings. Once we were all seated we joined hands, and it was Jalil's turn tonight to pray over the food. I smiled as I looked around at my family, and it saddened me that all of this was almost destroyed. Giving Jazz a wink, I began to serve the kids as they all told us about their day in school. I loved my life, and now that I had another chance at making it right I was determined that it was going to work. *I wouldn't give up this moment for anything in the world.*

Chapter 42

Jaydah B: Not That Easily Broken

How pissed was I that this bitch had the nerve to deny my visits after I helped her? I mean, for real? I loved her. Didn't she know that? I didn't even get the chance to apologize to her for what I did, and I was just so happy that she made it out alive. I was going through it, not knowing where she was at or if she had even survived the ordeal. Sheneka and I got into the biggest falling out behind this, and then she fell off the face of the earth. I didn't know what happened to her until the cops had informed me that she almost died in a drug house, and one of the fiends was kind enough to alert the authorities to come get her because she was crashing everyone's high. A damn mess.

Monica hasn't seen the last of me though. I still had her address, and since she wouldn't talk to me here, I would just wait for her to go back home. I was already looking into hotels and airfare so that I could get down there. The nurse wouldn't give me any information on her, but the cute little receptionist kindly informed me that Monica had been discharged when I called the hospital two weeks later. Monica loved me, she just didn't know it yet.

Once my travel arrangements were made I curled up on the couch with my laptop, eager to start my next novel. Monica would be the star, and I had a scandalous story that I was ready to tell. It would be about a woman who fell in love with this guy's wife and would do whatever possible to break them up. I wasn't sure of the title just yet, but it would definitely be a page-turner that I knew my fans would love. After all . . . Jaydah B always wrote the hot joints that bookstores couldn't keep on the shelves.

As my fingers flew across the keys I knew this one would be a bestseller, and I may even write a sequel to it. Either way, once I moved to Atlanta with my baby everything would be all good. *While she's painting her pictures I'll be writing my novels, and we will be like a power couple or something. My books will eventually be movies, and maybe we could eventually move to Hollywood to set that into motion.* I smiled at how bright my future was looking, and I couldn't wait to share the great news with Monica. Time waited for no one, and like it's been said in the past . . . don't put off tomorrow what can be done today. Let the games begin!